MURDER IN THE JAZZ BAND

A Golden Age Mystery

Murder in the Jazz Band

A Golden Age Mystery

G.G. Vandagriff

Murder in the Jazz Band: A Golden Age Mystery

Copyright ©2020 by G.G. Vandagriff

All rights reserved. No part of this book may be used or reproduced in any manner whatsoever without written permission of the author except in the case of brief quotations embodied in critical articles or reviews.

Cover Design by Melissa Williams Design

Interior Formatting by Melissa Williams Design

This is a work of fiction. The names, characters, and incidents are either the product of the author's imagination or are used fictitiously, and any resemblance to actual persons living or dead is entirely coincidental.

Published by Orson Whitney Press

For Karen Anderson
My enthusiastic Partner in Crime

Chapter One

Autumn, 1934

On the arm of Dr. Harry Bascombe, Catherine Tregowyn pulled her sable coat around her and exited Oxford's Sheldonian Theater into the chilly night.

"That was brilliant," she said. "George Ann made an inspired Ophelia. I'm so glad we came."

"Nothing like a remedial dose of Hamlet. At least they weren't costumed in pajamas this time," said Harry. He looked absolutely marvelous in evening clothes with his piratical Douglas Fairbanks appearance.

"Pajamas?"

"And dirty socks. The last time I saw the play—in Stratford, believe it or not—that was their idea of modern dress."

Catherine shuddered. Then she stopped. A hunched figure stood before her. "Wills! What are you doing here?"

Her brother, William, stood there, hands thrust in his coat pockets. "Cherry told me where to find you. I'm sorry to interrupt your evening, Cat, but I need your help. A friend of mine is in trouble." After kissing her on the cheek, he stuck his hand out toward her companion. "Harry. Good to see you. Sorry about this."

The men shook hands.

Catherine said, "How can I help?"

"It's Emily. Do you remember meeting her at the pub last month? The nurse from the Infirmary?"

"Oh, yes. The woman with the knock-out smile. I didn't know you were seeing her."

"We're just friends at the moment. She's been arrested for murder."

"My heavens!" said Catherine.

"A fellow she was keen on. Chap called James Westfield. Died of a drug overdose. Detective Chief Inspector Marsh came and arrested her from her flat." He kicked an invisible stone on the street. "Fortunately, I was there at the time. I don't know what the evidence is against her, but she didn't do it. She's not that sort of person at all."

By the lights still coming through the theater door, she could see Wills' classically handsome features, his lowering forehead reflecting his concern.

Her heart softened with worry for him. As far as she knew, her elder brother had never been in love. The idea of the police suspecting someone you knew so well of such a heinous crime must be a shock. "I'm not a solicitor, Wills," Catherine said. "What do you want me to do?"

"The same thing you did in the Chenowith business. Find out who the real culprit is."

Catherine felt the weight of this expectation settle on her shoulders like a shroud. She protested, "Are you serious? I'm no detective."

Harry said, "Let's go talk about this over a drink."

They took a cab from the theater to The Eagle and Child, and Wills led the way through the raucous crowd to a table in the back. A fug of cigarette smoke hung in the air as usual. Harry went for their drinks.

Catherine took off the fur that exactly matched her dark brown waved hair and hung it on the nearby hat tree. When she was facing her brother across the table, she said, "If you're serious, I guess you had better begin by telling me about Emily."

The gloom on her brother's face lifted a bit. His confidence in her abilities was daunting. "Well, you probably remember that Emily was born in Kenya. Her parents are ex-pats. They have a coffee plantation. But she went to boarding school and nursing school here." He paused and appeared to be searching for words. Wills was not comfortable discussing his feelings. Catherine had never had a discussion like this with him about a woman. He went on, "She decided to be a nurse for the same reason I'm pursuing pathology. The dying and sick children in Kenya. After she finishes her training, she wants to go back there and help. I've told you about all the disease there. Typhoid, cholera . . . you name it, we've seen it. It fairly broke my heart, and I'm a hardened case."

"You are certainly not hardened!" she exclaimed.

Harry returned with a pint of lager for himself and Wills and a shandy for Catherine. She caught him up on the conversation.

"I can see where you'd be attracted to someone like that," Harry said. "She shares your passion."

Catherine also remembered the girl's unusual beauty. Emily had large features and looked as though she belonged on the screen with her high cheekbones and perfect teeth.

Wills sipped his drink. "Her father is the younger son of a viscount who lives in Hertfordshire."

Since Wills was the only son of a baron, Catherine doubted this would be a problem in their relationship, if it were to progress.

"Is her grandfather still living?" asked Harry as he sat with his arm stretched along the back of the bench.

"I don't know," answered Wills.

"Maybe he or her uncle will see that she gets a solicitor," said Harry.

She knew her brother had been shaken up by his year in Kenya, but Catherine thought it a good thing. His life now had a direction and purpose that rescued him from idleness. He wouldn't end up like Rafe. But it troubled her to see him so upset.

"What do you know about the victim?" she asked.

"Not a lot," Wills said. "I know he's doing post-grad work somewhere in Oxford. I wouldn't think he took it too seriously, however. He plays saxophone in a dance band. You may have heard them on the weekends at the Town Hall." He pulled a face. "Buckets of charm. It always seemed to me that he was a player. I was hoping Emily would see that eventually. It's odd. She doesn't seem the sort who would be carried away by this chap's brand of charm."

"That doesn't seem like he'd be a good match for anyone," remarked Catherine, sipping her shandy.

"I know," said William. "I'm always waiting for her to wake up and see me standing there, but now this has happened."

"How do they figure he was murdered if he took an overdose?" asked Harry.

"He was knocked out and then given an overdose of morphine in his flat. Apparently, there was no syringe at the scene," said Wills. "He died a week ago, but they just got the full autopsy. He died of the morphine, not the blow to the head as they first thought. They didn't even realize it was murder at first. They thought he fell accidentally against the andirons and hit his head. Then the pathologist discovered bruising on his chin. It's all been reported in the *Mail*. They arrested Emily pretty quickly after getting the autopsy results. I don't know why. She couldn't have knocked the chap out. It's ludicrous."

Catherine said, "I don't know how much I'll be able to do, Wills. Will they even let her have visitors?"

"I checked, and they will. The police said they'd let the two of us in tonight, but after this, only one per day."

"Does that include her solicitor?"

"No. Emily's probably beside herself. Do you think we could go over to the jail now?"

Harry consulted his watch. "You do realize it's 11:00."

"I'm quite certain she's awake and will be relieved to have someone to talk to."

Catherine longed to tell Harry that all this wasn't a bit like Wills. Her brother kept his distance from relationships. She had always known him to be fully absorbed in his own interests.

But there was no opportunity for a private conversation. They walked down Cornmarket Street together to the Town Hall, where the police department and the jail were situated.

She thought of her brother's solemn face as he talked about the sick African children. Perhaps he had changed in Kenya as he learned to care more for other human beings. In some ways, it was like he had awakened and noticed the world for the first time.

* * *

Emily did indeed look dispirited when the police sergeant led her, handcuffed, into the interview room. Apparently, they were not to be allowed any privacy as the sergeant sat himself down in the corner. Only Wills and Catherine had been allowed in for this visit.

The young woman's large blue eyes wore a quenched look and immediately sought Wills.' Her nearly black hair was cut very short and looked as though she had been running her hands through it.

"This is so awful," Emily whispered. She sat on one side of the table. Catherine and Wills sat down on the other side. She knew it was difficult for him to refrain from giving the girl a reassuring touch of some sort, but they had been told to keep their distance.

"I brought my sister because she's a dab hand at solving crimes. She'll get you out of here," Wills said.

Catherine's heart fell at her brother's words. She said, "Suppose you tell us what happened. Why have they arrested you?"

"Morphine has gone missing from the Radcliffe Infirmary where I work, evidently. He was killed with an overdose. James and I didn't part on the best of terms, but why they think I killed him, I have no idea."

Emily looked down and away as she said this, and Catherine had the uncomfortable conviction that she was not telling the truth. About what, she wasn't certain.

"First of all," said Catherine. "You need to find yourself a solicitor if you haven't already done so."

"I rang my uncle. He is driving up tomorrow and promised to take care of that and have a word with the police. He wasn't pleased, however." She squirmed a bit in her chair. "It's all so beastly."

"You must buck up, Em," said Wills. "If you would feel more comfortable talking to Catherine alone, I will go out."

Emily nodded, and he stood. "Level with her," he instructed the girl.

Catherine watched as Emily kept her eyes on Wills until he was out of sight. When she spoke, the girl's eyes were cast down once again. "James and I were mad about each other. At least, I thought so until he broke things off. I spent nearly all my off-hours with him and his band."

"Tell me about the band."

"They're frightfully good. All the rage, here in Oxford. I expect they would have moved to London only most of the members are at university here. At St. John's. James was a post-grad there. Medieval History. What I don't know now about the War of the Roses would fit in a thimble."

Catherine followed Emily's gaze as she focused steadily on the blank wall to her left. She prodded the girl again. "Do the band members get along?"

"Not really. They're all very different. Tony—the drummer—he's a serious musician. Alfie plays the trumpet, and he's a whiz at maths. He's up for some sort of prize, but it's hard to believe because he's on cocaine half the time. Tony's after him all the time to quit because cocaine killed his older brother."

Catherine nodded. She took down these facts at the back of her appointment diary. "Go on," she said.

"Red—the leader—is a Communist. He's on the piano while he waits for the Revolution. Also, he studies something at St. John's. I'm not sure what." She paused. "He was frightfully condescending toward James."

"That's all?" asked Catherine. It seemed to be a very small band.

"No." She sighed. "There's Joe."

It wasn't hard to tell that Joe was someone special. Emily's eyes lit with the first touch of life she'd shown yet. Then she quickly looked down at her short, square fingernails. For all her glamorous looks, she had a nurse's competent hands. "He's an American. Frightfully talented on the trombone. It's a gift."

"And what does he study?"

She shrugged. "The trombone's Joe's life."

"They do sound like they're very different. Any motives for murder lurking there?"

Emily shrugged again but didn't say anything.

"Was James jealous of Joe, perhaps?" Catherine asked.

The girl glanced up, alarmed. "Jealous of Joe? Good heavens, no. Joe's black."

This information was so unexpected that Catherine was nearly struck dumb. "Black?" she echoed.

"Frightfully," Emily said. "You know. An American Negro."

"How . . . unusual," Catherine said.

"Not really. In the world of jazz, American Negroes are king. We are lucky to have him."

Catherine took in the information. She still found the fact odd. "Then, any idea why he's playing in Oxford instead of London?"

Emily shrugged again. "I don't imagine he could get a gig there. Oxford is far more progressive than London."

"Did his presence in the band make anyone uncomfortable?"

Emily stiffened. "What does that have to do with James's murder?"

Growing impatient, Catherine said, "Do you want my help? If so, you need to be a little more forthcoming. Did it make James uncomfortable?"

The girl's eyes flashed. "Yes, as a matter of fact, it did. But Joe is a lamb. He wouldn't have killed James," she said.

Catherine decided to leave the subject of the band for the present. "Tell me about James's family."

"They are frightfully wealthy. He's from the North. I think his father owns coal mines. But James didn't like to talk about where his money came from." To Catherine's surprise, the girl suddenly seemed a bit contemptuous.

"Does he have siblings?"

"A brother. He's here at Oxford. Christ Church. They don't get along. James is . . . was the eldest and Phillip is always after him for money. He goes through it like water."

"Their relations were rocky then?"

Emily pulled a face. "Frightfully. James thought him a beastly little tick."

At last, a straightforward motive.

"Is there anyone at all you know of that would have reason to kill James?"

"James was a pretty complicated person. I don't know everything about his life, but it would certainly be to Phillip's advantage for James to be out of the way."

Catherine found herself oddly reluctant to trust Emily or her impressions. There were powerful feelings there, but Catherine didn't think they were all about James. She felt uneasy. Unable to put her finger on the reason, she felt that it hadn't been a very satisfactory interview, but she didn't want to push the girl with the sergeant present.

"Is there anything else I should know?" she asked.

The girl studied her lap as she shook her head. Catherine didn't think she was a murderer, but she also didn't think Emily was telling her everything. If it weren't for Wills, she doubted if she would proceed with the matter. However, this was the first time Wills had ever asked for her help with anything, so she felt the matter was of first importance.

"I hope you can get some sleep now," she said, standing. "I'm very sorry this has happened to you. I hope your uncle can arrange for a solicitor tomorrow. Meanwhile, I will see what I can uncover."

Emily looked slightly alarmed at her sudden determination to leave. "Uh, would you see if William can come back in?"

Catherine agreed to this and left the young woman alone with her handcuffs. As she reentered the foyer of the police station, Wills looked up; his face pinched with anxiety.

"How did it go?"

"She was less than forthcoming, I think. But she would like to see you. I'll leave with Harry now. It's late. We'll talk tomorrow, all right?"

Her brother agreed and kissed her on the cheek. "You're a brick, Cat."

* * *

Catherine and Harry exited the police station into the cold night. She shivered, and Harry's arm went around her shoulders.

"So, she didn't tell you everything, eh?" he prompted.

"There was something off about her. I'm not sure what. I didn't exactly take to her. But, then, these weren't the best of circumstances."

She gave him the gist of her interview.

"Are we still going to look into it?" Harry asked as he hailed a cab.

"Yes. For Wills' sake, if nothing else. It hurts me to see him so upset."

In the cab, she told him about Phillip Westfield, who attended Christ Church, the college where Harry taught. He promised to look into James's brother the following day.

When the cab deposited them at her flat on Clarendon Street, she asked, "Are we still on for the picnic tomorrow? We can discuss it further then."

"By all means." He kissed her cheek. "Good night, now."

Chapter Two

Catherine woke late Saturday morning. It had been a while before she'd been able to sleep the night before. She had left Cherry, her maid, a note not to wake her.

As she drank her morning tea and ate a bun in the little dining nook by the window in her sitting room, she pondered what her first step in her investigation should be.

The whole incident struck her as odd. The death could so easily have been manslaughter—a punch to the jaw resulting in Mr. Westfield's cracking his head on the andiron. But the killer must have come prepared. Administering a lethal dose of morphine showed premeditation. And odd as she found Emily's behavior, she couldn't see her knocking the man out with her fists. Pushing him, maybe. Causing accidental death, maybe. She could even envision her administering the morphine. But, knocking a man out with her fists? No.

Cherry brought her the newspaper.

"Seems like there's been a murder, miss," she told Catherine.

"Yes," she answered. "I heard about it from Wills last night. He knew the victim."

"Cricky! It says he was the saxophonist for the band that plays at the Town Hall weekends. I've heard about them. They're supposed to be awfully good. Have you ever heard them?" the maid asked.

"Dr. Bascombe and I danced to a band there last summer, but I don't think it was this one, because they have a Negro trombonist. I would have remembered him. Apparently, he's sensational."

Cherry's eyes grew round. "I have to see that! I'll have to have Sam take me dancing sometime." Sam was Cherry's brother, who had followed her to Oxford and found a job as a chef at one of the colleges. He was a very good cook.

"What would you like me to do today?" the maid asked. "I spent yesterday putting everything to rights."

Catherine's Oxford flat was small, consisting of a sitting room, kitchen, two bedrooms, and a bath. Though Cherry hadn't done housework in the large London flat, when they had relocated here upon Catherine's taking her new post, she kept the flat in order. A char came in once a week for the heavy cleaning.

"Could you do the marketing? I'm concerning myself in this murder, as a matter of fact. There is a shopping list in the kitchen. I will be having lunch out with Dr. Bascombe."

"All right," Cherry said, her face lit with enthusiasm. The maid liked anything that took her out of the flat, which she considered gloomy after their London dwelling.

Catherine apologized, "There won't be any French lessons today; I'm afraid."

"Oh, that's all right, miss. Maybe I can help with the investigation?"

"Nothing yet. But I'll let you know," Catherine said with a smile as she took up the newspaper.

Cherry left for the market.

There was nothing in the paper about the murder that Catherine didn't already know. She would like to speak to the band members at St. John's, but she was a woman and had no standing that would allow her to call at a men's college. Besides, she had no surnames for the band members. Better leave that to Harry and his contacts.

After her bath, she dressed in her heather tweed suit and new aubergine cloche hat. She did a quick check in the mirror. There were circles under her large brown eyes. Along with her widow's peak, they made her look like an owl. Or so she thought. Harry told her that she didn't see her own beauty, and that was certainly true.

She decided she would go to the Oxford Town Hall to see what she could find out about the band. Her post as a tutor and lecturer of Modern English Literature kept her very busy throughout the week, so she knew she could not waste this free Saturday. She had essays to read and mark, but they could wait.

It was a lovely autumn day—clear with a blue sky and a nip in the air. The trees were in full color, and she thought as she had many times that there was no more picturesque place in all England. The architecture of the town was mostly Gothic, and she delighted in the profusion of golden stone walls and towers. Where else could you stroll among such a mass of ancient buildings, still busy and brilliant with purpose?

She and Harry would picnic in the Christ Church Meadows. Hopefully, they would both have news to impart regarding their investigations.

Catherine arrived at the Town Hall, with its profusion of neo-classical friezes. She was pink-cheeked and invigorated after her long walk down St. Giles Street, which became, in turn, Magdalen St., then Cornmarket. Luckily, she wore a stout pair of brogues.

The man in charge of bookings for the hall had a small office behind the police station in the building. He proved to be a lanky individual with heavily pomaded blond hair, which he wore combed straight back from a knobby forehead. The notice on his door said he was Mr. Webster.

"Hello," Catherine said with an ingratiating smile. "I wonder if you could spare me a moment of your time, Mr. Webster?"

"Come in. Come in. Always time for a lovely lady."

"Thank you." She sat down on a seat across from his desk.

"The fact is, someone I care for is a suspect in the murder of a Mr. James Westfield, the saxophonist who plays here?"

He studied her with interest. After a moment, he said, "Now, I'm sorry to hear that. I read this morning that it was a drug overdose. Don't like to be connected with murder of any kind, but drugs . . . that's going to give the band a bad name. Bad for business."

"A drug was the cause of death, but I don't think there was any evidence that he was an addict," she said. "It said in the *Mail* that there was no syringe found at the scene so they couldn't have taken it himself."

"Yes, yes. They have a suspect already, eh?"

"Yes. But she is completely innocent. I am confident of that. The police have made a mistake in this case."

"Well, then. How may I be of service?"

"Anything you could tell me about the other band members would be a help. They've been playing here for some time. I know that. They're a lovely band. I hope they can find another saxophonist and continue."

"Well, Westfield was the best saxophonist they've had. And an odder assortment of individuals it would be difficult to find in the Kingdom," he said. "What would you like to know?"

"Their names for a start. And possibly where they can be found. Oh . . . and well, anything you can tell me about them."

"I've already spilled all this to the police."

"But they'd hardly be likely to share it with me, would they?" She gave him another smile and pulled her diary out of her handbag along with a pencil. With a hopeful look at Mr. Webster, Catherine prepared to write.

"Well, I don't suppose it'll do any harm. I don't know much." Settling back in his chair, Mr. Webster folded his hands over his middle. "Red, now, he's the pianist and the leader. Called Red not because of his hair, but because of his politics. He makes no secret of the fact that he's a Communist. Leads protests all up and down the country at this and that factory." He leaned forward and pulled out a drawer in his desk. "Let's see. I've got his real name on the contract. More of a Toff than you would guess." He pulled out a file and opened it. "Yes, here, I've got it. Alexander de Fontaine."

Catherine wrote in her diary furiously.

"And how did Mr. de Fontaine get along with the others?" she asked.

"No idea. They played their pieces and kept their part of our agreement. The only reason I know so much about Red is that he's in the newspaper regularly, on account of the protest marches. Of course, there's Joe, the black. They tell me he's famous in America, but I had to think a bit before allowing him to play in the hall. Turns out I made the right decision. He's a real draw with that trombone of his. These days the band brings in customers by the cartload, so I've got no problem with Red or Joe."

"I heard Red was a student."

"Oh, they all are, except Joe. They study at St. John's."

"Are the others' names on the contract?" she asked.

"No. I just know them by their nicknames and their instruments."

She stifled her disappointment. "All right. I appreciate any help you can give me."

"There's Tony on the drums. Best drummer I've ever heard, by the way. He's talented. No question about it. Then there's Joe on the trombone and Alfie on the trumpet. If it'd been Alfie who died of an overdose, I could credit it more easily."

"So, he's an addict?"

"I have my suspicions. He's always twitching. Can't hold still."

She looked up from her writing. "I'm certain this will be a help. How does the rest of the band get along with Joe?"

"James came in to complain to me once about him. He and his sax were the band's biggest draw until Joe came along. He referred to him as the 'savage' and the 'nigger.' Wanted me to speak to Red and tell him Joe was bad for business. I refused, of course. It simply wasn't true."

Catherine thought it strange that Emily had failed to mention this.

"But the rest of the band seemed to accept Joe?"

"Musicians are a liberal-thinking lot. I never heard anything from Red about it if there were other problems."

* * *

When she left the Town Hall, musing over what she'd learned, it was time to go shopping for the picnic. The weather continued fine. She took the short walk to the covered market.

As Catherine shopped the market stalls, she was aware of the delicious smells—yeasty baked goods, citrus from Spain, fresh herbs, cheeses from all over the world. She bought a cottage loaf of fresh bread, some Camembert cheese, sliced prosciutto, oranges, and dusky red grapes. She had a breadknife and a cheese knife in her handbag. Harry was bringing the cider, rug, napkins, and mugs.

Looking forward to Harry's bracing company, she walked back the way she had come, past the Town Hall to the Christ Church porter's lodge. The porter knew her by sight.

"Good day, to you, Miss Tregowyn. I'll ring Dr. Bascombe, shall I?" he asked just as he always did.

"If you would be so kind," she replied just as she always did.

Harry joined her presently, dressed for a picnic in dark-colored slacks, a Fair Isle sweater, and a waterproof trench coat. Kissing her on the cheek, he said, "I'm famished."

She held up her shopping bag. "I've got the food. Have you got the rest?"

"I have. And I've been busy as a bee this morning."

Walking south on St. Aldates, they turned into Broad Walk and soon had reached Christ Church Meadows. The trees surrounding it were blazing with the red and gold colors of fall. A few other couples were taking advantage of the still fine weather with their own picnics.

Harry spread out the tartan rug, and they began to assemble the food.

"Oh, wonderful, you brought prosciutto," he said. "And Camembert!" He produced mugs and poured their cider. "So, I found out a bit about the egregious Phillip Westfield."

"Yes?" she asked, laying out the grapes and oranges.

"His roommate in college isn't exactly what you would call a fan. Name of Gerry Sloan."

"Oh?" she prompted as she cut a thick slice of the cottage loaf. "So, you didn't talk to Mr. Westfield himself?"

"Not yet. He's in London for the weekend. Some posh party, Gerry said."

"Bitter? Jealous?"

"More like disgusted. Apparently, Westfield's trying to pass himself off as an aristocrat. He's trying to iron out his Yorkshire accent. Very affected. Out-Toffs the Toffs. But then Gerry's father is a prize-winning journalist and he seems perfectly satisfied with his roots. Phillip makes him crazy with all his affectations."

"I don't blame him. Is Mr. Sloan a scholarship winner?"

"Yes. Studying medicine." Harry spread cheese on his bread and topped it with prosciutto. "He said Phillip loathed his brother whom he considered to have besmirched the family name by becoming a saxophonist. Believes *he* should be the heir. Moaned that his father didn't appreciate him and gave him only a stingy allowance when he could have afforded much more."

"Did this Gerry know very much about the Westfield family?" she asked, sipping her cider.

"Oodles of money, according to Gerry. Father's an industrialist. Coal mines, he thinks, but doesn't know for sure."

"And how has this Phillip reacted to his brother's death?"

"He's cheerful as a lark. Thinking about chucking Oxford and living a life of leisure in London."

"Hmm. That's rather interesting, don't you think?"

"Gerry doesn't know how Westfield's going to take the news that it's murder and not an accident. He left for London last night, so Gerry doesn't know if the bloke's seen the information given out in the paper," said Harry, popping a grape in his mouth.

"So, he doesn't know if the police have questioned him?"

"He says not. They were by to see him this morning. Gerry didn't know the whereabouts of this London 'do,' so his questioning will have to be delayed until he's back at Oxford."

A cool breeze blew over them, and she shivered. "Maybe he's the murderer. Though he doesn't seem to me to be the type that would like to soil his hands with something like that."

"He certainly has a financial motive."

"I really don't understand why the police latched on to Emily Norwood so quickly," Catherine said.

"What was your impression of her?"

"I got the feeling she was keeping something back," she said. "She did give me quite a bit of information, but she didn't tell me everything. It was odd because I felt she was a bit contemptuous of James. That didn't march well with the statement that they were crazy about one another."

"That's very odd," said Harry.

Catherine began peeling an orange. "Definitely. And here's something that will shake your world—there's a black in the band."

"I'd heard that. He's supposed to be sensational. Want to go dancing?"

"I'd love it." The one time she had been dancing with Harry, he had managed to change her antipathy toward him into something much warmer. It had been the beginning of the road to their present happy, if sometimes ambiguous, relationship.

She chewed an orange section. For a moment, they enjoyed their food. Then she said, "I questioned a certain Mr. Webster at the Town Hall."

"Oh? About the band? What did you find out?"

She related the information about the band that she had gained from both Emily and Webster. "According to Mr. Webster, James apparently had a strong antipathy to Joe. He called him a 'nigger' and tried to get him fired."

"That's actually not as surprising as the fact that he's performing at all. Given the feelings arising out of our African colonialism, we Brits definitely treat the blacks as the underclass. But I suppose a Communist band leader wouldn't have those feelings."

"And Mr. Webster said Joe has been good for business. An actual draw."

"Still," said Harry, "I don't see James's slurs as a real motive for murder on Joe's part. It's more interesting that Emily held back about that fact."

"I'd be interested to see what you can dig up by investigating at St. John's."

"And I think Westfield the Younger holds promise as a suspect. But the thing that's occurred to me about this murder is since it hasn't been given out when James Westfield died, no one can have an alibi," said Harry. "I say, Catherine, this bread is first-rate."

"Thank you."

His eyebrow raised, Harry said, "I rather fancy our undercover engagement dancing tonight. It will add a frisson to the occasion." There was a definite twinkle in his eye.

Her heart took off racing. "I wonder if they've found another saxophonist yet."

"They will sound deuced flat without one." Harry snatched up a handful of grass. "Dash it! I wish we knew what the police were thinking. Obviously, they've got evidence we haven't heard about Emily."

Catherine divided her orange into sections and fed one to Harry.

"This Emily must have a pretty face for a chap like William to be bowled over by her."

She scowled and said, "It's not just her face. William's fallen for her because supposedly, their passions about the Kenyan children coincide."

Harry smiled but didn't comment. *Men!* Catherine had an

uncomfortable moment. Was Harry's attraction to *her* based only on her face? The thought made her feel sour.

"Really! Wills has never shown a jot of interest in women before, and we've known some beauties."

"Sisters don't always know what their brothers are thinking." Harry changed his position on the rug and poured himself another mug of cider. "Heard from Rafe lately?" he asked.

She felt a twinge of distress. "What in the world made you think of him?" she asked. "We were speaking of Wills and Emily!"

"I was just thinking last night of all the years you've known and loved him. It must be hard for you to root that experience out of your life."

Her distress grew. "Harry, I can't help that he'll always be part of my memories."

"I remember what you told me about your bond to him—that it was more powerful than your bond with your family. Do you still feel that way?"

She had wondered that herself. How did one erase feelings so strong? Feelings one had had since childhood?

"To be honest, I don't really know. It's hard to write off someone completely when they are such a big part of your life. As long as he's gone, I'm fine. But I suppose I will always worry about him."

Harry began to pack up their picnic. She knew he didn't like talking about Rafe, but it was inevitably he who brought him into the conversation

"Wait! I haven't had any bread and cheese!" she said.

"Well, finish up. I'm going to have a go at my pet sergeant at the police station to try to find out if they've picked up Westfield yet."

"Go ahead," she said, her voice tight in her throat. "I'll just finish up here and take everything away with me."

"You can't juggle the rug and the mugs along with everything else. I'm sorry."

"I'm sorry, too. But you needn't be jealous of Rafe," she said, putting a hand on his knee. "I have my own insecurities, you know. I . . . well, what you said about Emily—it just made me wonder if your attraction to me goes beyond my face."

His bad mood appeared to evaporate as his expression cleared. Throwing back his head, he laughed. "And what about you and your attraction for me?"

She was startled by the question. "I hated you! You disparaged my poetry!"

"Well," he said, "A powerful physical attraction helps things along, but it won't keep things going forever. You sensed how jealous I was of your mind and talent. That's not a very admirable quality in a man. How did you overcome your dislike?"

"You were kind to me," she said instantly. "There is a dimension of respect in our relationship. It wasn't always there, but it is now."

"So. You've answered your own question. I love your beauty. I love looking at you. But there is a lot more to it than that. If that weren't so, I would be running after every beautiful woman I saw, wouldn't I?"

"I didn't think of it that way," she said, quailing at the idea of Harry being a skirt-chaser.

"To bring this back to the problem at hand, I rather think Westfield went about with Emily because of her beauty. But it obviously wasn't enough as he gave her the shove."

"Then don't be so dubious about Wills' feelings."

"I'm sorry. That was low of me. Now. Throw me one of those oranges."

"Move your sorry self and get one on your own. I'm busy making a sandwich." She suited her action to her words.

Chapter Three

Leaving Harry at his college, Catherine walked aimlessly for a while, trying to rid herself of the self-disgust she felt. Intentionally baiting Harry had been a schoolgirl reaction. Why had she done it? Was she that insecure and petty?

Since she had made the monumental discovery that the man she had loved since she was ten was a first-rate cad, she had become unsure of herself and her judgment. She might be intelligent, but she was capable of making a massive mistake in the understanding of character. That had to be the root of these feelings. If so, she had better take hold of herself.

Switching away from her self-centered musings, she wondered if maybe she should pay Emily Norwood another visit. Perhaps she could find out whatever the young woman was holding back.

* * *

"Miss Tregowyn!" Emily greeted her. "Do you have any news?"

"I'm afraid not. Phillip Westfield has gone to London for the weekend, but we don't know where. We're waiting for him to come back. Did your cousin come?"

"Yes. He's arrived with a solicitor in tow. I'm afraid we didn't take to each other much, but at least I have someone looking after my legal rights."

"I'm glad," said Catherine. "He doesn't have to be charming to do his job. My colleague, Dr. Bascombe, and I are going dancing tonight at the Town Hall and hope to make some observations about the band. I was wondering if, after sleeping on it, you might have some more information for me about James Westfield."

Instead of answering this question, the girl said, "Does William think I am a complete twit? He was rather distant last night."

"You have to make allowances for Wills. He doesn't know much about women and how they think."

Emily frowned. "Why is that? He's so handsome I would think he'd had heaps of girlfriends."

Catherine shook her head, smiling. "Nary a one, as far as I know. He's led quite a solitary life. Even as a child. There are reasons, none sinister, but I won't bore you with them. Let Wills tell you when he is ready. Now, is there anything you can think of that you haven't told me about Mr. Westfield?"

Emily studied her square fingernails. Finally, she said, "I've been remembering that he seemed very up and down of late. Moody. Sometimes he was so much fun, and he acted . . . well, like the world was his oyster. He was game for anything. Other times he was in a pure funk." She looked up. "When he ended it with me, he was in the middle of a funk. Then he was killed. I will always wonder if he would have changed his mind when he was feeling better."

Catherine thought for a moment. The warden at Somerville had just had a talk with her faculty about the symptoms Emily was describing. They were to watch for them in their students. They were typical of the cocaine abuser.

"When did you start noticing this behavior?"

"Let me see . . ." the young woman set down her cup and appeared to be casting her thoughts back into the past. "It would have been when the Michaelmas Term started. "What are you thinking?"

"I'm thinking about what you said about Alfie and his cocaine addiction. Could James have been an addict, too? I may be utterly wrong. What do you think, as a nurse?"

Emily put her fingers to her lips in a gesture of alarm. "I guess it's a possibility. I know that it's not unheard of for musicians to dabble."

"Do you think anyone in the band would have had a motive?" Catherine asked.

Catherine could see the shutter coming down over her eyes. She was back to the girl she had been the night before. Hiding something.

The young woman worried a piece of her short hair between her fingers. "I just can't see it," she said. "I think his brother is a more likely suspect. I know they didn't get on. James complained that he was always sponging off of him. And he was very self-righteous. I think he's a more likely murderer. Probably he has some self-justification for what he did and thinks he's above the law."

"My friend, Dr. Bascombe, is a professor at Christ Church and will be looking into the brother when he returns."

Emily put the heel of her hand to her forehead. "That's good. This is all just too awful for words," she said. "I just can't get myself to believe it. And here I am. In jail."

Catherine said, "I'm sorry you have to go through this on top of your grief. We promised Wills we would try to help you. I'll visit you again, I promise."

"Thanks awfully," the young woman said, pulling a handkerchief out of her pocket and wiping her eyes. "William said you solved a murder last summer. Can you tell me about it?"

Thinking it might encourage Emily to confide in her, Catherine spent the rest of her visit discussing the Chenowith murder case. It was a good diversion from thoughts of James Westfield.

* * *

"What do you think, Cherry?" Catherine asked, holding up her black evening dress with the jet beaded bodice.

"Let's have some music," said the maid, flipping on the wireless. While the apparatus warmed up, she took two more dresses out of the wardrobe. "I think this wine color is splendid with your hair," she said. "The black washes you out a bit."

As the strains of "Somebody Loves You" came on the wireless, Cherry began to croon along with it.

Catherine tossed the black dress across the bed and took the wine-colored one from Cherry. It had a graceful line, backless to the waist, then hugging her hips before flaring to the floor. While holding it up to herself, she began swanning about the room, joining Cherry in song. It was grand fun, and Catherine allowed herself to relax a bit, trying to forget the reason behind her date that evening.

"I think this one will do," she told the maid.

"Your voice is something special, miss. You ought to go on stage."

"I think Somerville might have something to say about that!" Catherine said with a laugh.

Nevertheless, when "Living in Clover" started up next, she sang along with the band.

* * *

It was heaven to be dancing in Harry's arms again. She wanted to put her head right down on his shoulder during a slow and smoky jazz tune. The band had added a female singer tonight, possibly to make up for the lack of a saxophone.

As for the trombonist, Joe, Catherine could scarcely keep from staring. He was one of the most handsome men she had ever seen. His smooth coffee-colored face had high cheekbones, a broad forehead, and a manly square jaw. Between sets, he allowed himself a smile—very white and broad in his dark face, with perfect teeth. As Emily had said, he was brilliant on the trombone.

"Joe's good, isn't he?" Catherine asked Harry.

"Marvelous," he agreed, tightening his hold on her trim waist. She enjoyed the feeling he gave her of being petite. At five foot seven, she looked most men in the eye, but Harry was over six feet tall.

"I had a visit with Emily this afternoon," she said, hoping her business-like tone would keep her from giving in to her urge to cuddle.

"Did you learn anything new?"

"Apparently, James was severely moody. From her description, it sounds like he might have been on cocaine. Since the beginning of the term."

He said, "I'm not surprised. I've been observing the band. I think the trumpet player has a habit, too. He's twitchy. Never still, even between numbers."

"Didn't I tell you? Alfie is an addict. In fact, the drummer, Tony, is after him to give it up. His brother died from an overdose." Catherine shifted her attention to Alfie. Unlike Joe's smooth, liquid movements, Alfie was jerky, as though he were trying to rein in a high-spirited horse.

"I took my pet sergeant out for a pint after work today," said Harry. It seems our Emily left something out of her unconvincing narrative," he said. "Unless you also forgot to tell me she visited the victim the day of his death."

Alarmed at the hard tone of his voice, Catherine drew back and looked at his face. "What?"

"She was seen visiting James's flat on Sunday."

Her heart fell, and for a few moments, she was silent. "Oh, dear. I did want to believe her. For Wills' sake."

"It doesn't auger well that she didn't volunteer the information," Harry said, then added, "Look, the band is going on break. This is our opportunity to do a little eavesdropping. Unless I miss my guess, they'll be off for a quick pint at the King's Arms across the street."

They gathered her fur from the coat check and made their way carefully across the High Street. As Harry had surmised, the band was there standing at the bar ordering. Minus Joe.

Once they had their drinks, Red, Alfie, and Tony moved to stand in a little triangle near the back of the pub. Harry ordered a shandy for Catherine and a pint for himself, and they maneuvered through the crowd into a position close to the now boisterous band members.

"Well, I do miss his sax, but I'm not exactly broken up that he's dead," the trumpet player was saying. "Blinking Nazi!"

The drummer gave him a little shove. "You think everyone who doesn't think like you is a Nazi."

"He didn't like Joe because he's a Negro," Alfie said, his raised voice belligerent. "Never mind that he's one of the best jazz trombones there is. It's thanks to James that they won't serve him in this pub."

"So?" said the drummer. "That doesn't make James a Nazi. You want to watch what you're saying. I'm warning you."

"Or what?" demanded the trumpeter. "I'd like to see you take me on."

"Like you took on James?" Tony taunted.

Catherine gave Harry a significant look at this. *Alfie and James had physically fought? Over Joe? Interesting.*

Red said, "Quit your boasting and bellyaching. Drink up. I'm no more fond of this place than Alfie is."

After that, they began talking about their singer that night who had not joined them. "She's good," said Red. "Too bad she has to go off to Liverpool."

"It's a great opportunity for her to sing with Bertini's band."

"Agreed," said Red. "But we still need a sax. Can't be a dance band these days without a sax."

They threw about a couple of names.

Catherine, full of sudden daring, cast a look toward Harry. "Watch this!" she said.

Walking over to the band, she said, "Excuse me, but we were just over there, and I couldn't help but hear about your singer dilemma. I'm called Cat. I can sing for you. I know all the tunes. It would only be temporary, of course. Maybe one or two weekends at the most."

"You're very bold," said Red. "What makes you think you can sing?"

She held her fisted hand up to her lips as though it were a microphone. Emitting the warmest, most syrupy tone she could manage, she pretended she was still fooling around with Cherry and sang:

"Living in clover,
Spilling all over
With love."

Red's skeptical face softened with admiration. "How about you take over for Gertie for one number when we get back? We'll give it a go, Cat."

She smiled with a radiance she could feel brimming up inside her. She'd done it! Wouldn't Cherry be proud?

"Finish up, lads," said Red. In moments they had drained their pints and headed back to their gig.

"That was interesting," said Harry when they had gone. "My dear girl, I had no idea you could sing like that!"

"You know I sing in the college choir."

He laughed. "You didn't sound like a choir girl believe me!"

"Cherry thinks I'm rather good. I think I can pull it off. And it will give me a chance to sleuth. And see something of how Joe interacts with the others. I imagine there'll be a practice or two."

"You're marvelous!" he said. Leaning towards her he kissed her on the lips.

"I think we've heard evidence that not all is happy between the boys in the band," said Catherine, her voice husky. "But we already knew that."

"Let's make our way over for your audition."

"Then more dancing?" she asked.

"Oh, yes," he said. "We haven't had our Tango yet."

* * *

When she ascended to the dais for her audition, Catherine's knees were knocking, but she managed a confident smile as she took the microphone. The band struck up "Living in Clover," and she began swaying her hips. When Red pointed to her, she began singing.

It was as though she had been doing it for years. The music poured out of her like warm honey. Looking down at Harry's face, she saw surprise and a wide smile of admiration. The room danced to the tune, appearing to be unaware that she was a neophyte.

She could do this!

When she was finished, Gertie smoothly took the microphone from her, and the band began playing "Good Night Deanna." Catherine walked down to join Harry.

"You were fabulous," he said. "I can't wait for next Friday!"

"I don't know if I've got the job yet."

"You've got it, believe me," he insisted. "Let's dance."

At one a.m., while the rest of the band packed up, Red came over to her, saying, "Have you done this before?"

"No, I promise you. But I can sing, and I love the tunes."

"Well, you have a job, Cat. If you can give us two weekends, we should be able to locate a sax or another singer by then. Rehearsal here on Wednesday night. Six o'clock. We have to get it in before the lecture series. Something about goats this week."

"I promise I'll be prompt," Catherine told him.

She and Harry headed for Carmichael's for champagne and oysters to celebrate.

"So that's all fixed up," she said with satisfaction. "Rehearsal on Wednesday night. We'll be listening to the wireless constantly at the flat, and Cherry will be my coach until then."

"How unexpected you are!" he said happily as their oysters arrived.

Carmichael's was a smoky restaurant with a low ceiling, a fireplace, lit by paper lanterns. It contrived an intimate atmosphere that Catherine enjoyed.

It would be so easy to let her barriers down with Harry. But she had once trusted too easily. That wasn't going to happen this time. Luckily, they had this mystery to investigate. Who knew what other strange paths it would take them down?

"This has been a lovely evening," she said. "Especially the Tango."

"You were at your most seductive, Señorita."

"I took my cue from you," she said with a little smile.

"It has definitely been too long since we've been dancing, but next weekend will be all work for you."

"I only hope it proves to be worth it," Catherine said. "Now tell me what you think about this business with Joe."

"I think Negroes frighten people because they look so obviously different. We English are terribly insular and feel so above anyone else. And while it's true that our civilization is more advanced than present-day African societies, people tend to forget that Egypt was the first great civilization in our hemisphere, and it existed for thousands of years."

"How do Americans behave toward blacks?"

"Superior. Why do you think slavery was tolerated there for so many years? Everything is segregated there. Restaurants, WC's, buses, schools, the military. In fact, the only things that aren't segregated are jazz bands. And, in that respect, black jazz musicians are considered the founders of jazz. They've made a breakthrough there. But even though their musicians are famous, they're still discriminated against in every other way, just like Joe is here."

"I wonder where he lives, then," mused Catherine.

"I'll be willing to bet he has a fair-minded flatmate who doesn't let his landlord know Joe is living there with him."

"It's a wonder the police haven't arrested him for James's murder, then," Catherine said.

"Perhaps that's what Emily's afraid of. Perhaps she's holding back evidence that may tell against him," said Harry thoughtfully.

"She lights up when she talks about Joe."

"There you have it, then," said Harry. Catherine detected a weariness in his voice.

"Do you think it's possible he's the killer?"

"We don't know anything about him yet. But he's a suspect."

Catherine sobered. "I don't like this case."

"There is always the brother, Phillip," said Harry. "And probably other suspects we've never encountered yet."

"But James's defining passion was the jazz band."

"As far as we know. He may have had a passion for another woman, and that's the reason he gave Emily the push. And there's the whole cocaine issue."

"I suppose that's true enough." She gave a prodigious yawn. "I suggest we call it a night. Remember, in my other life, I sing in the choir at eleven a.m. I can't sway when I do that."

Chapter Four

Nine o'clock came early the following morning. Cherry woke her with her tea.

"You came in very late, miss," she said.

Catherine stretched, putting her hands above her head. "I had a lovely evening." She sat up in bed and took the tray on her lap. "We have our work cut out for us. I took your advice, and I'm going on stage."

At Cherry's startled look, she said, "Only temporarily. Two weekends at most. It's part of the investigation. I'm going to sing with James Westfield's band. You have only a couple of days to bring me up to snuff."

"We'll manage, miss. What fun!"

"Now, it's off to sing in the choir."

After her tea, she took a warm bath and dressed in her navy wool suit and an ice blue silk blouse. Once she was at the church, she would don her black choir robe.

She and Cherry walked to the Somerville College chapel. It was newly built, with a white interior and a modern stained-glass window. Making her way into her choir seat, she shivered as she always did when she remembered discovering Dr. Chenowith's strangled body under these very seats.

Before long, however, she was lost in the music she loved.

Singing in this choir every Sunday was an unexpected bonus to her employment by the college. There was something very cleansing and renewing about swelling her voice and heart in song and participating in this lovely blend of voices. "Nightclub singing," was going to be altogether different, that was certain.

The homily that morning was taken from Philippians, Chapter Four. She listened to the vicar's sermon on Paul's finding joy and strength in prison as she cast her eyes over the students sitting below in the well of the chapel's nave. She paused at the sight of Miss Beryl Favringham, one of the four students she tutored on Tuesdays, which jerked her out of her preoccupation. The girl was clearly upset, wiping her reddened eyes and shaking in silent sobs.

The comely blonde Miss Favringham had invited her to sit with her at Sunday dinner in the hall today to meet her father, Baron Favringham. The last Catherine had seen of the girl; she had been happy and enthusiastic about a tennis match. Her father had been coming up from London on Saturday to watch her play. The girl was something of a tennis champion and had hopes of playing in the Olympics. Catherine had no idea what kind of event could cause the girl to become so publicly upset.

As the service continued with a congregational hymn, she watched Miss Favringham master her emotions. She didn't see any sign of her father here in church. Catherine thought of her friend and former scout, Jennie. The college servant had helped her in her last investigation. Though Catherine didn't live at college now, she still kept the rooms allocated her. It was there that she worked and held her tutorials. Maybe Jennie would mention Miss Favringham to her. Catherine didn't want to pry, but she couldn't help wondering if there was something she could do. Scouts knew everything.

After the choir sang the closing hymn, the congregation rose. Catherine went to the vestry, where she disrobed and met Cherry. Her maid took the robe from her.

"Did you see Jennie today?" Catherine asked. The scout and Cherry were friends.

"No. I didn't," said Cherry. "I hope she's not ill. Perhaps I'll call on her this afternoon."

Sunday was Cherry's half day.

"Take her my best wishes."

* * *

When Catherine joined Miss Favringham and her father, the Baron, she couldn't detect any trace of tears on the girl's cheeks; however her eyelids were a bit swollen over her too bright blue eyes.

"Miss Tregowyn!" the girl said. "I would like to present my father, Baron Favringham. Father, this is my tutor, Miss Tregowyn."

"Yes, my dear lady," said the baron. "I have been so wanting to meet you. You have awakened my daughter's mind!"

His enthusiasm was welcome to Catherine. "She stimulates my mind, as well. I think you have a budding poet here."

They sat on either side of her at the long table.

"I am so pleased," he said. He began to recite:

> *Do not forget that 'limpet' rhymes*
> *With 'strumpet' in these troubled times,*
> *And commas are the worst of crimes;*
> *Few understand the works of Cummings,*
> *And few James Joyce's mental slummings,*
> *And few young Auden's coded chatter;*
> *But then it is the few that matter.*

Catherine was puzzled. He was obviously quoting a modern poem, but not one she knew. Was it possible the baron was an aspiring poet?

"I'm afraid you have the advantage of me, Baron. I don't know the poem or the poet."

The baron beamed, and Miss Favringham said, "He's Father's new pet, Dylan Thomas."

The baron said, "He's not published yet. A friend of mine, Pamela Hansford Johnson, sent me that. It tickled me."

"She's also sent us other, more serious poems," said Miss Favringham. "He writes a bit too much about death for my taste."

"Poets are often obsessed with their own mortality," said Catherine. "They seem to lack that bulwark that most of us use to keep such ideas at bay."

"I think we will all hear of this youngster before he is finished. He's out of Wales."

"I will keep my ear tuned," said Catherine with a laugh.

"I enjoy your poetry very much," the baron said with the air of bestowing a great prize.

"Thank you," Catherine said. She never knew quite how to respond to praise of her work. "Has your daughter showed you any of her poems?"

"She has promised to eventually. I think she is a bit shy of me. And we have been entirely caught up in her tennis. But now that the match is over, we shall move on to other things."

"I lost," said the girl, pulling a face.

The server set steaming plates of roast beef and Yorkshire pudding before them.

"I'm sorry to hear it," said Catherine. *Surely that can't be the reason she was crying. She's always seemed so sensible.* "I'm sure you'll be back in top form soon. You are so dedicated."

"One must be," the baron declared firmly against the rising swell of female voices, "If one is going to achieve anything."

Miss Favringham rolled her eyes. "I've been hearing that all my life," she said. "Give it a rest, Father."

The baron began to eat as though he hadn't seen food in a year. He was a portly gent, slightly balding, with his daughter's bright blue eyes.

"Your home is in Yorkshire, I believe?" asked Catherine.

"It is," he said. "Though when Parliament is in session, I spend a good bit of time in London. I come up to Oxford often to see my daughter."

"Father is my tennis instructor," the girl said. "And, of course, he has to check up on me. Make certain I haven't kicked over the traces."

"She's one of my steadier students," Catherine assured the baron. "Always prepared, always insightful."

"I'm glad to hear it. We've had some bad patches lately, but hopefully that is in the past," he said.

As she heard those words, Catherine concluded that the Baron was a hovering parent of the worst sort. They could be the bane of a child's existence. Not to mention the child's tutors. She hoped it wasn't he who had driven his daughter to tears.

Miss Favringham was quiet, cutting up her beef and pushing it about on her plate.

Catherine sought to keep the baron's attention off his daughter.

"Besides this Mr. Thomas, who is your favorite modern poet?" she asked him.

"I am very fond of T.S. Eliot. He takes my mind such interesting places. He is a Brit at heart, I think, having immigrated here before the war."

"Yes. I am quite fond of him myself. I also like E.E. Cummings, though he is also an American and doesn't pretend anything else. 'Somewhere I Have Never Traveled' is a favorite of mine."

The baron looked into the middle distance and then, with a flash of drama, against the din of the dining hall, he quoted:

> *"somewhere i have never traveled, gladly beyond*
> *any experience, your eyes have their silence.*
> *in your most frail gesture are things which enclose me,*
> *or which I cannot touch because they are too near"*

"How splendid!" she said. "We should have a poetry reading where you can perform Cummings. You do it perfectly!"

"I would be honored," he said.

"I'll see what I can arrange."

She initiated a discussion of other modern poets and kept the baron's eyes off his daughter's plate.

After a splendid trifle for pudding, the diners enjoyed a cup of coffee. Miss Favringham entered the conversation once more.

"I'm very glad I came to Somerville," she said. "I wasn't sure about it, at first. But I did so want to come to Oxford."

"What were you unsure about?" Catherine asked.

"The mountains of work. I didn't know if I could stick it. But now I quite enjoy it."

"I'm glad," said Catherine. "Your work is quite good."

"Now that you're over your bad patch . . ." the baron started when his daughter interrupted, "Not that again, Father."

"Just so," he concluded. "Well, I'm afraid I must get back down to London. The baroness is arriving on the late afternoon train. Coming to London for shopping."

They stood.

"It was delightful to meet you, Baron," Catherine said, shaking his hand. "I so enjoy having your daughter to work with. I'll be in touch through her about the poetry reading."

After praise of her tutoring, he left Catherine alone with her student. Miss Favringham said, "Pay no attention to Father. I don't."

Catherine smiled kindly. "I'm certain he wants the best for you. Are you his only child?"

"Unfortunately. All his hopes and dreams are centered on me."

"I imagine you find that a bit of a weight," Catherine said.

"Oh, I stagger under it. But fortunately, he is also always there to pick me up."

"I'm available, as well, if you find you need to talk," said Catherine, rooting about in her clutch bag for her visiting card.

"Thank you. I will remember that," Miss Favringham said as Catherine wrote her telephone number on the card and handed it to her.

Catherine hoped she would. It had disturbed her to see the girl crying.

* * *

She was dabbing at a poem she had been reworking when Cherry returned that evening.

"Did you have a good day?" she asked her maid.

"Oh, yes. I went to the pictures. It was lovely. And I talked to Jennie. She has a head cold."

"Bother for her," said Catherine. "I hope she gets over it soon."

There came a brisk knock on the door. Cherry went to answer it while Catherine ran a comb through her hair and freshened her lipstick.

"It's Mr. Tregowyn, miss," Cherry told her.

Catherine hastened into her black and white sitting room, "Wills! Come by for a report, have you?"

"I heard you've taken up jazz singing," he said, his eyes sparkling with mischief. "With Westfield's band, no less."

"Well, you know how I love to sing. I might as well do a little investigating while I'm at it."

"I didn't realize you had quite so much daring! As a matter of fact, the chap who told me said you were rather good."

"I'm glad to hear it. It was a bit nerve-wracking to tell you the truth. I didn't know if I could pull it off, but it seemed worth a try."

She sat on her black leather sofa and patted the place next to her for Wills to sit. "Come, tell me if you have any idea what Emily saw in Mr. Westfield."

"Aside from his matinee idol looks, I haven't a clue. I have figured out that Emily's the sort of woman who likes to be needed, but I can't for the life of me decide exactly how he needed her," Wills said with a scowl.

"Hmm. Interesting. That makes sense given her choice of profession."

He leaned forward, his elbows on his knees. Can you really see a person like that murdering Westfield?"

"Not under ordinary circumstances. But maybe the circumstances were extraordinary for some reason," Catherine said.

"I thought you were on her side!" he said, furrowing his brow in anger.

She put a hand on his shoulder. Though she was reluctant, it had to be said. "Wills, there's something you should know."

"What?" he demanded.

"The police have a witness who saw her go into James's flat on the Sunday he was killed."

Wills leaped up from the sofa as though he had been scalded. "Impossible!"

"So, you didn't know? She hasn't told you?"

"Of course not. I would have told you if I'd known anything like that." He began pacing her carpet.

"I haven't decided if we should confront her about this," said Catherine, hurting for her brother. Did he feel betrayed? "What do you think? I imagine that's why the police think she might have done it."

"It's just circumstantial," he said. "She must have had a good reason. Maybe he was already dead when she got there. I think we should ask her about it."

Wills went to her drinks tray and poured himself a whiskey. "I don't know why she hasn't said anything," he said. "And I also don't know how she expects us to help her if she doesn't tell us everything."

Catherine was glad he was taking that attitude. If she were going to help Emily, they had to face the realities of the situation. Blind devotion on her brother's part wouldn't help.

"I still believe she's innocent," he said. "But it seems to me it must be less straightforward than we thought."

"It would be a great mistake to adopt the notion that the police are fools," she said gently. "Come, sit down, Wills. Your pacing is making me dizzy. How is your work coming?"

They discussed the latest experiment Wills was conducting at his lab. Catherine pretended to understand, though his ideas were in a realm totally foreign to her way of thinking.

"I'm convinced that water purification in the Kenyan villages can be a simple matter if we just discover the right chemistry and delivery system to bring it about," he said in summary. Now that she had gotten him on the topic of his work, he seemed more relaxed. He chattered along earnestly for a good twenty minutes before rising to leave.

"When shall you talk to Em?" he asked at the door.

"It will have to be tomorrow night. Remember, we can only visit one at a time. And one visitor per day. You and I could have a pub dinner first, and then I could go 'round to see her."

"She doesn't want us to know whatever it is she's hiding. I'll let you know about dinner," he said, gloom darkening his brow once again. "I may be working."

"Try not to worry too much," she said, her hand on his sleeve. "We're doing all we can, Wills."

"I know you are, Kitty." He kissed her cheek.

His use of her childhood name warmed her. He hadn't called her Kitty in many years. Maybe working together to help Emily would bring them closer together as brother and sister. They had both tended to go their own way before now. Since childhood, they had each fought their very real need to lean on another person.

But she had allowed herself to lean on Rafe, hadn't she? And that had proved a big mistake.

Chapter Five

Monday morning, Catherine knew must be spent in reading her student's essays on the influence of the Great War on poetry. She settled with a cup of tea at her desk in the sitting room and got to work.

Generally, she was impressed with her students' writing. Her Tuesday group were all in their first year, and their talents were varied. Miss Favringham's essay was surprisingly superficial and poorly executed. This was unusual. Especially with such a meaty subject.

Had the girl been putting all her time into tennis in preparation for her match last Saturday? But what about the evenings? Was she too tired? Or was this all part of whatever had made her break down at Sunday services?

She wondered if Miss Favringham had a young man. That could surely be the problem and the reason for her "rough patch." She would have to ask Jennie.

After Catherine had read all the essays, made notes for the tutorial for tomorrow, and had cheese and a bun for lunch, it was time for Cherry's French lesson. They had begun the lessons at Cherry's request when they had moved up to Oxford. Catherine knew her maid to be intelligent and quick but was still surprised at how well she was doing. The maid was preparing for their next journey to the South of France over the Christmas holidays. Catherine now had hopes that Wills might join them.

The French lesson went well. After they had finished, Cherry lingered, clearly wanting to speak to her. Finally, Catherine asked, "Were you wanting something, Cherry?"

"It's a personal question, miss. One I have been wondering about for a long time."

She gave her maid a half-smile. "Out with it." Cherry had never contented herself with the post of lady's maid. She was too egalitarian, which was unusual, for she came from a long line of house servants. And the truth of the matter was, Catherine had indulged her. Her mother would never approve.

"Why do we never go to your family in Cornwall for Christmas?" the maid asked.

Catherine frowned. "You're right. That is a personal question. I'm going to exercise my prerogative as your employer and not answer it."

Cherry pursed her lips. "All right then. I had to try."

"I'm out for dinner tonight," Catherine said. "You may have the evening off if you like."

* * *

Late afternoon found Catherine searching out Jennie at Somerville. She started in the scout's retiring room, where Mary, another scout, told her Jennie had gone home to nurse her cold. As Jennie was not on the telephone, and Catherine did not wish to disturb her at home, she knew her question about Miss Favringham would have to wait.

It looked like rain, but she needed to be out of the flat for a bit, so she decided upon a walk to the iconic Blackwell's Book Shop with her umbrella securely tucked under her arm. Once she was in the bookstore, which had its merchandise crowded everywhere except on the ceiling, she headed downstairs to the underground labyrinth, where the poetry books were.

There was a healthy selection, and she took her time prowling among the new authors, where her own book appeared. Her new one would be out at Christmastime. She felt butterflies at the thought of another round of reviews. Would it be well-received?

The time between submitting her final manuscript and publication was always filled with anxiety. Everything was out of her hands. She hated waiting on something so personal.

Would Harry like it better than her first one?

He had confessed to her recently that the antipathy between them over her earlier *Life of Edith Penwyth* had colored his view of her poetry. The Life had been written while she was still an undergraduate. She had strayed onto his turf and scooped him with information to which he had not had access.

Her academic success and her first book of poems had paved the way for her present post. However, Catherine had to earn her post-graduate degree in a distinguished fashion over the next three years to secure it. It was time she decided on a subject for her dissertation.

Pulling out an occasional book by a poet who was new to her, she leafed through them idly and then put them back. They weren't unique enough to hold her interest.

She had just come upon one which piqued her curiosity when she felt a tap on her shoulder. Startled, she turned around and found herself looking into the blue eyes of the drummer for her new band. He was dressed in the black mortarboard cap and gown of a student.

"Cat? Hello, again," he said, thrusting out his hand. "I'm Anthony Bridgegate—Tony, the drummer."

"Yes, I recognized you," Catherine said. "How good of you to say hello."

"Most singers I know don't patronize Blackwell's," he said.

"Nor do most drummers," she said, laughing. "I'm actually a tutor and lecturer at Somerville."

His expression changed to one of respect. "And I'm at St. John's. Studying music. What's your specialty?" he asked.

"Modern British Lit.," she said.

He chuckled. He was a very good-looking young man. His hair was dark, his features regular, and his eyes sky blue fringed with heavy black lashes. "Bit of a change from James Joyce, your singing with a band."

"It's one of those things I've always wanted to do, like dying my hair red or something."

"You're a natural performer. Care for a cuppa?"

She couldn't pass up the chance to see what the drummer had to say. "Let me just purchase this book, and then that would be lovely."

They adjourned to a tea shop around the corner on Parks Road, featuring indoor plants on the sills and tables. It had the feeling of a greenhouse. Rain had just begun to sluice down outside, lending coziness to the atmosphere. Tony ordered not only tea but a plate of pastries, of which she was only happy to partake. The cherry tart melted in her mouth.

"You're very good at drums," she said. "When did you start playing?"

"When I was a little fellow. Mum's saucepans." Though his laugh was easy, she detected signs of strain on his face. When it was at rest, there was a crease between his brows, and his eyes looked as though they were set in deep hollows. She remembered what Emily had said about Tony. He had a brother who had died of a cocaine overdose.

"What happened to your saxophonist? Did he go with another band?" she asked ingenuously.

His brow lowered. "No. He was killed. You must have read about it in the *Mail*."

"Oh! Sorry. I didn't make the connection. How dreadful for you."

"Yes. We were mates. I was the one who recruited him for the band."

Catherine noticed that the young man had a West Country

burr to his speech differentiating him from most Oxford students, even Red, the bandleader. He was not quite out of the top drawer.

"The newspaper said he was a student at St. John's, as I recall."

"Post-grad. Just to pass the time. The sax was his real love. But his dad held the purse strings, so he had to do something else to show he was serious-minded. Not that he wasn't smart as a whip. He was."

"I'm sorry," she said. "It must be painful to talk about."

"Well, you probably need to know. Since you'll be singing with us."

"Was there a girlfriend or anyone like that?" she asked, hoping the question sounded off-hand enough.

A palpable veil descended between them immediately. "Emily, the one who has been arrested, was never a serious interest," he said, standing suddenly. "Other than that, I won't say. Finish the pastries. I'll see you on Wednesday."

He was gone before she could even reply. *Won't say*. Not *can't say*. Was there someone other than Emily then? Someone who had caused him to break things off with the nurse? And if so, what was preventing Tony from bringing it up? And why was he suddenly in such a hurry to be gone?

She stood and watched the rain which had not abated. Sighing, she looked at her watch. Time to go home and get ready for dinner with Wills.

* * *

Her brother came for her at seven o'clock, and because it was still raining, they taxied together to a restaurant on the first floor of a building overlooking the High.

She told Wills about her encounter with Tony at Blackwell's and their strange tea together. "He grew very uncomfortable and left in a hurry. There was something he was not telling me, either about Emily or someone else entirely. What I can't figure out is why."

"It sounds like he was trying to divert attention from Emily. Perhaps he has a soft spot for her? And doesn't want her to be a suspect? Or . . . hold on! Maybe he doesn't want you to know, but he has more than a soft spot. Maybe it's a passion, and he ended up killing James because of it. Emily doesn't want him suspected, so she doesn't tell us that it was really her who broke up the relationship. Because of Tony."

"I say, Wills. You're getting the hang of this! That's brilliant. I can ask a few leading questions tonight and see what Emily's reaction is."

He frowned suddenly. "It's not right to set her up like this."

"Wills! She's been arrested! We're trying to get her released. I also need to find out what time she visited the victim. Maybe someone saw him alive after that."

With this cheerful thought, they both tackled their excellent steak and potatoes.

* * *

Emily looked wary when Catherine was shown into the interrogation room to see her.

"How are you coping?" Catherine asked the young woman.

"Today was hard," Emily admitted. "There's nothing to do to take my mind off James. I spend most of my time staring into space, going round and round. First, I'm unable to believe he's dead, and then I wonder who could have killed him. I keep being surprised by the fact that the police think it was me."

"About that," said Catherine. "You left a little something out of your account. You didn't tell us that you went to see James the day he was killed."

The girl hung her head. "I didn't want William to know."

"I don't need to tell you that that's most likely one of the reasons they've locked you up. Can you tell me what time it was when you went to see him?"

"Early afternoon. Around 1:00, I think."

"Can you tell me why you went there?"

"I'd rather not," she said.

"Is that what you told the police?"

"Yes." Her eyes went to the detective sergeant, who sat in the corner, taking notes.

"You realize I can't help you if you don't level with me."

"It has nothing to do with the murder, and James was alive when I left."

Catherine sat back in her chair and looked at the girl's bowed head. She hadn't been wrong. There was something the girl was keeping back. Was she protecting someone?

"It might help us if you told me more about him," said Catherine. "You seem something of an odd couple to me."

Emily looked up and swallowed before she began. "I met James at the Infirmary when he came in for surgery. He had an emergency appendectomy. He was there for a week. Tony was the only one who came to visit him, so I tried to keep his spirits up. You'd be surprised how many patients connect with their nurses. That was last summer."

"And he looked you up when he got out of the Infirmary?" Catherine guessed.

"Yes. This was all before Tony convinced him to join the band. James had a motor, and we used to go down to London to the jazz clubs. We danced."

Emily's account seemed nothing more than a remote recital to Catherine.

"After he started with the band, I found out how terrific he was on the saxophone. I used to go with my flatmates to hear him. Pretty soon, I became absorbed with the band. I spent all my free time with them. We would go out to the pub and talk."

"But what about Joe?" Catherine couldn't help asking.

"The Eagle and Child is high-minded. The pub owner is a fan of Joe's. We spent a lot of time there—all of us together."

"From something I heard Tony say last Saturday, James and Joe didn't get along."

"Oh." Emily's eyes slid away from Catherine and focused on the empty wall. "Well, I don't know what you heard, but though they weren't exactly best mates, they got along all right."

Catherine knew this wasn't true. "Tell me more about Tony," she prodded.

Her eyes came back to Catherine's, and she actually smiled. "Well, they *were* best mates. I think it was because they were both from wealthy middle-class families, and they each rather had a chip on their shoulders about it. Especially about their accents. James confided that most of the other students found him vulgar, and that made him more so. He threw money around like water. But being members of a jazz band gave them a bit of cachet. Red and Alfie are from the gentry."

"I can't even imagine how Joe would feel," Catherine said.

Emily frowned but said nothing. Catherine thought that perhaps now she understood the girl's attraction to playboy James. She fancied society had misused him, and she was a young woman with a tender heart looking for a cause.

"And you still won't tell me why you went to see James on Sunday," Catherine said.

"No." She pressed her lips together as though she were fastening them.

"Well, hopefully, I'll know more about the band members after Wednesday. I'm undertaking a clandestine operation," said Catherine.

"What do you mean?" asked Emily.

Catherine told her about singing with the band.

The account of her hiring surprised Emily into a giggle. "You are brave! I could never in a million years do anything like that!"

Now that Emily's mood was somewhat lightened, Catherine didn't mind leaving her. She looked at her watch.

"Oh! I must be on my way. I have a tutorial tomorrow and a lecture on Wednesday. Wills sends his regards."

All in all, she hadn't learned much.

* * *

Tuesday morning, she went early to her rooms at Somerville, hoping to catch Jennie. She felt a bit guilty seeking out gossip, but Miss Favringham's studies were being affected by whatever was going on in her personal life.

The scout was setting up Catherine's sitting room for her tutorial when she arrived.

"Jennie! Just the person I need to see."

"Always lovely to see you, miss."

"The room looks spiffing. Thank you." She bade the scout be seated for a moment. "There is something I wanted to ask you, as a matter of fact. "Do you do for Miss Favringham?"

"That'd be Mary, miss."

"Has Mary said anything about her? Her work was not quite up to snuff this week. It's not like her. I wondered if there was something I should know."

"I think her young man is giving her a bit of trouble, miss. Mary said how she put his photo away in a drawer. She is usually such a lively thing, laughing and joking with her friends. But she has been that solemn. Like all the stuffing got knocked right out of her."

"Well, I'm sorry to hear it. I'll go easy on her today, and maybe just have a word with her afterward."

First, Emily, and now Miss Favringham. Oh! The dramas we women endure, all on account of men! Catherine thought back to last summer when she had been embroiled in drama over Rafe. Could she say anything to help Miss Favringham? No. It wouldn't do to let her know others had been gossiping about her.

The tutorial was rough going, because Miss Favringham seemed to be elsewhere, and the other three girls were well aware of it. Their discussion never really got off the ground, which was a pity because the topic of the War's influence on literature was an especially fertile one.

At the end of the ninety minutes, she said, "Well, I think we've barely scraped the surface of this topic today. I'm going to give you another week, and I expect you to be better prepared next time. I would like you each to take a particular poet writing during or immediately after the Great War and prepare a paper on him. Come prepared to participate more actively with comments about your chosen poet next Tuesday. You may leave your papers with me now."

The girls all filed out, Miss Favringham being the first to go. Shrugging her shoulders, Catherine collected the papers from the round table she used for her tutorials. Paging through them briefly, she saw that the troubled girl's was shorter than usual. Shorter than required. If this continued, she was going to have to have what would be an awkward conversation with the young woman.

Spending the rest of the morning concluding her preparation for her lecture the next day on Rupert Brooke, the handsome young war poet who always captured the women's attention, Catherine took lunch in the hall. As she watched the excited chatter among the students, she thought how sad it was that Miss Favringham had withdrawn. She wasn't at luncheon. Where did Catherine's duty lie as a tutor? Was she strictly an academic counselor? As such, she could only intervene if it was a matter of academic consequence. She had best read the essay first and then call the student in for a visit on those grounds.

When she went back upstairs to her rooms, she separated Miss Favringham's paper and sat down to concentrate on it. It showed no trace of the original thought which she had come to expect from the young woman. It parroted other people's opinions and those sparsely. There was more about how horrible the war was than about how the war had affected the art of poetry.

After weighing the pros and cons of confrontation, Catherine finally rang the hall where Miss Favringham had her rooms and asked to speak to her. She wasn't in. Sighing deeply, Catherine replaced the receiver on the hook and went back to Rupert Brooke.

Chapter Six

Harry called her office that afternoon with big news. According to his friendly sergeant, with whom he had shared a pub lunch, Emily had been released from jail, and William had been brought into the station that morning for questioning. They intended to hold him for twenty-four hours, at least.

Her heart threatened to leap from her chest. "What! But why?"

"It might have something to do with the fact that he told the police last night that Emily couldn't have killed Westfield Sunday afternoon because he, William, visited him later, finding him very much alive. And though William has never mentioned the meeting, he hasn't exactly made a secret about what he thought of the deceased," said Harry.

"Do you think I ought to call our solicitor?" she asked.

"I think this is just a fishing expedition."

"All the same, I don't like it," she said. "I hope my parents don't come to hear of it."

"I didn't imagine that you would. I'm sorry to be the one to tell you, but I knew you would want to know as soon as possible."

"I am going to see Detective Chief Inspector Marsh and ask him what he thinks he's about."

"I'm sure that won't come as any surprise to him."

Catherine tried to calm down. She asked, "Did the sergeant mention any other suspects?"

"No. So far, it's just Phillip Westfield, who didn't show up for his lecture today. And the members of the band, of course."

She told him about meeting with Emily the night before. "I don't think she's nearly as broken up as she should be in the circumstances, and she flatly refused to tell me why she'd gone to see Mr. Westfield the day he died."

"Not good," he said.

"I agree. I also ran into a member of the band—Tony. Oh, and by the way, Emily says Tony and James were particular friends. Tony told me that there was no woman important in Mr. Westfield's life. He was quite uncomfortable about the whole idea, however. Wills seems to think it was Tony that Emily was thick with, and James found out and was jealous."

"That's rather convoluted," Harry said.

"It could be true, I suppose. It could be Tony she's protecting."

Harry asked, "Are you going to see your brother this afternoon?"

"I am," she said. "And the Detective Chief Inspector." She could almost feel the steam shooting out of her ears at the prospect.

"Stop by the college afterward, and I'll take you to dinner."

"I will. Thanks for letting me know about Wills."

"You're welcome. I'll see you later."

* * *

All Catherine could do was pace her small office. She had scarcely ever been so unnerved. Until this murder and the danger to Emily, she and her brother had not been particularly close. He was older, and they had each spent their formative years at separate boarding schools. When he came home for the hols, he had brought Rafe. It was Rafe she had been close to, not Wills who was quiet and self-contained. Rafe had been full of fun and adventure.

Her parents had lost their firstborn, Michael, to polio when she and Wills were just babies. It was her and Wills' theory that this loss had so affected their parents that they were afraid to risk an emotional bond with their younger children. Their home was a shrine to Michael. Every time Wills or Catherine had a birthday, the parents had always said, "Michael would have been seventeen years old" or "Michael would be taking his A levels." "Michael would be going to Oxford." "Michael would have had his Rugger Blue." She and Wills had lived in the shadow of the imagined life of an older brother they couldn't even remember.

She didn't want to blame her parents. They continued to be devastated by their loss. But, like Wills, she had learned to be very self-contained and self-sufficient, aside from her closeness with Rafe. The latter strategy had ended badly only last summer.

Now she felt like she was making some progress in her relationship with her brother. She certainly wasn't going to let the police trump up some case against him. She knew that the Detective Chief Inspector was capable of going off half-cocked. He had certainly started his investigation into Agatha Chenowith's death wrong by accusing her and Harry last summer merely because they had discovered the body.

She had worked herself up into such a lather; she couldn't stay away any longer. Leaving her office, she went back to her flat. Cherry was out at the market, according to the note she had left. Catherine changed into her sober navy suit with a white blouse and her red and blue striped tie. She covered her waved hair with a red cloche hat. There. She looked reasonably serious. Wearing her walking shoes, she began to walk quickly down to the police station.

It was a gloomy afternoon. She didn't enjoy the journey down St. Giles and the Cornmarket the way she usually did. Not only was she angry, but she had misjudged the weather and failed to wear her fur coat. She was cold.

Finally arriving at the Town Hall, she asked the sergeant at the

53

desk to see Chief Detective Inspector Marsh. Apparently, he was finished with Wills, for he came out to greet her.

"Miss Tregowyn! I expected you. Come back to my office. It's better suited for fireworks."

Once the door was closed to the policeman's office, she wasted no time. "How could you possibly suspect my brother?"

"I am under no obligation to discuss this case with you, Miss Tregowyn. Let us say that certain evidence led us to suspect a man with a violent dislike of Mr. Westfield."

"Violent? You think Wills is violent? He's studying to be a pathologist, for heaven's sake!"

"He is in love with Mr. Westfield's girl. Mr. Westfield treated her badly. Your brother's knuckles are still bruised from their fight."

Catherine's eyes grew large as she clenched her teeth to keep her jaw from dropping. "How do you know they fought? That doesn't even sound like Wills!"

"I don't need to tell you that, Miss Tregowyn," he said. She could tell he was very pleased with himself.

Anxiety clutched at her stomach. "Are you holding him?"

"I'm afraid we are. We have other evidence, you see. I would advise you to get him a good solicitor."

"Have you arrested him?"

"No. We are just holding him for questioning. As I'm sure you know, we are entitled to do that for twenty-four hours without charging him."

Catherine fired back, "You've made a huge mistake."

"Suffice it to say, Miss Tregowyn, I am reasonably sure of my ground."

"Well, I'm not! You haven't even talked to Mr. Westfield's brother yet! The brother who despised him, and who stood to gain an inheritance!"

"Contrary to what you believe, I do not need you to tell me how to do my job. Do I need to remind you that you nearly died the last time you played policeman?"

She couldn't restrain herself, "Are you aware that the band was anything but one happy family?"

The policeman looked taken aback but said nothing.

"I wouldn't be in such a hurry to blame my brother if I were you!"

"I will look into it. Which band member are you speaking of?"

"Everyone of them will bear looking into. Which is just what I intend to when I leave here. Now, may I see my brother, please?"

* * *

Wills was looking as he used to after being closeted with his sire in his study for an hour between terms. His hair was standing up in the front where he had run his fingers through it. He had a sour aspect, and his hands shook. But she knew she wouldn't learn anything relevant from him while the sergeant sat in the corner taking notes.

"Wills!" she cried. "I'm going to London right now to arrange for a solicitor."

"That's a little extreme," he said. "I haven't done anything wrong."

"The Detective Chief Inspector seems to feel he has a case. It was he who told me you needed representation."

He sighed heavily and ran a hand through his hair. "I got Emily off, anyway," he said.

"I had no idea you'd been to see Mr. Westfield the day of the murder."

"I didn't realize that's what they had against Emily, or I would have come forward sooner. No one had even questioned me. I went to see him about Emily and how badly he continued to treat her. But I never got to say my piece. We had drinks, and I was working my way up to it when he suddenly announced he was on his way out to dinner."

Catherine felt a swelling anger against the police. "I don't think they've even questioned the band much. They had their suspicions set on Emily and weren't looking any further. The Detective Chief Inspector said you bruised your knuckles. I refuse to believe you were fighting. How did that happen?"

His color rose, and he said, "Huh. I hit a wall in my flat when they arrested Emily."

"Golly! I've never known you to do anything like that before."

"I've never felt this way about a woman before. It's jolly uncomfortable."

"Never mind," Catherine told him. "We'll see you through." She stood. "I'm off to secure you a solicitor."

"Thank you, Kitty. Sorry to be such a bother, but I'm glad you know something about how the police carry out their business."

She touched his cheek fondly. "You're my brother."

* * *

Catherine and Harry walked to the car park to pick up Harry's motor. He was more than willing to drive her to London to speak to Mr. Gowing, the Tregowyn family solicitor, but he said, "Catherine, I think you need someone who practices criminal law. Perhaps Mr. Gowing can recommend someone."

"I don't want Wills spending the night in jail."

"Has he been arrested?"

"No. But he's being held for twenty-four hours for questioning. I think they're bringing pressure on him to confess. I told Marsh he needed to be questioning the band, not Wills."

She told him about Wills's bruised knuckles. "The police have other evidence, too, but they're not sharing."

"William doesn't strike me as the type of repressed lover who would bludgeon a wall!"

"Still waters and all that," she said, feeling miserable.

"I wonder how the police found out about William's feelings for Emily?"

"He did visit her faithfully in jail, and that bothersome sergeant was taking everything down."

They reached Harry's Morris Motor, and he helped Catherine to climb in. Soon they were on their way to London.

"Marsh said they had other evidence. What if he left fingerprints on some incriminating object?" she asked.

"Why didn't he tell us he went there?" asked Harry.

"It's his nature to keep mum. I imagine he didn't see any point until he realized he could help Emily."

"Oh, the repressed and reticent British!" Harry said. "He probably didn't want to discuss it because he didn't want her to know the strength of his feelings for her."

"What a lunkhead," Catherine said. "But I didn't even ask you—do you have a lecture or a tutorial tomorrow?"

"A lecture. But not until eleven. How about you?"

"I have one at the same time. And a rehearsal with the band tomorrow night, lest you forget."

"It's marked on my calendar in red," he said. "I wouldn't miss that for anything."

They made good time to London, and it was half-past seven when they arrived at Catherine's flat. She rang Mr. Gowing at his home. His firm had been solicitors to the Tregowyns for a hundred years, at least.

"Mr. Gowing? Catherine Tregowyn here. Listen, I'm sorry to bother you at home, but something rather serious has happened, and we need your advice. May I come 'round?"

"Certainly, my dear. Say in half an hour? We are just finishing our dinner."

"Oh, I'm terribly sorry. I didn't think!"

"That's all right. I'll see you in half an hour."

When she had rung off, she put her hands up to her burning cheeks. "I can't believe I did that. I am lost to all propriety, it seems."

"Your brother isn't held by the police every day, Catherine. Calm yourself. Where does he live?"

"Here in Mayfair. It won't take us any time to get there."

Catherine collapsed on the sofa. Soon, she heard Harry

clanging pots and pans in the kitchen. She looked about at the deep charcoal gray walls and white crown molding. She missed these high ceilings. The flat in Oxford always seemed so cramped.

"I am heating us some tinned stew," he called. "I don't know about you, but I'm famished."

"I don't think I could eat," she said.

"You must. I don't want you collapsing before you get William taken care of."

After a minute, he brought several tins of fruit through to the sitting room for her inspection. "I'll have the applesauce," she said. "That's the only thing I can imagine eating. You go ahead and eat whatever you can scrounge. Sorry we missed our dinner. You are a brick for bringing me to Town."

She had finished her applesauce and Harry his stew in half an hour. She did the washing up quickly, and they left the flat for Mr. Gowing's home.

The solicitor's London residence was imposing Georgian brick. His butler took them back to Mr. Gowing's cozy study lit only by the fire, some wall sconces, and a green-shaded banker's lamp. Catherine had never been there before.

He wasn't an imposing man. A little stooped, he stood to greet them, his thin grey hair thinner and grayer than the last time she had seen him.

"Mr. Gowing, it is so good of you to let me come. Please forgive me for interrupting your dinner. This is my colleague, Harry Bascombe. He kindly motored me down here from Oxford where I'm living now. Harry, this is our family solicitor, Mr. Gowing."

The men shook hands and murmured greetings.

"You said it was urgent," Mr. Gowing said.

"It is. The police in Oxford are holding my brother in connection with a murder. They haven't charged him yet, but the Detective Chief Inspector suggested that I contact our solicitor." She kneaded her hands in her lap. "I am positive he is innocent. I came down here to London straightaway."

"That does sound serious, Miss Tregowyn. I am not surprised

you are concerned. Why don't you acquaint me a little with the circumstances?"

She endeavored to calm herself. Beginning with William's entreaty to help his friend, Emily, she told him about the murder and Emily's involvement. She concluded with her conversations with Wills and Chief Detective Inspector Marsh late that afternoon.

Mr. Gowing said, "I think it would be best if I rang a couple of solicitors who specialize in criminal matters. If you would like to be seated in the drawing room, I will let you know when I have this sorted. Don't worry. I know William, and I know he wouldn't get up to that kind of thing."

"Thank you so much. I knew you would know just what to do."

In a moment, the butler came through the door and showed her and Harry through to the drawing room where a huge fire burned in the grate. Harry sat next to her on the floral-patterned sofa before the fireplace. She rubbed her hands together, trying to get warm.

"Stupid of me to leave my fur at home. I'm freezing."

He put a hand over her clasped ones. "He seems very competent, darling," he said. "I hope you feel a bit better, having given it to him to handle."

"It is a relief, yes. Thank you so much for bringing me. I'm quite frazzled, I'm afraid."

She stared into the fire, and slowly her panic began to lessen. It wasn't long before Mr. Gowing entered the room.

"Miss Tregowyn, I managed to engage Mr. Gregory Spence on your behalf. He is quite capable. Spence seemed to think time to be of the essence under the circumstances and will leave shortly for Oxford. I told him you would meet him at the Oxford Police Station."

She stood up immediately but found she was a bit dizzy. Harry steadied her by placing his hand at her elbow. "Thank you so much, Mr. Gowing. I knew you would know just what to do."

Catherine began to feel a bit steadier. "I would prefer that you not bother my parents about this."

"I understand. No need for them to know about things unless they become a lot more serious."

"They won't. William didn't do it. Thank you."

"Keep your head, my dear, and I'm certain all will come right. Now, you must get on your way if you are to meet Mr. Spence."

* * *

When they had begun their journey out of London toward Oxford, Harry said, "Why, if I may ask, did you not want your solicitor to contact your parents?"

Catherine sighed. "Father is hard on William. My brother has as little to do with him as possible. Our parents have never been a positive in our lives."

"That is sad."

"Yes, it is. I think the whole reason William has gone into pathology is that he hopes to find a cure for polio and win my father's approval finally."

"Polio?"

She sighed again. "We had an elder brother neither of us can remember. Michael. He died of polio, and my parents have never recovered from the loss. They've paid our school and college fees, but other than that, we've been pretty much left to raise ourselves."

"Hmm. I see now why you said you never bonded with anyone but were always separate. Until Rafe."

"What happened with Rafe last summer upset things at a very profound level. I put far too much faith in him for far too many years. It has made me skittish about involving myself with anyone else. How can I possibly trust my judgment after making such a big mistake? I'm sorry, but you have been very patient with me."

"You're worth it," he said. He kissed his fingertips and placed them on her cheek. "Thank you for bringing me to London. I am so dreadfully afraid of losing Wills."

"You won't lose him. Everything the police seem to have on him is circumstantial evidence. My money is on the bloke he had dinner with. Someone may have seen them somewhere."

As they neared Oxford an hour later, Catherine hoped the new solicitor would believe in Wills. So much depended on it.

Chapter Seven

Mr. Spence was a solid man of medium height with a wealth of prematurely white hair. He greeted Catherine and Harry with firm handshakes. The on-duty police sergeant was obliging enough to offer them an interview room not in use at eleven o'clock at night.

"Suppose you tell me about this crime, Miss Tregowyn. Everything you know and how you learned it."

Catherine began the tale with William and Emily and related everything she could remember up until she heard Wills had been called in for questioning. "They say he has bruised knuckles. I don't know what the other evidence is that they say they have against him. I don't think my brother has told me everything. But he is a sober and law-abiding man," she told Mr. Spence. "I have confidence in him. He didn't murder Mr. Westfield."

She also sketched an outline of the band members and their volatile relationships. "The Chief Detective Inspector hasn't even begun to question the band. First, they thought they had the murderer in Emily; now they think they have him in my brother."

"What about family members? Does anyone stand to gain from his death?"

Catherine told him about James Westfield's elusive brother/heir, Phillip. "It's absurd that they are concentrating on William when there is such an obvious suspect," she said.

"Absurd. I agree. I believe I am ready to see Mr. Tregowyn. I think it will go better if I do so in private. I may be able to find out what he's not telling you when he realizes how serious the matter is. Then he needs to decide if he is going to retain me."

"All right," Catherine said, suddenly feeling exhausted. Mr. Gowing trusted Mr. Spence, so she must, too. "I'll leave everything in your hands." She took a calling card out of her clutch bag and wrote her telephone numbers on the back. "This is the telephone at my flat and at my office. There should always be people at both places who will take a message. I hope you will keep in touch with me."

"And I will be staying at the Randolph," he said. "If you need to leave a message for me. Here is my professional card with my London address and telephone number."

She took it and offered her hand. "Thank you, Mr. Spence."

* * *

When Harry walked her to the door of her flat, she thanked him again. "You have been my white knight," she said. "I don't know what's going to happen with Wills, and it scares me to death, but I'm glad you were with me tonight."

"I'm glad I was, too." He kissed her gently, his hands on her shoulders. "Now you are freezing and completely done up. Go in and get some sleep. You need to be in fine fettle for your rehearsal tomorrow night."

Reaching up, she kissed him again. "Thanks."

* * *

Catherine slept soundly until nine in the morning. Chagrined when she realized the time, she knew she wouldn't be able to visit Wills before her lecture.

She ate the bun and drank the tea Cherry brought her, bathed, and dressed in a tweed suit and turtleneck jumper. The weather had turned colder.

"Don't skimp on the coal, Cherry," she said. "I feel like I haven't been warm for days."

Sitting at the table in her sitting room, she went over her notes once again. She was only slowly getting into the habit of lecturing. Catherine much preferred the tutorial part of her duties, and she knew the students did, too. The subject of the war and its effect on all facets of British life was a sobering one, well reflected in the literature produced since that time. Catherine considered it something of a sacred trust to convey those thoughts and reflections to young women who were coming of age in a world substantially different from their parent's time.

The hall where she taught was cold. Students arrived dressed in layers of wool and fur. Catherine began her lecture with the question, "Had Rupert Brooke survived the war, would his idealism have survived, also?"

Drawing on Brooke's poetry, which had endeared him to the likes of Winston Churchill and landed him in the navy instead of the trenches, she still surmised that he, like the others of his generation, would have been completely unprepared to be anything but patriotic. His death of sepsis from a mosquito bite in 1917, which year proved to be a turning point in many a soldier's view of the war, kept him from disillusion. However, citing his pre-war nervous collapse over a love affair, she doubted very much that this sensitive young man's idealism could have survived after that year. As it stood, however, his poetry served as a seminal example of the viewpoint of his generation when they first embarked on their military service in 1914.

The lecture seemed to keep the young women awake and engaged, but she was glad when it was over. Miss Favringham had been absent, though, and Catherine knew that before she went to see Wills, she needed to make an effort to talk to the young woman. Once she had returned to her office, she rang the girl's dormitory and waited while someone went to fetch her.

A sleepy voice answered, "Hello?"

"Miss Favringham?"

"Yes. Is that you, Miss Tregowyn?"

"It is. I wonder if you might come over to my office after luncheon. I would like to talk to you."

"I'm not feeling very well," the girl said, after a pause.

"Are you ill?"

"I'm just not myself."

"Your work is suffering, Miss Favringham. I hate to see this happen to you. I would like to help if I can."

"No one can help me. I just need to get hold of myself. I shall be all right in a day or two, I'm sure of it."

Catherine couldn't compel the young woman to confide in her. "I'll leave it up to you then to get the lecture notes for today from a friend. And I expect your next paper for our tutorial to be an improvement upon the last one."

"Yes. I understand," the girl said.

"Please ring me if you need to talk to someone."

"I shall," the girl promised.

Catherine knew she would do no such thing.

* * *

After luncheon in the student's hall, Catherine left for the police station. The morning was cold and clear, perfect for a brisk walk. By the time she passed the Martyr's Memorial, she felt warm for the first time since before she heard the news of Wills's arrest. When she arrived at the station, she felt composed and ready to talk to her brother.

The sergeant allowed her request to speak to him and arranged a small, windowless room for their meeting. It came equipped with the ubiquitous sergeant, ready to note down her conversation. Her first glimpse of her brother, who looked unkempt and miserable, brought back all her misgivings.

"Wills!" she walked to him and grasped his listless hands. "My dear, you look positively dismal!"

She led him to a chair and then took one next to his, taking one of his hands in both of hers. It was cold and lifeless.

"I'm sorry, Cat. Thank you for arranging for Mr. Spence to represent me. He's a decent sort."

"What does he think?" she asked.

"The strongest evidence they have against me is my fingerprints on a whiskey glass. Westfield's jaw was bruised, as are my knuckles, but there is no admissible proof that I was the one who hit him. You know I wouldn't get into a fight."

She knew she couldn't question Wills with the sergeant there taking notes, but her brother would have been allowed private conversation with his solicitor, so she had to have faith in Mr. Spence. She longed to know more about why Wills had visited James Westfield and why he had been drinking whiskey with him.

"I suppose it's too much to hope that you damaged that wall you hit. Is there any proof of it?"

Gazing down at his offending knuckles, he looked uncomfortable. "No. The wall is solid. Not even a dent. But I wish I had clobbered the bloke. You should have heard the way he described Emily! He was a rotter and no mistake." He massaged his knuckles ruefully.

"Tell me about Mr. Spence. how did you get on?" Catherine asked.

"All right. Bit early for all that, though."

"Not according to the police. I told you. They suggested a solicitor, Wills." She tried to keep the worry out of her voice.

"Rum go," he said.

"They must think they have a case against you," she said gently.

"They asked me if I'd ever used a syringe," he said, his voice hollow.

"Of course! You use them at work all the time, don't you?"

"I do. Every time I transfer substances to a petri dish, for starters. It's what I do all day."

"Blast! We've got to find the murderer fast! Maybe tonight."

"What's happening tonight?" asked Wills.

"I'm making my debut as a jazz singer. Actually, it's just a rehearsal," she said. "Wish me luck."

"Oh I forgot all about that," said William.

"It will be fun. Now. Down to business. You retained Mr. Spence, I hope."

"I did. If they haven't arrested me by 3:00, they have to let me go. Mr. Spence is waiting at the Randolph to hear one way or the other."

"I will be home. Either you ring and let me know they've let you go, or Mr. Spence rings to tell me they've arrested you. I'll be waiting."

Leaning forward, she kissed his unshaven cheek.

"God bless you, Wills," she whispered.

"And you, Kitty," he whispered back.

* * *

Catherine walked back to her flat, realizing halfway she should have taken the bus. The meeting with Wills had tired her. However, she needed the exercise, so she pressed on. She didn't feel the usual lift of her spirits at the Church of St. Mary Magdalen. She was worried.

Cherry greeted her from where she sat at the sitting room table, studying her French. Catherine realized she'd missed their lesson.

"Oh, Cherry, forgive me. I was out on an urgent errand. We can have your lesson now if you like."

"Please, miss if you aren't too busy."

They spent the time studying irregular French verbs until the telephone finally rang.

Her heart fell when she heard Mr. Spence's voice.

"They've arrested him, Miss Tregowyn."

"Have they even talked to Mr. Westfield's brother?" she asked.

"Apparently, the man's disappeared. I have in my mind that the police have arrested your brother with the intent of lulling Phillip Westfield into a false sense of security."

"But that's beastly!" she said.

"Nothing to prevent it. However, all the evidence is circumstantial. If it ever comes to court, I doubt the Crown would have a very strong case."

She collapsed onto a chair. Court. The Crown. Case. It was all was too, too real. "We can't let it come to that," she said. "I know he's innocent, and I'm going to prove it."

"How do you plan to do that?"

"I'm going to find out who did it. And before you take that lightly, you should know that I've done this before and succeeded."

"Your brother has told me. He's rather counting on you, as a matter of fact."

"I won't let him down," Catherine said with dogged determination.

"Keep in touch with me." He gave her his office number. "I'm going to raise the devil to try to get Mr. Tregowyn released."

"I hope you succeed."

For a while, she couldn't even leave her chair. Having her brother arrested for murder was the worst thing that had ever happened in her life. Catherine tried to get hold of herself, but she began to shake. First, it was just her hands, and then it was her whole body.

Cherry asked, "Miss, what's wrong? You've gone all white!"

"My brother," she said. "Wills has been arrested for murder."

"That's not right!" Cherry said, her anger evident as she stood with her hands on her hips. "Who would ever believe Mr. William would do something like that?"

"A conniving policeman," she answered, her voice dull, all the spirit gone out of it.

"You need a nice cup of tea," the maid said.

* * *

Now it was even more imperative that she make a success of it tonight. Catherine dressed carefully for her rehearsal, all the time practicing her singing as she listened to the wireless. The last thing she felt like doing was singing, but she kept telling herself it was for her brother. To her surprise, soon the soothing jazz with its syrupy lyrics took the edge off her anxiety.

She needed to look a bit daring, she thought. Out of the ordinary. Even though this was just a rehearsal, jazz singers were a little outré. Deciding upon her white silk trouser suit, she tried several shirts before settling on one the color of midnight. Cherry used the iron to wave her dark brown hair. For jewelry, she wore a Chinese red cloisonné choker and matching drop earrings. She was liberal with the kohl emphasizing her deep brown eyes.

Wills was depending on her, and she was preparing to infiltrate what she thought of as the enemy camp. Her personal favorite for the role of the murderer was the suspected cocaine addict, Alfie. She knew next to nothing about him but suspected (because of his addiction) that he lacked moral fiber. Also, if he had access to cocaine, he would probably have access to other drugs. Who knew whether or not the trumpeter had suffered some kind of violent manic episode while on his drug? Was he James's supplier?

Harry rang as she was trying to eat dinner. Cherry was experimenting with curry dishes, and this one was not a success. It was not really Cherry's fault. She hadn't trained as a cook.

"Darling?" Harry inquired.

"Wills has been arrested," she said. "We've got to take this sleuthing seriously."

"Well, I shan't allow you to go off to that rehearsal by yourself then."

"You really haven't any right to tell me what to do, but under the circumstances, I will forgive you. I would be glad of the company."

He called for her in the Morris motor, which was good since that meant she needn't take a cab.

"You look suitably glamorous, darling. How are you holding up?" he asked.

"I'm jumpy. I'm hoping I'll find out something tonight."

"I hope so, too. But you're going to knock 'em dead, as the Americans say."

"Thanks."

As they pulled up in front of the Town Hall, Catherine knew a moment's nerves. Inhaling deeply, she took Harry's hand and climbed out of the vehicle.

She could do this.

Chapter Eight

Red greeted them perfunctorily and introduced the band.

"You can just call me Red," he said. "The kid with the trumpet is Alfie. Tony, you've met, I hear. Joe's on the trombone."

Tony nodded at her. Alfie lifted his chin, his whole attitude pugnacious. Does he have some idea of what I'm up to? Joe gave a single hoot of the trombone.

"I'm Cat, as you know. My friend is Harry." She sketched a curtsey. The band bowed as one.

Red asked, "What's your favorite tune?"

"' No Harm in Hoping,'" answered Catherine.

"All right. Let's start with that and run through the routine." He sat down at the piano, played an introduction, and the band launched into the first song.

Catherine let them play a stanza, and then came in with her most wistful, sultry voice.

> *"No harm in hoping*
> *You can care about me.*
> *No harm in thinking*
> *How happy we'd be . . ."*

After some initial nerves, Catherine settled into the rhythm and was soon swaying and gesturing as though she'd been singing jazz all her life. It was an adventure using her talent in this new way. As Cherry had told her, her voice was made for jazz. A feeling of well-being enveloped her.

When they had run through a dozen or so numbers, Mr. Webster came out of his office and told them their rehearsal time was up.

"You did fine," said Red. "Let's go up the road to The Bird and the Baby and have a pint."

She was glad they had chosen the pub where Joe was accepted. She wanted to get to know the trombonist. The band packed up their instruments and left the Hall.

Harry joined them. "You were unbelievable," he said. "If I didn't know better, I'd think you were made for this."

They negotiated the crossing of the High Street, Harry's hand at her back, and after a short walk, they entered the cozy, warm pub. Harry ordered their drinks while the others got their own.

They all sat at a high table back in the corner.

"Sure you've never done anything like this before?" The good-looking Tony asked her. She was still bowled over by his black fringed, sky-blue eyes. "You're a natural."

"No," I haven't," said Catherine. "It's great fun. I'm looking forward to this weekend."

"Tony says you're a tutor," said Alfie. "I can't feature that in my mind. What is your subject?"

"Mod Brit Lit," said Catherine. "Harry does Nineteenth-Century Brit Lit at Christ Church. You all go to St. John's, I understand. What are you reading? Music, like Tony?"

"Maths," said Alfie.

"He's brilliant," said Red. "Politics and philosophy for me, of course. No doubt you've heard my nickname doesn't relate to my hair."

"I had heard that," said Catherine with a little laugh. "You're famous."

"I do what I can," the bandleader said. "Joe here is my mate, but he's not at Oxford yet. We're working on it."

Joe smiled his gleaming smile, looking just past her. She realized the smile was for someone else—Emily. Apparently, she knew the band's habits and had just arrived. She was making her way through the crowd to their table, looking striking now that she was no longer confined to a jail cell. Her black hair was waved, her big blue eyes encircled with a heavy line of kohl. She wore red.

Catherine was suddenly angry. How dare Emily stride into the pub happy and looking gorgeous when Wills was under arrest? Who was she trying to impress? Tony?

The only person even aware of her arrival, however, was Joe. When the others noticed her, they all perked up a bit, except for Red, who remained impervious to her charms. She kissed them all on the cheek, even Joe. To her surprise, Catherine received a kiss as well.

Emily carried a basket. Inside was something covered with a tea towel. Like a child in expectation of a treat, Tony whipped off the towel and revealed the shortbread and currant biscuits underneath.

"You've been baking again!" he said. "Didn't you have to work today, Em?"

She pulled a face. "I'm still under investigation at the Radcliffe regarding the stolen morphine. I'm suspended for the rest of the week."

"Too bad of them," said Alfie. He was in a morose mood, but the sight of the biscuits brightened his face. His heavily pomaded hair was so fragrant of lilacs, Catherine could smell it from where she sat.

Red just rolled his eyes in Catherine's direction.

Joe said, "I'll have to give you the recipe for my grandmother's oatmeal-raisin cookies."

"You make biscuits out of oatmeal?" asked Emily aghast.

"They're tasty," Joe said, biting into his shortbread. "But I must admit, these aren't bad."

"Is that supposed to be a compliment?" teased Emily. Catherine noted the flush on the girl's cheeks.

Red said, "Thank you for these, Em. Now, lads, how did you think the rehearsal went?"

Joe answered, "Cat is a great addition. Are you sure you're all white, girl?"

Startled, Catherine realized he was giving her a compliment. She laughed. "So, my parents tell me."

"Sure we can't convince you to give up your day job?" Red asked.

"Sorry," Catherine said. "But I'm glad you're pleased."

Harry, who had been quietly nursing his pint, now said, "Anybody know where Westfield was getting his cocaine?"

The four remaining band members simultaneously looked at one another and then sipped their drinks in unison.

"No," said Alfie, his voice cold. "How did you know he was taking cocaine?"

Since the information had come from Emily, Catherine wondered how Harry was going to answer.

He said, "Something the police said."

"I never heard," said Joe. "I can't take the stuff, myself. It gives me hives."

Red and Tony remained silent. They were all looking at Emily, however, and Catherine felt suddenly that they all knew the answer to Alfie's question. Did they know the answer to Harry's? Did they think it had something to do with the murder?

Red went off to get another pint. She decided it was time to change the topic, "So, Alfie, I suppose you're a whiz at Maths."

Alfie quickly moved his eyes back down to his lager, but not before she had noticed his large black pupils almost obliterating his irises, which gave him an odd look. Was that a characteristic of a cocaine user? She would have to ask Harry.

"He's blinking brilliant," said Tony.

"That's interesting. I've read that researchers think there's a link in the brain between music and maths," said Catherine. "Does that seem right to you, Alfie?"

He shrugged a bit, clearly annoyed by Tony's praise. Catherine wondered why. Maybe because Tony wasn't a mathematician?

The drummer continued, "The trumpet's second nature to him. He took to it like a duck to water."

"I guess that answers my question," said Catherine. "Unfortunately, I'm dismal at maths."

"But you have a great voice for jazz. Sure you've never performed before?" asked Tony.

"I must confess that I sing in the church choir, and I've always loved it." She smiled at their shocked looks. "But, of course, that's much different than what we're doing."

Harry spoke up. "Cat's one of those people who shines at most things they take up. She published her first academic work when she was an undergraduate. And she's a published poet. I say, darling, have you ever thought of writing songs?"

"Don't listen to him," she said. "We have an unfortunate academic history we're trying to work through. He's always trying to rile me. And no, I wouldn't know the first thing about writing a song."

Red had returned during this exchange and now looked at her as though he were seeing her for the first time. "Maybe you ought to give it a go. Alfie or I could write the tune. All you would have to do is come up with the lyrics."

She put her mug on the table as she thought it over. "All right. You write the tune, and maybe I'll try my wings at some words. But I'm not promising anything."

This decided, the group suddenly felt more solid to her. It enfolded her. She no longer sat on the outside. Only Alfie didn't accept her. He seemed to be not quite there. He fiddled with the zip on his jacket, turned his drink this way and that, flew furtive glances at the patrons at other tables as though he were watching for someone.

"Who is your favorite bandleader?" she asked.

They became lost in a discussion of current jazz in England and the States, Tony being the most knowledgeable and enthusiastic. It lasted well into the ten o'clock hour. When they broke at the end of it, Catherine felt that she had been accepted into their ranks. It was promising, even though it hadn't yielded anything too new that night.

Harry was of a different opinion, however. On their drive home, he said, "There is a definite cocaine connection in that band. I don't know how many others of them are using it, but Alfie certainly is. It's a pity, because he shows promise. Tony's right. He's brilliant on the trumpet." He appeared to consider. "But of all the players, I was watching Joe the most. He's very innovative on the trombone. I was impressed."

"I didn't know you were a jazz aficionado," Catherine said.

"I went through a phase. Before I met you. I used to go down to the clubs in London all the time."

"Why did you stop?"

"I have a reason to spend my evenings in Oxford these days," he said, taking her hand.

She smiled at him. They were silent as they drove through the evening traffic. Oxford was never quiet, even in the evenings.

Harry said, "I was wondering if you had told Emily of Wills' arrest. I know you were knocked sideways by it, and she was the last person on your mind. She should know. She may know other things she hasn't told us."

Catherine smote her forehead with the heel of her hand. "Of course. I'll phone her tomorrow. Only that may be too late. What if it's in the papers?"

"You'd best ring her tonight."

"All right. Will you come in? I can fix you some cocoa. It's beastly cold out tonight."

"I will, thank you. We can discuss our perceptions of the band."

* * *

Emily's very irritated flatmate informed Catherine when she rang that Emily was out for the evening.

Catherine made cocoa, and they sat in her sitting room, which she was in the process of decorating in an Art Deco manner. Over her black leather sofa hung a chrome-framed poster of an ocean liner standing at quayside with people going up the gangplank.

"All right," she said. "So, what clues did you pick up tonight?"

"Alfie was coming off a high, I believe. You noticed his pupils?"

"Yes. And I think something is going on between Emily and someone in the band. Tony or Joe, I think."

"Joe?" said Harry, obviously astounded at the idea. "But she's from Kenya. You can't tell me she would be attracted to a black man!"

"He's a beautiful man. And an American, not a Kenyan."

"I'm surprised the police haven't latched onto him. I foresee that you are going to need to do a little cozying up to Red. He likes you. Tony, too. I'm less sure about Alfie. With the cocaine and everything, he just seems a bit off. I'm not sure he isn't dangerous, too."

She shivered a bit, and putting down his cocoa cup, he drew her into his arms.

"It bothers me that there's a cocaine connection with that band and that they all know it," she said.

"It may not be anything sinister. Alfie may be the son of a chemist. He may get it from him."

"But you don't think so," she said, putting her head down on his lapel.

"It's not the most likely scenario. You are going to have to take the very greatest of care. I don't get the feeling that anyone in that group was particularly fond of me." He stroked the back of her hair. "I don't like it, but you're going to be on your own with them."

"I feel like a goose just walked over my grave. Let's not talk about it anymore. Kiss me," she said, looking into his warm brown eyes.

"I'm always happy to oblige," he said, his voice husky.

He kissed her thoroughly and expertly, starting at her hairline and working his way to her lips. It was lovely in a toe-curling sort of way.

Chapter Nine

Catherine slept late again the following morning. Cherry, impatient to hear a report on her band practice, woke her at nine with a tea tray.

"How was it, miss?" she asked when Catherine was scarcely awake.

"It was lovely, Cherry. Now let me go back to sleep."

"You have a tutorial at eleven. You have to get your day started."

Grumbling to herself about ever allowing her maid to think she could dictate her schedule, Catherine drank her tea, ate her bun, and tried to get her head in order. What was it she was planning to do today?

Oh, yes. She needed to talk to Emily about Wills being in jail. But first, she had her second-year student's tutorial. It was the same subject for them as it had been for her Tuesday students. Had she even looked over their essays?

Good heavens! She hadn't touched them. There had been the little matter of her brother's arrest.

Dressing quickly in her black suit and white silk shirt with its high collar and stock, she donned her black professor's gown, so she'd be ready to dash out the door. Then she sat down to read the thousand-word essays in an hour and a half. Fortunately, there were only three students in this tutorial.

When she was all but finished, she asked Cherry to call a cab and made it to her sitting room at Somerville just in time. Her students arrived, and they commenced a surprisingly productive ninety minutes discussing the English poetry landscape after the Great War. She had found the essays to be surprisingly good and had given each of her girls full marks. She gave their assignment and then walked down to luncheon with them.

She was happy to see Miss Favringham there with an empty seat beside her.

"Feeling more the thing?" she asked her as she took the available chair.

"Getting there," said the young woman. "I got the lecture notes from Anna for yesterday. Sorry I missed. It seemed like it must have been good."

"It did go well," Catherine said. "Do you have any tennis matches coming up?"

"No. Last weekend was it until spring. I'm going down to London this weekend though to see Mum. We're going to do some shopping, which is always great fun."

Catherine could tell the girl was trying on the impression of someone for whom shopping was an unmitigated delight. Catherine didn't buy it. Something was still troubling the girl. Her eyelids were heavy, and the ashy circles under her eyes pronounced. She ate only soup. She hoped the girl wasn't headed for a crisis of the nerves.

"Do you like jazz?" Catherine asked suddenly.

Miss Favringham looked at her tutor as though she had lost her mind. "Why do you ask?"

"I'm filling in for a jazz singer this weekend. I thought you might be due for a night's frivolity and would get a kick out of it."

The young woman returned to her soup. "I don't particularly care for jazz," she said.

Catherine was at a loss. What young person today didn't like jazz?

Miss Favringham pushed back her chair and got up. "I'll see you next week in your tutorial. And I promise my essay will be up to snuff."

"Have a good time with your mum," said Catherine.

* * *

Catherine rang Emily's flat. One of her flatmates answered and informed Catherine that she was out.

"Do you know if she has read the newspaper this morning?" she asked.

"We don't receive the *Oxford Mail*," the flatmate told her.

Catherine thanked the girl and rang off.

Maybe it was just as well she wasn't going out. She had promised herself that she would put in time in her office preparing the next month's tutorials and lectures she had outlined in her syllabus. Since it was her first year of teaching, she didn't have old notes to rely upon.

She put in three hours reviewing *Testament of Youth* by Vera Brittain. The book was profoundly moving but depressing. Would there ever be another war? Surely the best way to avoid that was to reveal the faulty mindset that had resulted in the last war, as Brittain did so beautifully. It had been a war of empires. But what if Germany tried to reclaim what they had lost?

Catherine reminded herself of the pocket of British fascists she had uncovered at Oxford last summer and shook off a sudden feeling of weariness. No wonder the sentimental tunes of modern jazz had an appeal. To her, listening to the mellow jazz tunes was like wearing a pair of silk pajamas.

Sketching out a lecture based on Brittain's book, she tried to infuse it with warnings and the tradition of warnings in literature. When she had completed that bracing task, it was close to five o'clock, and she rang Emily again.

The girl was in and said she would be happy to see Catherine. She put on her coat and hat and set off for Cranham Street, where Emily had her flat.

* * *

The girl was once again beautifully groomed and seemed to be in top form when she greeted Catherine at the door. As she viewed Catherine's demeanor, however, her face fell.

"What is it? Is something wrong?" She showed her guest into the plain, functional sitting room.

Catherine sat on the sofa underneath an insipid painted reproduction of an English cottage.

"It's Wills. He's been arrested," she said.

The girl's hand flew to her mouth. "When?"

"Yesterday."

"But William wouldn't hurt anyone! It's preposterous!"

"Didn't the police tell you that the reason you were released was that he came forward and told them that he had called on James after you had been seen there and found him alive?"

"No! They didn't tell me. How frightfully gallant of him!"

"It was the truth. And they found Wills's fingerprints at the scene." Catherine intentionally left out the details of his bruised hand.

"But why would William visit James? He didn't like him."

"I presume it had something to do with how he had treated you."

Emily looked blank. "Treated me? Oh! You mean breaking things off. Why should that concern William?"

Catherine was suddenly impatient. "Don't be dense, Emily. Surely you realize he cares for you!"

The girl's eyes grew large. "We're friends, that's all."

"Is it? Obviously, you don't know him very well, or you would realize he's head over ears."

"With me? But he's so good looking and wealthy and comes in for a title. What would he see in me?"

"I believe he feels a kinship with you over your joint concern for the Kenyan children's physical well-being."

"Really? Golly! I had no idea."

"Truly?" Catherine asked.

"Truly."

Catherine wondered if she could believe Emily's incredulity. How could she not have had any idea?

"Well," she said to the young woman, "I think it would do him a tremendous amount of good if you would pay him a visit."

"I will do it," Emily said. "First thing tomorrow morning. I'm afraid I already have plans for this evening."

Catherine hoped her disappointment didn't show on her face. "He will be happy to see you." She stood. "I'm off then."

"Thank you for coming and letting me know. And thank you for helping me when I was arrested."

"You have Wills to thank for that," Catherine said.

* * *

When she arrived back at her own flat, she was discouraged. She would visit Wills that night. He needed bucking up.

Had Phillip Westfield come back to college? She decided to ring Harry to find out. Before she could carry this out, however, she sorted through her mail and came upon a letter from Kenya. *Rafe.*

Should she open it? Habit was strong, and she almost gave in. But before she could, Catherine threw it on the fire. She had to root him out of her life whenever he cropped up. The seeds he had planted there were much too hardy. Until last summer, she had been in and out of love with him since she was ten years old. She was not going to resume that pattern. This time he was out of her life for good. No compromises.

Defiantly, she dialed Harry's number. He was not in. She left a message with the Christ Church College porter.

Fiddlesticks!

Cherry had prepared a cheese omelet for dinner, which she served along with fresh croissants from the local bakery. Between her depressing reading and reflections, Rafe's letter, and Harry's absence, she was in a black humor. She asked Cherry to tune into Harry Hall and the BBC dance orchestra. She couldn't visit Wills in this frame of mind.

After listening to half an hour of the relaxing sounds, she decided she needed to change out of her black. Catherine perused her wardrobe, looking for something warm but cheery. She decided on the red wool trousers which matched her red coat with the stand-up fur collar. Cherry freshly waved her hair, and Catherine reapplied her makeup. Spraying herself with Lily of the Valley scent, she called a cab and set off for the Police Department's jail and Wills.

* * *

Her brother's mood was surprisingly upbeat. To Catherine's surprise, Emily had visited him. She had scarcely left. Why had the police let her in when Wills had already had one visitor? Someone must have a soft heart. Detective Chief Inspector Marsh?

Wills was full of Emily. "She blamed herself for my situation. Idiotic, of course. Of all the crazy things, she says she had no idea I cared for her. She thought we were just pals. Thank you for enlightening her. I don't seem to know my way where women are concerned."

She felt like saying, "Jolly good, but her affection won't do you much good if you hang," but instead, she entertained him with the story of her rehearsal for the band.

"Tony and Joe seem to be thoroughly good chaps, but the other two are a bit suspect. Red is a thorough-going Communist and Alfie, a drug addict." With a bit of melodrama, she asked, "Who knows what motives lie within the hearts of such unsavory characters?"

He gave a wry smile. "Were you able to convince them you could sing?"

She preened herself. "They were completely bowled over. I was an utter and complete success. Mother and Father would have been horrified and invoked the spirit of Michael and his perfect taste in music a thousand times."

That time, he laughed. "Any luck with Westfield's brother?"

"He's disappeared or something. Perhaps now that you've been arrested, he'll come out of hiding."

"One can only hope," William said, his face serious again.

"Wills, promise me you'll keep your spirits up. Harry and I are doing everything we can to prove the police wrong on this."

"I'll certainly try. It's rather a bore, you know."

"I'll visit you often, and I'm certain Emily will, too. I must push off now. I want to catch Harry before it's too terribly late."

* * *

After leaving the police station, Catherine walked around the corner of the High Street onto St. Aldate's and down to Christ Church College. The porter greeted her, "Dr. Bascombe?"

"Yes, please."

The porter rang Harry's rooms, and in a few minutes, he had joined her. As they walked north to The Eagle and Child, she told him about her visit with Wills. Then she said, "We've got to find the brother somehow. He's an even better suspect than the band members."

"I think I've got a line on him," said Harry. "The roommate, Gerry, has found out where he was last weekend. It was a house party in London. I managed to get an address."

"Good. I don't have anything scheduled for tomorrow, do you?"

"You want to go down to London?"

"Yes, please. And we can meet Dot for lunch. Maybe we can

enlist her help." She spoke of her closest friend, who worked in an advertising agency off Fleet Street.

"Let's make a day of it."

"Remember, I have to get back for my spot of singing tomorrow night. It'll take me some time to get ready, too."

"Maybe Dot would like to come up to hear you sing," Harry suggested.

"As she would say, that would be smashing. It'll give you someone to dance with tomorrow night while I'm slaving away at the microphone. I'll ring her when I get back to the flat."

* * *

Dot was thrilled with the news that Catherine and Harry would be coming to London the next day.

"I have a surprise for you," Catherine said. "Do you have any hard and fast plans for the weekend?"

"Not really," her friend said. "I'm between chaps at the moment. Nothing going on there."

"Well, it's a long story which I'll fill you in about tomorrow, but Harry and I have gotten ourselves involved in another bit of detecting. Wills has been arrested for murder."

"Oh, Cricky! That's dreadful."

"It's all connected somehow to the local jazz band, so I've infiltrated them. I'm singing with them starting tomorrow night. Can you come and stay with me at the flat for the weekend?"

"You're singing with a band? How frightfully smashing! I'd love to come — what fun. I haven't been up to Oxford for an age. Not since the Chenowith business."

"It will be lovely to have you here for moral support while I warble. And Wills could do with a visit."

"Meet me at the Spot for luncheon. I'll take the afternoon off tomorrow. I have it coming to me. I've been working terrible hours with a new soap campaign I just pushed out the door. I deserve to celebrate!"

"I can't wait to see you. Ta!"

Catherine's spirits had improved mightily when she rang off. She and Dot had so much to catch up on. Since Michaelmas term had started, she had become a rotten correspondent, and Dot wasn't much better.

She and Harry had agreed to leave at nine in the morning to begin their search for Phillip Westfield, so she took a soothing hot bath and was in bed by eleven. Catherine had difficulty falling asleep, however.

She was worried about Wills. She and Harry must find the murderer. She was under no illusions about Detective Cheif Inspector Marsh. Now that he had Wills under lock and key, he would be unlikely to look for anyone else. Unless Phillip turned up. Would they be able to find him?

* * *

Somehow Cherry managed to wake her at eight o'clock though Catherine had slept only fitfully. After tea, she began the process of resurrection. Cherry waved her hair, chattering away about getting things ready for Dot.

"I will go to the market and get that chutney she likes," said the maid. "And ginger biscuits. She adores ginger biscuits!"

Catherine dressed in a smart forest green suit for London. Her pillbox hat had a peek-a-boo veil. She was wrapping herself in fur when Harry tooted for her out at the curb.

He greeted her with a kiss on the cheek and admired her ensemble. "You look good enough to eat."

"You're kind, but I've got bags under my eyes, I'm certain. I haven't had much sleep. Poor Wills. It will do him good to see Dot. She's a regular tonic. I've always cherished hopes that they would marry." Catherine told him about their plans to meet at the Spotted Pig, a Fleet Street pub.

"This place we're headed for is in Chelsea. Quite a way from Fleet Street. I hope we make it on time."

"Dot's taking the afternoon off from work. It will be fine whenever we arrive."

They spoke about her new book of poems, *Harvesting the Light*, which would be published for the Christmas Holiday market. Harry was very happy because he also had a book coming out, Catherine having referred him to her publisher. She asked him if he'd ever heard of Dylan Thomas, the new Welsh poet Baron Favringham had told her about.

"He's supposed to be a Diamond in the Rough, I've heard," said Harry. "The word is that he's going to rock the world of poetry someday. I have a friend in Swansea who's had a look at the chap's notebook. It's a marvel, apparently."

"The baron thinks a lot of him," she said. "I'm worried about Miss Favringham, though."

"Why is that?"

She told him of Beryl Favringham's careless behavior and the difficulties she seemed to be having. "I think a lot of her. She's one of my most brilliant students. But she's under a dark cloud right now. I wouldn't be surprised if she were one of those manic-depressive types, though I certainly hope not."

"It's one of the hardest things for a faculty mentor when you don't see a bright student living up to his or her potential. I wonder if Alfie from the band doesn't fall into that category."

"I'm glad I'm not his tutor," she said.

Chapter Ten

The address in Chelsea proved to be a block of three posh flats. Only the top floor tenant responded to Harry's knock.

"I say," he said to the manservant who answered the door. "I'm looking for a friend. I believe he was a houseguest last weekend. Name of Phillip Westfield. Oxford chap."

"You'd have to speak to the master," the manservant said. "He's at breakfast. Do you have a card?"

Harry handed him his visiting card. They were invited into the vestibule. It was painted stark white with a vase of some feathery grass in the corner and what Catherine thought to be an original Van Gogh painting on the wall.

When the manservant returned, he took them into the breakfast room where his master sat drinking coffee. The man was about Harry's age with a prematurely receding hairline. He was dressed for a ride in jodhpurs, a blue jacket, and an ascot at his neck. Catherine felt his slightly protuberant eyes on her as he studied her from head to toe. She gritted her teeth.

"Richard Stephens," their host said, standing and shaking each of their hands. "May I offer you a cup of coffee?"

She had passed muster.

To her surprise, Harry accepted the coffee as he introduced the two of them. The manservant poured two cups. They sat at the table.

"I'm Phillip's tutor," Harry said. "We're looking for him on a matter of some urgency."

"I'm afraid I can't help you much. Vicious little tick. He stayed with me through the Sunday, and then he went off with another chap in somewhat of a hurry, as I recall. After breakfast. Something in the paper upset him, I think. I was glad to see the back of him; I can tell you. He didn't treat my staff well. Not out of the top drawer, if you know what I mean."

"Yes," said Catherine.

"Just for the sake of conversation, how do you come to know Phillip?" asked Harry.

"I don't know him well, nor do I want to. He's the friend of a friend. You know how these things go. The friend he left with, as a matter of fact—Samuel Reed." Their host clapped his hands together and said in a brighter tone, "I'm having another party tonight. Would be more than happy if you'd come."

Catherine felt uncomfortable. "I'm sorry. I'm afraid this is just a day trip. We have plans back in Oxford this evening. We're sorry to have interrupted your breakfast."

"It was a welcome interruption," Mr. Stephens said smoothly. "I have these parties most Fridays, and I hereby issue you a standing invitation, Miss Tregowyn. You, too, of course, Dr. Bascombe."

"Thank you," Harry said. "That is most kind. We'll let you dine in peace now."

Mr. Stephens stood and shook their hands again. He lingered over Catherine's hand, and she was afraid for a moment that he was going to kiss it. He eventually let it go.

"Bounder," Harry said once they were back out on the street.

"He was, rather," Catherine agreed. "At least we have a name. Samuel Reed."

"If I hadn't had you with me, I doubt he would have told us a thing," said Harry. "But how the devil do we find this Samuel

Reed? I doubt he's in London, or they wouldn't have been houseguests."

"Do you suppose he's an Oxford man?"

"Possibly. If he is, I can look him up at my club."

Catherine knew Harry was a member of the Christ Church College Alumni Club.

"They have records of all the colleges there?"

"Yes. Volumes and volumes going back to the War."

"That's handy."

"Can I drop you at Harrod's while I go have a squint? We can meet at noon at the Spot."

"Yes. That's a lovely idea. I want some little thing suitable for my hair for tonight, so that works out splendidly."

* * *

If jazz was like silk pajamas, Harrod's was like the finest Shetland wool scarf. She loved the Knightsbridge Department Store. It made her feel elegant and safe at the same time.

Making her way to millinery, she noticed the ever-present scent of French perfume pervading the ground floor. Maybe she would buy some of that, as well. She had a full hour before she needed to find a taxi.

Among the hats, she found exactly what she wanted—a jeweled creation made mostly of black feathers. It was worn on the side of the head, curving down just to the outer edge of her large brown eyes. It was exceedingly provocative.

Once it was packaged for her, she moved off to the perfume department. She had long had a desire for the scent Shalimar. She felt her gig with a jazz band deserved something suitably dramatic, and the exotic perfume qualified perfectly.

Enveloped in scent, she carried her purchases out to the taxi stand, where the doorman helped her into a waiting cab. It was time to meet Dot and Harry.

* * *

Catherine's spirits rose at the sight of her friend striding through the door of the pub carrying a small suitcase. It had been way too long since she'd seen Dot. Short and curvy with a head of red hair, Dorothy Nichols had been her best friend since boarding school. They had attended Somerville together.

Catherine walked to meet her friend and kissed her cheek. "I'm over here," she said, weaving through the crowd and fug of cigarette smoke until they reached her table where her shandy awaited.

"I thought Harry was with you," Dot said.

"He's meeting us. He had to look something up at the club." The one fly in the ointment of this weekend was that Catherine harbored an idea that Dot had a secret pash for Harry. It bothered her a bit that Harry and Dot were going to be spending the evening dancing together even if she had suggested it.

"I'm so looking forward to hearing you sing tonight, Cat," said her friend. "But tell me about this murder Wills has gotten mixed up in."

Catherine gave her an outline of the case.

"And who's this Emily?" Dot asked. "Is Wills in love with her?"

"I think he thinks so, but I don't know how she feels. She grew up in Kenya. They share a passion for improving the plight of the Kenyan children. But I rather think she has hopes of one of the musicians in the band. Much more glamorous."

"Oh, I do hope they find the brother soon, and that he turns out to be guilty. I can't bear the thought of Wills locked up in some moldy old jail."

"It's dreadful," agreed Catherine. "Oh, Dot, it's so good to see you. Harry must be held up. Let's order lunch."

They decided on fish and chips, and Catherine went to the bar to order for them. When she returned with the steaming food, she filled Dot in on the members of the band as they ate.

"It sounds like a bit of a rum crew, all right. Imagine! A Negro American Shades of Louis Armstrong! I can't believe you're really singing with a jazz band. What fun! Are you nervous?" asked Dot.

"I'm quaking, actually. But I'm so glad you're going to be there. And I'll take you to see Wills. It'll cheer him up no end."

"Maybe we can do that this afternoon if we get back to Oxford in time. Wills is a pet," Dot pronounced.

Harry joined them then and hung his overcoat and hat on the tree next to them.

"Hello, Dot," he said, leaning down to kiss her cheek. "You are a welcome sight."

"Do you have news?" asked Catherine.

"Rather. It took me a while to find, but Samuel Reed did indeed go to Oxford. He was at Merton College. His address is in Hampshire near Winchester. If we rouse ourselves early tomorrow after our night of debauchery at the Town Hall, we should be able to make the drive tomorrow. We might even look in on the parents."

Catherine felt a tiny spurt of nerves. Meet Harry's parents? Was she ready for that? She had stayed at their Hampshire home last summer, but they had been at the seaside at the time.

Harry stole a chip from Catherine's plate. She rapped his wrist.

"All right. I'll go get my own," he said.

Dot gave her an arch look as Harry wandered off in search of food. "How are things with Dr. Harry?"

"Progressing slowly," said Catherine. "I like him awfully, but I'm finding it difficult going. It's hard to trust another man when Rafe let me down so badly."

"You still have feelings for Rafe?" Dot was incredulous.

"No. Just for the boy I loved as a girl. He's like a missing tooth. He's been part of my life for so long, and it's hard to let go of who I thought he was. I loved him awfully." Catherine pushed away her lunch.

"Do you hear from him?" Dot asked.

"Yes. But I don't read his letters. I put them on the fire."

"Good."

Harry was back with his food. He questioned Dot about her job, which Catherine had neglected to do.

Dot said, "I got a promotion after my last campaign. I'm an account supervisor now!"

"Well done!" said Catherine.

"Smashing!" said Harry, using Dot's favorite word.

The three friends toasted. "To success in our many endeavors!" said Harry.

* * *

Wills was allowed only one visitor, and Catherine decided that it should be Dot. They had brought him some sporting magazines and a box of chocolates. The chocolates had been confiscated by the desk sergeant, but he did let Dot take the magazine back.

She was gone some time before Catherine saw her come out.

"Poor Wills!" her friend said. "I don't like that Emily on principle. I think she is the reason he's stuck in here."

"I know what you mean. I feel the same," said Catherine.

"I'm to watch over you and see that you don't get yourself killed."

"So, I imagine. I don't like Wills worrying about me. I hope you were able to ease his mind."

"I gave it a go. Told him we have a line on the brother and that we're going down to Hampshire tomorrow to look into it. That cheered him."

* * *

To the tunes of Harry Hall and the BBC Dance Orchestra, Dot and Cherry collaborated to dress Catherine in her most stunning black evening gown. Its fitted velvet skirt flared at the knees, and the beaded bodice was cap-sleeved, with a sheer lace overlay fitted down to her wrists. Catherine did vocal exercises as she dressed.

Cherry waved her hair, and Dot fixed the new feathered headpiece in place perfectly. The maid did an exaggerated make-up since she would be on stage. Catherine's chocolate brown eyes appeared large and dramatic, and the makeup emphasized her high cheekbones and full lips.

Dot dressed in a lovely gown of royal blue that matched her eyes. They both spritzed themselves with Shalimar and were ready when Harry picked them up in the Morris.

"A man would kill for such beautiful women," he remarked with a smile.

"You don't look so bad yourself," said Catherine. "Very Douglas Fairbanks this evening."

"I left my saber at home, though," he said, grinning.

Catherine's nerves were in a tangle by the time they reached the Town Hall. She was afraid nothing but a squeak would emerge when she opened her mouth to sing. Harry walked her to the edge of the dais, and she climbed up the stairs. The band was already playing as couples began to stream in through the just-opened doors.

She moved carefully to where the microphone stood and heard the opening notes of "Paradise." Channeling her inner siren, she began to sing. To her relief, her voice emerged low and full-throated. Soon, Catherine lost herself in the moment and began to sway and gesture with her hands. Applause followed at the end of the song, and she felt herself relax. She could do this.

She had never pictured herself in such a role, but Catherine found that she enjoyed it. She almost forgot her other job as an infiltrator. When their first break came, Red escorted her off the stage with his arm around her waist. Tony helped her down the steps. Joe fetched her fur from the coat check, and Alfie even offered his arm as they crossed the street. She felt herself slowly enter the real offstage world.

To her surprise, they hailed a couple of cabs. "We're boycotting the King's Arms," Red said, referring to their customary nearby break pub which wouldn't seat Joe. They taxied to The Eagle and Child instead.

When they got settled with drinks, the compliments began.

"You're a blinking marvel, you are!" said Tony, imitating a Cockney accent.

Red said, "Soon, we'll have you on the BBC."

He and Joe had gone to pick up her hot tea order. Catherine hadn't wanted to put anything cold on her throat. She wondered if the burly Red thought Joe needed his protection.

"Nights like tonight and I could play in a jazz band forever," said Tony.

"I think I could sing until my voice went, but alas, I am first a scholar," she said.

"And I am a serious music student who must do the impossible and find a job conducting a major orchestra."

"Surely you can play jazz if you want to!" she said.

"There's a girl involved," he said. "And her parents frown on band musicians."

"That's a rotten shame," she said emphatically. She whispered in his ear, "Your band is good, but I think you and Joe are the best of the bunch."

Tony beamed. Then he leaned toward her and away from Alfie. He whispered back, "Thanks. Just between us, I've got an offer from a posh band in London. But it would be every night, so I'd have to quit college."

"And you need your degree to get the job as a conductor. I see your dilemma. Is the girl that important?" she asked.

"She would be. She's not even mine. It's all wishful thinking on my part."

Red and Bertie joined them. Alfie remained in a world of his own, singing under his breath as he rolled a cigarette.

It wasn't the time or place to continue the discussion with Tony. Catherine wanted to tell the talented young man that there were plenty of women in the world, and he shouldn't make life's most important decisions based on a relationship that was so uncertain. But the arrival of others prevented her from imparting this wisdom. And she knew that where love was involved, she was a poor judge.

Red was saying, "He's a great sax player, I grant you that. But he's undependable. The only thing he can focus on is when he's going to get his next fix. I need someone who will be on their game and here every Friday and Saturday night."

Joe replied, "Alfie seems to manage."

Alfie looked up at the mention of his name. "Manage what?"

Joe handed Catherine her tea. She thanked him and concentrated on drinking it, trying to appear unaware of the tension that swirled through the group.

"Alfie has been with us since the beginning," said Red. "He knows the routine. Let's drop this discussion for now."

A large man in a rugby shirt appeared at their table. "What's he doing here?" he asked, looking at Joe with a sneer.

"Looking for a fight?" asked Red. "I must warn you; he's a middleweight boxing champ in the States."

Joe stood up. Catherine had never realized how tall he was. His color had blinded her to it. How many other things had she not noticed about him?

Joe's would-be accoster backed off, saying, "I'll take my business elsewhere. Your kind dirties up the place."

Joe sat back down.

"Sorry about that," said Red. "Come the Revolution, I promise you that guy had better leave the country."

"Believe me, that was mild," said Joe with a smile. "Don't shoot him on my account."

Catherine noticed that Alfie was giving Joe a nasty look. As soon as he saw her looking at him, he shuttered it. A chill went down her spine.

Red said, "It's time we were getting back. Drink up."

Catherine thought that between Alfie and Joe, Red had his hands full with this group.

When they returned to the stage, Catherine looked down from the dais at the mingling crowd trying to find her friends. Dot and Harry were talking to a couple of people she didn't recognize. The woman was a knockout—blonde, with shoulder-length hair worn long and wavy. A red dress covered in sequins accented her gorgeous figure.

Red said to her, "Before we get you started singing again, we're going to play a Tango to get this crowd back into it. Maybe you'd like to dance. I know you love a good Tango."

Catherine did. And she and Harry especially enjoyed a good Tango. She descended onto the dance floor and was approaching Harry when the band struck up.

To her chagrin, he pulled the blonde out onto the floor with him, and they began dancing with a drama that was immediately evident. Their eyes locked, then they turned their heads sharply and changed direction. Soon the spectacle had the other dancers clearing the floor to watch the breathtaking pair. Catherine's heart sank to her middle. Who was this woman? She was certainly en rapport with Harry.

The sight hurt. The Tango was Catherine and Harry's dance. She had begun to fall for him the first time they had danced it. Had he and the mystery woman danced together before? It certainly looked like it.

And what about Dot? Had he left her to fend for herself?

Looking about the room, she spotted Dot dancing with the man who had been standing with Harry and the blonde. She was smiling and having a wonderful time. By the time the dance ended, Catherine was shaking. She was scarcely able to climb the stairs back to the band. How was she going to sing for the next two hours while Harry was carrying on with someone else?

In fact, her anguish worked to her advantage. The first song she sang was a ballad of heartbreak—"Stormy Weather." Once she got past that, she had caught the knack of putting her very real emotions into her singing. She was glad the spotlight on the band prevented her from seeing what was going on down on the dance floor, but the images of that Tango wouldn't leave her.

The band played for another two hours, and then, to Catherine's relief, they packed it in at midnight. Performing for four hours when she wasn't used to it on top of the extra emotion was exhausting.

Red came over to her while the others were putting away their instruments. "You were magnificent tonight. I'm sorry, I meant to tell you at the break, but the fact is, you were even better the second half."

"It was fun," she lied. "I really had a good time."

"Tomorrow night, then?"

"I'm planning on it," Catherine said.

* * *

Harry and Dot were waiting for her by the coat check with the woman in red and her companion.

"Are you going out with the band?" Harry asked.

"I wasn't invited. They have some business they want to discuss without me around, I think."

"Here, I'd like you to meet some friends of mine. They're students from the States. They're here studying Nineteenth-Century Brit Lit, and we've been working together. Madeleine and Max, meet Catherine Tregowyn. She teaches Mod Brit Lit at Somerville. Catherine, Madeleine Foster and Max Jones."

She offered them her hand, and they shook. The American woman was looking at her curiously.

"Oysters?" Harry asked.

She had no intention of being a fifth wheel. Besides that, she was totally wrung out.

"You go on ahead. I'm exhausted, and we have a long day ahead of us tomorrow, so I want an early night. I'll take a cab home."

Harry said, "I can take you home."

Catherine demurred, "No. You go ahead. This is Dot's big weekend. I don't want to cut your night short."

"You were smashing by the way," said Dot. "Absolutely fabulous."

"Thanks."

There was a cold wind whistling down High Street. Catherine buried herself up to her eyes in her sable collar as she walked toward the cab queue. The quartet accompanied her, and Harry saw her into a cab before going off to Carmichael's with the others.

She was acutely miserable by the time she reached the flat.

Dot will keep them in line. Maybe I can't trust Harry, but I can surely trust Dot.

Chapter Eleven

Morning came early. Cherry had been up and waiting when Catherine got home the night before. As she helped to prepare her mistress for bed, she had been full of questions about her performance. Catherine had answered them all, given Cherry instructions to wake her at eight, and then, when she was finally in bed, had only been able to toss and turn and wonder what was going on at Carmichael's.

It was not until Dot came in at 3:00 that she was able to fall asleep.

Dot groaned at the early hour when Catherine awakened her in the morning. "I think I got in at dawn," she protested.

"We're meant to leave for Hampshire in an hour," Catherine said. "Up, up, up."

After bathing, Catherine breakfasted on kippers, a bun, and a cup of tea. She dressed in tweeds and a soft pink jumper.

Dot emerged, nearly breathless, to drink a quick cup of tea before Harry arrived. Catherine found she couldn't even ask about the woman in red. Even to Dot, she couldn't betray her insecurity.

When Harry arrived, he was in tearing spirits. "How are the ladies this lovely morning?" he asked as he helped them into the motor.

"I'm doing well," Catherine said. "I understand you got in

rather late." She was planning on taking the back seat but was preempted by Dot, who said she wanted to snooze.

Harry laughed. "Dot knew she was going to have difficulty getting up this morning."

"I don't know what you're laughing about, Dr. Harry Bascombe," said Dot grumpily. "What did you do, drink a gallon of coffee?"

"Almost," he said. "I'm feeling very frisky and anxious to get on with things this morning. Now, Catherine, tell us what you learned last night."

That you are a cad.

"It was a bit disappointing." In a neutral voice, she reported the short conflict between Joe and the rugby player. "I may not agree with Red's politics, but he doesn't hesitate to champion the underdog."

"That's all?" asked Harry.

"That's all that's new. I suspect they wanted to talk about candidates for the sax, and that's why they didn't invite me out last night. Alfie was completely buzzed. Tony was pleasant. He's had an offer from a London band but doesn't know whether he's going to take it or not."

"Well, you may well have a new career awaiting you if you decide your Somerville job isn't to your taste. You were incredible. I saw a completely different side to you last night."

As I did you.

"Oh, I am full of surprises," she said. She heard her friend softly snoring in the back seat. "Did you and Dot have a good time?"

"Dot's always a good time. When she'd had a little too much champagne, she began doing impressions of her boss. What a shatter!"

"Dot should go on stage. She played with the OUDs when she was at Somerville. Comic parts, always," she paused and asked, "What about your new friends?"

"Oh, they aren't particularly *new* friends. I've been working with them since the beginning of term. Madeleine may not look it, but she's fiercely bright. She's a Brontë scholar. She has a grant from the Carnegie Trust. Max, too. He's studying Conrad."

Catherine couldn't think of anything to say. Her heart was hurting. For a little while, they rode in silence while she wondered just how much Harry had been seeing Madeleine and if she was always with Max.

This was absurd! She chided herself. What was she, an adolescent? She had a job to do. Wills was in jail. Completely changing the mood, she asked, "What are we going to say if we find this Phillip Westfield?"

"I'm confident something will come to me in the moment," he said. "I'm a great believer in spontaneity."

"Yes, I've noticed that about you. You live in the moment," said Catherine.

She tried to banish her unwelcome thoughts. Where had this insecurity sprung from? Was it all because of Rafe? It was true that he had left her wondering if she really knew anyone close to her. But she had known Rafe for fourteen years! She had only been seeing Harry for a few months. How could he have so much power to hurt her? Catherine had deliberately kept the relationship casual.

Except for the odd night we've spent canoodling on the sofa. I slipped up there.

She was quiet as they traveled toward Hampshire, looking out the window at the trees that were becoming bare. She didn't like it when the landscape became stark and the sky gray. Catherine didn't function well emotionally when the world outside was dormant. It reminded her of the long cold winters at boarding school.

Then she thought of her brother again. Wills was stuck in a jail cell and wasn't even allowed a look outside, dormant or not. She had better pull herself together and get on with this investigation.

"I think we ought just to verify Phillip's whereabouts," she said. "If we talk to him, he will just bolt again, and the police will never be able to find him. I don't think we ought to talk to him at all."

"You're probably right about him bolting. But perhaps we can talk to him a bit without his knowing who we are."

"How do we do that?"

"We'll just have to see if there is an opportunity. Reed's family home is just outside a small town. It probably has a pub. We should start there. I'm betting that it will be known if he has a visitor."

The town of Redford was small. It had a short High Street sporting a pub, two shops, a post office, a school, and a church. The pub, The Duck and Drake, was welcoming and warm when the party of three entered. A fire burned in the grate, and there were gas lanterns on the tables—lit since the day was dark.

It was near midday, and the pub had about a dozen patrons. Harry asked Catherine and Dot what they wanted for lunch.

Catherine decided on the lamb stew, the savory aroma of which had hit her as soon as she entered. Harry went to the bar, and she heard him having a pleasant conversation with the barkeep, a stout, bald man with a white tablecloth wrapped about his waist.

Catherine asked Dot if she had gotten much rest in the car.

"I'm still knackered. I'll probably fall back to sleep as soon as we get back in the car."

"Did you have fun last night?" asked Catherine.

"More fun than I've had in ages. Thanks so much for inviting me up. I wouldn't have missed hearing you sing for anything."

"It was good for me. I've never done anything quite like it," she said. "Oh, here comes Harry. I hope he got the goods."

Harry had got the goods. "Reed is in residence. And he has a visitor that sounds like Westfield. They're doing some shooting this morning. He thought they might stop in for a bite, so he expects them anytime. Apparently, Reed is a fan of his lamb stew."

"We're sparking on all cylinders then," said Dot. "Excellent."

"He'll be bringing our stew in a moment," said Harry, who

had brought three mugs—two pints of bitter and a hot cider for Catherine.

"You know, they must have had a funeral for James Westfield by now," said Catherine. "His parents must have thought it odd that his brother didn't attend."

"Didn't I tell you?" asked Harry. "They had the funeral before the toxicology results came back. So it was that first week—up in Yorkshire. They didn't know it was anything but an accident then."

"Oh. All right. That makes sense then."

The barkeep approached them with a tray upon which sat three bowls of lamb and vegetable stew topped with baked crusts. For Catherine, it was just what the doctor ordered.

She was in the middle of enjoying the savory dish when the door opened, and together with a gust of cold wind, two gentlemen entered. They were both handsome, dark-haired, and red-cheeked from the cold. Pulling off their leather gloves, they went up to the bar.

"Is that our quarry, do you think?" whispered Dot.

"Probably," said Catherine.

Carrying pints, the two men went to sit a couple of tables away, but they did not attempt to lower their voices. They were reliving their shoot and glorying over the number of birds they had bagged.

"Great idea of yours to come down here," said the taller of the two gentlemen. His accent was a bit off, and Catherine could hear traces of the Tyne.

She said in a low voice to Harry. "The tall one is from Yorkshire. Listen."

"You're missing a good bit of the term, you know," said the other, who must be Samuel Reed.

"I don't need my degree now with James gone. Good thing. I couldn't stick it at university. Don't know what made me choose Mod Brit Lit. Too much writing by half."

"I miss university," said Reed. "Happiest time of my life. It gets dull down here in the back of beyond."

"You should travel," said Westfield. "We could go together. To Monte for starters."

They began talking about all the places they would travel together. Mr. Westfield was going to get a shock when the police turned up to question him about his brother's murder. Catherine thought him rather obnoxious.

Harry echoed her feelings. "He's doing it a bit too rich. That's obviously his impression of a landed gentleman. I certainly hope I'm never guilty of that. If I am, kick me smartly under the table."

Dot giggled. Catherine smiled. "The only time I'm likely to kick you is when we start discussing poetry."

"Haven't you made your peace about that yet?" asked Dot.

"Harry doesn't care for the post-war poets," said Catherine. "Luckily, he doesn't teach them."

The men they were observing had finished their stew and were lingering over a second pint of ale.

"I'll see if mine host will allow me to make a trunk call from his telephone. These chaps might decide to leave for 'Monte' any minute now."

After a brief conversation at the bar, Harry disappeared into the back regions of the pub.

While he was gone, the barkeep came over to Westfield's table and had a few words with him in a low voice. Phillip Westfield flashed a look at Catherine and Dot and said something to Reed. They stood up quickly and left the pub.

Harry didn't return for ten minutes. He looked chagrined when he noticed the men had left.

Catherine said, "The barkeep tipped them off about us. Phillip Westfield looked really alarmed, and they left immediately. What did Detective Chief Inspector Marsh say?"

"He was going to get in touch with the local Chief Constable and have him hold Westfield for questioning until he could get here himself. Looks like I made a large-sized error. The barkeep must be a pal of Reed's and Westfield's. He must have listened in on my conversation and warned them I was calling the police."

Dot said, "So we came all this way only to warn them off. I bet they scarper off to Monte Carlo or some such place."

"Maybe we can intercept them," said Catherine. "When you talked to the barkeep the first time, did he tell you where Samuel Reed's house is situated?"

"Yes. Let's go," said Harry.

They paid their shot, left the pub, and piled once more into the Morris. Harry took the High Street until it headed out of town and then followed the first right. Soon Deepings came into view. It was a large brown and white Tudor dwelling with an untidy garden in the front of the house.

"You're the only one he hasn't seen," Catherine said to Harry. "You go to the door."

But they were to be disappointed. The butler told Harry that his master was not at home.

"Do we go to the nearest train station? Or try to guess which way they went and follow in the car?" he asked.

"I have a singing engagement tonight," Catherine said. "And what could we do if we caught them? We can't arrest them!" She was irritated with Harry for not being more circumspect. "Dot's right. I'll bet they're headed for Monte Carlo. Why would he flee like this unless he was guilty, though?"

Harry swore and then begged their pardon. He pounded his steering wheel to vent his feelings instead. "The only thing we can do is wait here for the Chief Constable. Name of Caldwell, Marsh said. I suppose we had better tell him what's happened."

Catherine said, "You're right. I'm going to step out of the car and get some air."

She paced through the untended garden. Could Reed not afford a gardener? If he was short on funds, a trip to Monte Carlo might not be in the cards, so to speak. Was Westfield flush? Had his father already started paying him the allowance he had paid his brother?

At length, she grew cold and got back into the car. Harry was smoking his pipe and talking to Dot.

"Max was taken with you. I had to break it to him that you live in London in real life," he was saying.

"If he wants to see me again, he can jolly well come down to London."

Catherine asked, "Did you like him?"

"He was a lot of fun," Dot said. "Americans know how to have a good time."

"I noticed," Catherine said dryly. "I watched Harry and Madeleine doing the Tango."

Harry didn't say anything in reply to this dig, and at that moment, a Lagonda pulled into the circle drive. He got out of the car, and Catherine watched him explaining things to the Chief Constable. The older man—a tall, spare fellow in a top hat—looked vexed. He returned to his motor and drove off, his wheels spitting gravel.

"He's going to try to catch Marsh on the telephone before he leaves Oxford."

"Well, we might as well go back," said Catherine, hoping Harry had forgotten his scheme to take them to meet his parents.

Evidently, he had, for he struck out for the highway in the direction of Oxford. She was vastly relieved. She wasn't in the right frame of mind to worry about making a good impression. And she was extremely tired after her short night.

Conversation was strained on the way back. Harry was angry with himself and Catherine not in any mood to salve his feelings. Dot was asleep.

Would Max and Madeleine be at the Town Hall this evening? Taking a deep breath, she told herself that she was not a green girl. She would cope. Harry had made no commitments to her.

When at last they reached Oxford, it was after three. Harry took her straight to her flat. She said good-bye and told him she would take care of getting herself to the Town Hall that night, so he needn't bother.

"I'm sorry I've been such rotten company. I've been castigating myself. But I'd be happy to accompany you tonight," he said. "I was looking forward to it. What will Dot do?"

She had forgotten about Dot. Her friend looked from one of them to the other and said, "I'll go with Catherine. You don't need to tend me, Harry."

"Fine," he said, his voice terse. "I'll spend the evening ringing the airports to see if our suspect booked a flight through to the South of France. They would have to drive to Monte Carlo from there."

When they got inside the flat, Catherine excused herself to Dot. "I need to take a nap. I'm sorry."

"I slept my fill in the car. I'll go down to the police station and visit Wills. He's probably wondering what we got up to today."

"Thank you," said Catherine, her eyelids growing heavy. "You're the best of friends."

* * *

That evening, much rested, Catherine dressed in another of her evening gowns—this one ice pink with white marabou feathers as soft as down at the shoulders and hem. As Cherry applied the heavy makeup once again, she chatted with Dot.

"Are you certain you will be all right on your own without Harry?" she asked.

"Oh, yes! Max was planning to come tonight."

Her friend's eyes sparkled.

"Now don't you go running off with him to America," Catherine cautioned. "How long will he be here?"

"He leaves at the end of term."

"Good," said Catherine, thinking not so much of Max, but of Madeleine.

Chapter Twelve

Her singing gig went a lot better that night without Harry on the dance floor. She poured her soul into her songs, letting out all her frustration and anxiety like steam from a tea kettle.

When the break came, she was determined to make some headway in the investigation even if she had to ask leading questions. No more sitting around and waiting for someone to utter a chance comment.

She waited for them to settle at the high table in the corner of the Eagle and Child with their beverages and said, "Tell me about your sax player. I'm curious. Have you got any ideas about who murdered him?"

Alfie looked up sharply and met her gaze. "They've already found his murderer. Chap called Tregowyn. He's in love with James's girl. Didn't like the way James was treating her and thought he'd get her to himself."

She was very glad they only knew her as Cat. Hearing William spoken of as the murderer gave her a bad moment, but she pressed on, looking at Tony. "I thought you said he didn't have a girl."

Tony corrected her, "I said, 'no one important.' And Emily wasn't. She is nothing more than a hanger-on."

This gave Catherine another bad moment. Emily had never seen herself that way, surely.

"I wonder why Tregowyn murdered James then," she said. "If this Emily wasn't important to him."

"There's no accounting for people when they're in love," said Tony.

Red spoke up for the first time. "He was a great sax. Best I've ever known, but I'm not sure about Tregowyn. I think his arrest is just a matter of police incompetence."

Catherine turned to him, hoping her gratitude for this comment was not showing in her face. "So, who do you think is guilty, then?"

"Probably that worthless brother of his," said Red. "He has delusions of becoming a Toff. Always touching James for money. Regular leech."

"Sounds unpleasant," said Catherine. No one else was forthcoming, so she said, "I guess it's time we were getting back."

Red put his hand at her waist this time as they crossed the street to the Town Hall. The gesture was unexpectedly protective. She was disappointed that her question had not born more fruit, but perhaps no one had wanted to speak up in the presence of the others. It hadn't escaped her that Tony had said little.

"No boyfriend tonight?" Red asked.

"Harry's just a friend," she said, hoping her voice sounded careless enough.

"No one could sing with your passion unless she was in love," Red said with a smile. It was a very attractive smile, lighting up what she had always seen as a stern visage.

"I know what it's like to be in love," she said. "I parted ways with him last July."

"Hmm," he responded. "Go with me for a drink tonight?"

"I'd like that," she said.

* * *

The second half of the evening went very fast. Catherine found that she was thinking of other things as she sang. It was in danger of becoming a rote performance. With difficulty, she persuaded her thoughts away from Wills and Harry and concentrated on what she was doing.

Red helped her down the steps after their performance and shepherded her to the coat check. Once she was wrapped in her sable fur, they left the Hall and began walking east down High Street. "You know Carmichael's?" he asked.

"I adore Carmichael's," she said, knowing a moment's fear. What if Harry was there with Madeleine?

She saw no Harry there, but Max and Dot were sitting in a cozy corner. It was one of her and Harry's haunts, and she felt a stab of pain as she was shown to a table with Red.

"Do you like fondue? They do it very well here," he said.

"I adore it," she told him. "I just remembered I didn't eat dinner."

After he had placed their order, which included a bottle of wine, he sat back and appeared to relax.

"You seem to be more than a bandleader," she said. "You are like a band 'father.'"

"Sometimes, it feels that way. Thank heavens we only play on the weekends. Sometimes I feel like I'm trying to herd cats."

"There are some distinct personalities. But then I'm sure musicians are a temperamental lot."

"Some more than others," he said.

The waiter brought their wine and poured a sample for Red to taste. After sipping, the bandleader nodded his head. The waiter poured each of them a glass.

"Was Mr. Westfield temperamental?" she asked.

"He was the complete musician. I think it was the only thing he was really serious about in life. In his daily pursuits—university and women—he could be a bit careless. A bit of a playboy. But when it came to his sax, he was all business."

"I wish I had known him," she said.

"He was a strange duck," said Red. "Had a chip on his shoulder the size of London. All the money anyone could want, but he was not content. It wasn't that he wanted to be a Toff like his brother does. It was more like he resented that he didn't get the respect that a Toff would."

"Right up your street, I would think," she said, sipping her wine. For the first time, she realized that Red was an attractive man. His eyes were bright blue, and he had that brilliant smile with straight, even teeth. He just didn't use it very often.

"Yeah. But he wasn't interested in politics. He was stuck in Medieval History. He would have liked to live when men proved themselves by the sword and gained titles and land by virtue of their service to the Crown."

She appreciated his analysis. "But you're a Toff, aren't you?"

"I've given up my birthright to my parent's everlasting scorn. My father's an earl, but I've refused to be his heir. Everything will go to my younger brother. I've even made it legal. I get an allowance, but I use it for rent on the house for Joe and me and the rest for the cause."

The waiter delivered their fondue, and Catherine almost grinned. Was feeding her expensive wine and fondue part of the "cause?"

"I've read about you in the newspaper. When's your next protest march scheduled?" She put a bit of torn bread on the end of her fondue fork and dragged it through the melted cheese in its fondue pot.

"We like to take the business owners by surprise, so we don't talk about that except among ourselves. What are your politics?" He helped himself to the fondue.

"I'm an old fashioned Liberal," she said. "I don't go to extremes. I think extremes lead to war, and I certainly don't want another war."

"What about a revolution?" he asked.

"Surely your goals can be reached without bloodshed?" she asked, her mind abhorring the idea of bloodletting of any kind. She put down her fork.

"All we want is for the ordinary people to have equal power

with the aristocracy. It should be decided by a vote, but I can't see the Toffs letting that happen."

"Oh, let's not have this conversation," she pleaded. "I don't want to argue with you."

"You're going to have to choose one day, come the Revolution," his brow furrowed in earnestness.

"Why do you have a jazz band?" she asked.

"Because I love it," he said simply. "It is something people of all classes enjoy. Who else could get away with employing Joe?"

"Would you consider staying on with the band?" he asked as she dipped her bread in the cheese mixture.

"I love singing, but my real passion is poetry, so I don't think so."

"That's right. You're a poet. You're going to write me a song."

"I might give it a try. I am actually employed teaching Mod Brit Lit, but I focus heavily on poetry."

"You can't be that much older than I am," he said.

"I was lucky enough to be published early. I have two books in print and one coming out at Christmas. There were two vacancies in my department, so they offered me the post with the proviso that I get my doctorate within three years. I am only committed to the teaching for this year, though. We'll see how things progress."

"I might as well tell you that I know your surname."

She felt her cheeks heat.

"You know I'm William's sister?"

"Yes. You're looking into this murder, aren't you? That's why you joined the band."

Her heart speeded up. Red had a clear, uncompromising gaze. It was now fixed on her.

"Yes," she said. "But I don't think you had anything to do with it."

"Whom do you suspect, then?" Red wanted to know.

"Well, truthfully, I haven't ruled out Joe or Alfie."

"What about Tony?" he asked.

"He doesn't have it in him; I don't think. Besides, James was his good friend. He's honestly mourning him."

"They had their disagreements," Red said.

"Do you know any details?" This was a new wrinkle.

"No. Most likely, it was over a woman. It seems like it always is. I know nothing about the love life of either one of them, though."

"Hmm. I wonder if it was Emily, and Tony is trying to protect her by downplaying their relationship."

"It's possible," Red said. "Now how about some chocolate fondue for dessert?" he asked, pouring her another glass of wine.

"I couldn't," she said. "I'm replete with bread and cheese. It was wonderful."

"I'm glad you enjoyed it."

"Do you think Joe or Alfie could be guilty?" she asked.

"At the risk of upsetting my band, yes. Either of them. I have a feeling James was blackmailing Alfie in exchange for cocaine. Threatening to turn him over to the police for unlawful distribution. And Joe might not seem like it, but he's a hothead. He really despised James, and the feeling was mutual. And, of course, there's the fact that he's a middleweight boxing champ. But I won't give evidence against either of them, just so you know."

"Do either of them have an alibi?" Catherine asked.

"I haven't the slightest idea."

"Well, that certainly is interesting. Thanks, Red. And thanks for the delicious meal."

"I take it you're ready to go now?"

"Yes. I'm exhausted. But this has been lovely. And thank you for not giving me away to the rest of the band."

"You're still going to sing next weekend?"

"Yes. I'm looking forward to it."

"Rehearsal on Wednesday? We have a few new numbers."

"That will be fine."

Red signed the check, recovered her fur from the coat check, and led her downstairs onto the High Street.

He flagged down a cab and handed her in.

"For a Communist, you have nice manners," she said.

"Don't breathe a word," he said, smiling as he got in beside her.

Catherine gave her address to the driver. While sitting in such close proximity to Red, she was amused to note that he also wore a spicy men's cologne.

When they arrived at her flat, she said, "You needn't see me to the door. Thank you for the lovely evening."

"It was good to talk," he said. "Good night."

* * *

There was a lot for Catherine to think about, but Dot was waiting up for her.

"You were smashing tonight," her friend told her. "Was that the bandleader you were cozying up to at Carmichael's?"

"I wasn't cozying up to him, but yes, that was Red, the bandleader."

"Did you find out anything?"

"Not really. I added to my suspects instead of eliminating anyone. Red doesn't think I should go so far as to discount Tony. Now I'm wondering if Tony has been disguising his interest in Emily to protect her."

"What do you mean?"

"According to Tony, she wasn't anyone important in James Westfield's life."

"Hmm. That does vary a bit from what she told you and William," Dot said. "Of course, he doesn't know you have anything to do with Emily."

"Right," said Catherine. "He also told me Joe is a hothead, and James might have been blackmailing Alfie. But he said he wouldn't give evidence against them. How was your evening with Max, the American?"

"Umm," said Dot. "Lovely. I wish I weren't going back to

London tomorrow. He's an interesting chap. From a place called Julesburg. That's in Colorado, but I'm not even sure where that is. He grew up on a cattle ranch."

"So, he's a genuine cowboy?"

"Not now. He wants to be a college professor. He and Madeleine study at UCLA. That's in Los Angeles."

"What else do you know about Madeleine?" Catherine asked.

"She's a diva, according to Max. He's had enough of her to last a lifetime, he says. She grew up in a place called Beverly Hills, which sounds quite posh. Why do you care about Madeleine?"

"Harry seemed quite taken with her," Catherine said carefully. She yawned and checked her watch. "I've got to sing in the choir tomorrow, so I had better get to bed. I want to hear more about the un-cowboy, but it'll have to wait 'til morning if you don't mind."

"Cricky!" exclaimed Dot. "I had no idea of the time. I want to catch the 10:40 to Town tomorrow. It's gone two a.m."

Catherine said, "You may have the bathroom first. I must get out of this gown."

Chapter Thirteen

Max surprised Dot and Catherine by arriving in his motor at ten o'clock in the morning to drive Dot back to London.

"I didn't know you had a motor," cried Dot.

"You must know you can't separate an American from his car," said Max. "I rented it for the duration."

"Well, it's very kind of you to rescue me from the train," Dot said.

"This way, I'll know right where to find you," he said.

Catherine was happy to see Dot beaming back at Max.

Dot said, "I'll be ready in just a moment."

Catherine was all ready for church, so she sat down to entertain the American. "May I get you a cup of tea? I'm sorry we don't have coffee."

"No, I'm just fine," Max said.

Catherine liked the cut of the American. He was blond and blue-eyed with a healthy dose of freckles. No doubt, cowboys spent a lot of time in the sun.

"What made you decide to come to Oxford to study?" she asked.

"Are you kidding? My field is Nineteenth-Century British literature. Where else would I go?"

She laughed. "Cambridge, maybe?"

"I like Oxford better. Cambridge is too quiet for me."

"Did you know Madeleine at UCLA?" she asked, trying to sound casual.

"Yeah. She and I had a lot of the same classes, but we're more competitors than friends."

"Oh?"

"I'm here on a grant. She's here on her own dime. There were a lot of other candidates for the program. We just happened to be the ones who were accepted, but we were competing all the way."

"She's very bright then?" asked Catherine.

"She has to be. They don't award many places in the program to women. She's already published a book on Emily Brontë." Max seemed more resigned than impressed by his colleague's success.

"And you both work with Harry, er Dr. Bascombe?" Catherine asked.

"Yeah. He's a major voice in the field, you know."

"Has it been valuable?"

"You must know the work he's done on the psychoanalysis of the Victorian authors. It's been especially helpful to Madeleine. The Brontës were all head cases, as I'm sure you know. As a matter of fact, Harry and Madeleine were supposed to go up to up to the family home in Haworth this weekend, but something came up, and Harry wasn't able to go."

Catherine was so surprised by this information that she didn't immediately reply. Dot chose that moment to emerge with her suitcase.

"All ready," Dot said.

"Swell," said Max. "Let's go. Nice to chat with you, Catherine."

"It was nice. Hopefully, I'll see you again before you go back to the States."

"Now that Harry's introduced us to the jazz band, I imagine we will."

Catherine was agitated after Max and Dot left. Harry had planned to leave town for a weekend with Madeleine, and he had never said a word to her about it. Then, when they couldn't go, he'd invited Madeleine (and Max) to come to the Town Hall to dance when he knew Catherine wouldn't be dancing. It wasn't a chance meeting.

So, his interest in Madeleine would appear to be more than scholarly. Catherine didn't know what to think. But now she was going to be late for the choir if she didn't hurry.

* * *

After the church service, Cherry and Catherine went for their Sunday meal at Somerville Dining Hall. She tried to find Miss Favringham in the throng, but she evidently wasn't there. Perhaps she was still in London, staying with her parents.

She wondered what they gave poor Wills to eat for Sunday dinner at the jail. She had hoped to have him out by now.

When they returned to the flat, she changed into her charcoal-colored trousers and a long black cashmere jumper and cardigan. Adding her fur, she decided to walk to the jail. Sunday buses were few and far between and she could use the exercise.

The afternoon air was brisk, and the streets were full of Sunday strollers, taking advantage of the dwindling days of above-freezing temperatures. The church bells were tolling in competition with one another all over Oxford.

Wills was happy to see her.

Catherine greeted him, "Have you heard from Mr. Spence?"

"Yes. He's coming up this afternoon. It seems that he's managed to convince the Chief Constable that they don't have enough to hold me."

"That's good news!" Catherine's heart lightened. "I think your arrest was all a ploy to give Phillip Westfield a false sense of security. We found him down in Hampshire, but he got the wind up and escaped before the police could question him. I think that speaks to his guilt. Maybe the police agree. We don't know where he is now."

Wills said, "You have no idea how much I appreciate it, Cat. It's good to have you and Harry in my corner. And Emily, of course."

"I'm just glad your solicitor is getting you out today."

Wills said, "Harry was in last night."

"Oh?" she said, keeping her tone light.

"He actually told me about your doings yesterday. Said he'd found out Westfield flew to Nice. He suspected they were bound for Monte Carlo."

"Oh. That's more than I know. But then I was with the band last night."

Wills asked, "Have you found out anything about the band?"

"A little here and there. Nothing huge." She told her brother about Alfie's cocaine habit, Joe's being a middleweight boxing champ, and James's taunts of him. "Either of them could have easily gotten on the wrong side of James. Then there's Red. A bona fide Communist who has demonstrated against James's father's coal mines. I don't see any direct personal conflict, though."

"Isn't there another member?" asked Wills.

"Yes. Tony. I don't see any actual evidence against Tony, though Red thinks they may have been after the same woman."

"Emily?" Wills looked pained.

She nodded.

At that point, Mr. Spence strode in and said, "I just secured your release, Mr. Tregowyn."

The sergeant followed him, and with little ceremony, unlocked his handcuffs and Wills was free to go. Catherine felt such a tremendous relief she couldn't think how to express it, except to say, "Thank you so much, Mr. Spence."

"Do either of you have a motor?" asked the solicitor.

When they both said no, he said to Wills, "Come along then, and I'll take you home. May I offer anyone else a ride?"

"Thank you. I'd appreciate a ride," said Catherine.

* * *

Catherine didn't know whether or not to call Harry to tell him about Wills' release. She had never had to think twice about calling him before. But now she had to admit to herself that she was unsure about their relationship.

She decided to wait for him to call her. They usually got together on Sunday afternoons. But it was also Cherry's half-day, and so the maid had not been there to answer the telephone. Bother!

She spent the rest of the afternoon reading essays and planning tutorials, as well as her lecture on Wilfred Owen. Reviewing his poetry threw her into a melancholy.

> *What passing-bells for these who die as cattle?*
> *Only the monstrous anger of the guns.*
> *Only the stuttering rifles' rapid rattle*
> *Can patter out their hasty orisons.*

Surely there could never be another war! It might be painful for her students, but she didn't plan on missing any opportunity to preach the horrors of the last conflict. They were beyond anyone's comprehension who hadn't been there, but the testimonies left in poetry were solemn and heart-rending.

Her dark mood was only added to by the knowledge that Owen was Harry's favorite of the war poets. He didn't telephone during the afternoon or the evening. Was he with Madeleine?

* * *

Monday it rained. The storm lashed at the windows of the flat. Cherry hummed about cheerfully as she dusted the flat. Catherine finished her lecture notes that morning, and she taught Cherry's French lesson that afternoon.

They dined on her maid's lamb chops, fried potatoes, and the last of the season's green beans. Catherine had a long, hot soak in the bathtub, and donned her silk pajamas.

But creature comforts could only take her so far. She

acknowledged to herself that she was miserable. Writing a long letter to Dot, she confided everything and felt better having gotten it off her chest.

Then at 9:00, the telephone rang. Cherry came to her bedroom to tell her that Dr. Bascombe had rung. Catherine's heart gave a leap, and she went to the sitting room to take the call.

"Harry?"

"Catherine. I'm sorry to ring so late, but I've just returned from Monte Carlo."

"Oh! As Dot would say: Cricky!"

"After all that sleuthing and traveling, it was no good, I'm afraid."

Her hopes fell. "What do you mean. Couldn't you find them?"

"I found them, but Westfield hadn't anything to say to me except that he didn't kill his brother. He had no intention of providing an alibi. He said he owed me nothing. I was an absolute fool. I don't know what I was thinking to hare off like that."

Catherine was frustrated. "But have you told the police where they are? Isn't there such a thing as extradition?"

"Only if you have proof of guilt. The police have less than nothing."

"So, Phillip Westfield can stay abroad as long as he likes, unless a case is proved against him."

"Yes. And he knows it."

"Do you think he's guilty, Harry?" She couldn't accept that his long journey had been for nothing.

"He's afraid of something. But he seemed to dismiss his brother's murder as if it were of no account."

"That's odd."

"Sorry, I can't be of more help."

Catherine realized Harry didn't know about Wills. She said, "Wills is free. He's back home. Mr. Spence appealed to the Chief Constable, and convinced him they didn't have sufficient evidence to arrest him."

"Oh. Well, that's good then. Jolly good. I'm glad," he said, sounding relieved.

"I feel rotten that you had that long trip for nothing," she said.

"It was my own fault. I overestimated my ability to frighten the fellow. He was unflappable as it turned out."

"But he obviously doesn't want to face the police."

"Yes. He's gone to some length to prove that."

"Well, I'm sorry I have nothing concrete to report from the band. Nothing new."

There was a pause on Harry's end. She wondered if he was thinking about Madeleine. "How was Saturday night?" he asked finally.

"I didn't learn anything new. The singing went all right."

"Good. That's good. Well, I must go and put together a tutorial for tomorrow. I'll see you soon, I'm certain."

"Good night, Harry," she said. "And thank you for trying to help Wills."

"Right. Well, good night."

Ringing off, Catherine wasn't sure how she felt. Harry had gone to phenomenal lengths to help her brother. Surely that was a sign of caring for her?

Of course, he cared for her. Catherine just didn't know if he cared for Madeleine, as well.

Chapter Fourteen

Catherine slept better that night and arose with thoughts of Wills. She decided to ring him, though it was early.

"Your arrest isn't going to have any effect on your standing with the Dunn School, is it?" she asked him.

"I rang my professor last night," he said. "They're going to give me the benefit of the doubt for the time being, but they don't want me in the lab. I'm strictly limited to book research until proof of someone else's guilt comes to light."

"Oh, Wills!" said Catherine. "I'm so sorry."

"Well, my professor's a scientist, remember. He wouldn't make a permanent move without proof, I don't think. But the best proof is to find the real murderer. I don't think I can count on the police for that at this point."

"And Harry and I are committed to finding that if possible." She told him about Harry's trip to Monte Carlo. "So, James Westfield's brother is likely to remain a question mark, at least for the time being. He is dependent on his father for money. I can't help but think his father is going to be displeased at his leaving school and decamping to Monte Carlo, presumably to gamble."

"At least Emily seems to be in the clear," he said.

"That reminds me," Catherine said, smiting her forehead with the heel of her hand. "I still need to find that witness that saw Emily at Mr. Westfield's flat. Maybe she saw something else later."

"What do you hope to learn from the witness?"

"I don't know. It's just a matter of leaving no stone unturned. Can you tell me where his flat was?"

"It was on Clarendon Street. James was your neighbor. Two doors down from the University Press."

"Thanks, Wills. I'll keep you informed about my progress. Try not to worry."

She needed to speak to Emily about Tony, as well, but she didn't share that with her brother.

"Thanks for everything, Cat. Especially for hiring Mr. Spence. It's good to be out of that place."

"I'll see what else I can manage so that you can get back to work," she said.

After they rang off, she decided to try finding the witness before she had her 11:00 tutorial. Cherry told her it was cold out, so she dressed in her warmest tweed suit, a heather-colored jumper, and her fur coat with the large collar that stood around her head.

She walked swiftly down the street through a freezing fog. Knocking on the flat doors across from the victims flat, she found only one person home—a tiny elderly lady in a flowered housedress wearing a heavy shawl.

"I'm sorry to bother you, ma'am. My name is Catherine Tregowyn, and I would like to know if you are the lady who spoke to the police about the murder across the street?"

The lady's gleamed with interest. "I am."

"I am looking into this case. Would you mind if I spoke with you for a few moments?"

"You had better come it," she said, opening the door wider.

Catherine walked into a flat that was overly warm and smelled of Mentholatum. There was a fire in the grate.

"Won't you have a seat?" the lady invited.

Catherine removed her fur and held it over one arm.

"I understand that you identified Miss Emily Norwood visiting

Mr. Westfield's flat on the day of the murder. How did you identify her?" she asked.

"The police had pictures. There was one of Miss Norwood taken from the Radcliffe Infirmary file. I remembered her, especially because she is so beautiful. She ought to be in films." A slight flush of excitement colored the woman's cheeks. "She used to visit the murdered man in his flat quite a lot. Sometimes she was in her nurse's uniform."

"Did you know the victim?" she asked.

"I knew his name and face because he was in that jazz band. His photo was in the *Oxford Mail* sometimes."

This was definitely one of those ladies whose chief form of entertainment was her neighbors. A veritable Miss Marple. "Was there anyone else you saw who visited him the Sunday he was murdered?"

The lady played with the fringe on her shawl with nervous fingers. "In the evening, there was a gent, but I think poor Mr. Westfield was already dead because he didn't answer his door."

She had missed William then. "Did you recognize the gentleman?"

The lady didn't answer at once. "It was dark and a bit foggy. All I could make out was his top hat. That's how I knew he was a gent."

"Very astute of you, then. Thank you so much. As you probably know, Miss Norwood has been released from jail. I'm hoping to find the real culprit. I appreciate your help. Can you tell me anything about the people who customarily visited Mr. Westfield?"

"Well, yes. I especially noticed it, you see. A black man came to see him once. Probably the one in the band. You don't see black men too often. I almost rang the police. I was that frightened."

Catherine felt a stab of sympathy for Joe. "Did you recognize any other band members?"

"They could have visited, but he wasn't home much. He didn't have too many visitors. I certainly wish you luck on finding whoever it was that killed him."

Catherine quelled her disappointment and took her leave after complimenting the woman on her profusion of houseplants. No doubt, they flourished because of the tropical climate in the flat.

Almost relieved to be out in the chilly fog once more, she crossed carefully over to the other side of the street. There was a small alley that traveled along beside the Westfield flat. She followed it back to a small yard behind James Westfield's flat. From that viewpoint, she was able to see that the flat possessed a back door.

Hmm. That's interesting. Perhaps Mr. Westfield wasn't dead when the "gent" came but had gone out. And just who was he?

Catherine checked her watch. It was close to the time for her tutorial. Increasing her pace, she walked to the college through the fog, pulling her collar close about her neck. After greeting Hobbs, the porter, in his lodge by the entrance, she went to her rooms and donned her black scholar's gown, just in time to receive her students.

Miss Favringham was present today, but Catherine noticed that her color was pale, and she had lost that animation that had made her so attractive. As they discussed *Testament of Youth,* she was quiet, not involving herself in the discussion.

Catherine finally asked, "Miss Favringham, assuming you read the book, how did it appeal to you?"

"I found it horribly depressing," the young woman said. "Now I know why my father never talks about the war."

"He was an officer, I imagine?" Catherine asked.

The girl looked down at her fingernails that Catherine now noticed were bitten to the quick. "Yes. But that's all I know."

She seemed disinclined to speak any longer, so Catherine didn't press her.

"Next week, we'll discuss May Wedderburn Canaan, who worked as a V.A.D. during the war as well as for MI6. She's an interesting woman. The only woman among the major War Poets. We'll also discuss Wilfred Owen, the subject of tomorrow's lecture. Two very different perspectives."

She dictated the reading assignments—poems to be found in their anthology. "Your essay for next week is to compare and contrast Owen and Wedderburn Canaan, particularly taking into account their genders."

Miss Favringham was the first out the door. Catherine had intended to inquire after her health and wondered if the young woman had escaped intentionally. It was quite obvious she didn't want to be questioned.

Catherine went down to luncheon in the hall and was dismayed when her Miss Favringham didn't come in to eat. Her concern for the young woman was to the point where she decided she must talk to the new Dean of Students.

After she returned from luncheon, she rang the dean's secretary for an appointment. After securing one for three o'clock, she rang the Radcliffe Infirmary and inquired what time the Emily Norwood would be off her shift. She was told that Nurse Norwood did not come in until 4:00 that afternoon.

Since her lecture for tomorrow was prepared, and she had two hours before her appointment with the dean, she decided to go to Emily's flat and ask her about Tony. Red's comment about the drummer's possible conflict with James Westfield was a loose end she felt she needed to either tie off or unravel, whatever the case may be. If there was tension over a woman, she needed to know for certain who that woman was. She felt as though she were missing a piece to her puzzle. Why had Emily never mentioned Tony if he had such a pash for her?

The fog had finally lifted, so her walk to Emily's flat in nearby Cranham Street was more pleasant than her morning outing, but still cold. There was no sun today. Cheerless November days were just around the bend.

Emily was in, fortunately, and looked especially pretty. Catherine's feelings for the young woman were jumbled. Which of all the men in her life did she truly favor?

"Is William all right?" Emily asked.

"He's very relieved to be out of jail, but he has been barred from his lab for the time being," Catherine said.

"Oh, I am so sorry. That's rotten."

"I wonder if I could talk with you for a few moments, Emily," Catherine inquired.

"Certainly," the young woman replied.

They sat on the beige sofa. Catherine took off her gloves and hat and laid them beside her on the seat.

"I know I've asked you about Tony before, but someone was telling me that James Westfield and Tony were at odds over a woman. It seems pretty obvious that woman would be you."

Emily frowned. "I'm afraid I don't know what you mean."

"Tony hasn't shown any interest in you? He doesn't tease you or flirt in any way? Even slightly?"

She smiled. "I'm sort of a mascot for the band. Everyone flirts with me a little. Except for Alfie."

"Tony has told me on two different occasions that there was no woman in James's life. Of course, you know that wasn't true. Is there any chance he harbors a secret pash for you? Maybe by downplaying your relationship with James, he is trying to protect you from suspicion in the murder?"

"That doesn't make sense!" Emily protested. "Why on earth would he do that?"

"I guess I should tell you that he mentioned that he has secret feelings for a young woman that he hasn't revealed to her yet. Red told me that at the time of James's death, he and Tony were feuding. It is Red's opinion that it was over a woman. The only woman in the picture so far is you."

"Oh, golly!" said Emily. "Tony? I never thought . . ." She wound her fingers together in her lap as she considered this possibility.

"I'm not questioning you about *your* feelings, Emily. I just want to know if you have ever thought that Tony might be attracted to you."

"I suppose it's possible, but I never picked up any sign of it. I admit that sometimes I'm a bit dense. All this time, I never guessed that William . . ." her voice faded, and she blushed.

Catherine smiled at the girl. "Well, I guess I'd better ask Tony straight out," she said. "I hate to embarrass him."

"I can't imagine him with a secret pash. I mean, he's a fantastic drummer in a popular band, and he's very good-looking. What girl wouldn't return his feelings?"

Catherine hoped she had not nixed William's chances with the girl. She had brightened and seemed enamored of the idea of Tony. But, as she had said, who wouldn't be?

Emily had gone from being rejected by James to being flush with suitors. It must be a heady time for the young woman. But Catherine couldn't help but feel that William's not being in the band put him at a distinct disadvantage in the quest for the girl's affections.

* * *

Catherine did not know the new dean, Miss Godfrey, well, but the woman was comparatively young and enthusiastic. She made an effort to know the two hundred students, but she had only started at the beginning of the Michaelmas Term.

"How can I help you, Miss Tregowyn?" she asked. She was short and slim with wavy blonde hair, looking more like a film star than the Dean of Students. Catherine imagined that this would appeal to the students.

"I'm quite worried about one of my students, Miss Favringham. Her father was here a couple of weeks ago and intimated that she was going through a 'rough patch.' Her behavior, since then, has been completely uncharacteristic. I think she may be in the midst of a nerve storm of some type. I'm not qualified in this area, but I should hate to see her have a breakdown."

"Tell me about her," invited the dean.

Catherine explained Miss Favringham's family background, her new seeming disinterest in her schoolwork when she had formerly been so enthusiastic, her pallor and nervousness, lack of animation, and failure to be present at meals.

"And this all started when?" the dean asked.

Catherine thought for a moment. "It dated from when she lost a tennis match a couple of Saturdays ago. Her father was here for the match. For any other student, it wouldn't be that momentous, but Miss Favringham has Olympic ambitions and doesn't lose tennis matches. I ate dinner with them on the day after. Two Sundays ago. She was unusually nervous and didn't eat her dinner. I put it down to her father's presence."

"And what was your opinion of the father?"

"He's a bit pompous, but not unkind. She didn't seem afraid of him or anything like that. Just nervous."

"How can I help?" asked the dean.

"I'm certain the parents are already aware of the situation. She was going to spend this last weekend in London with them. But she gives the impression of staggering under a load that is too heavy for her right now. Something has changed in her life. I don't have the least idea of what it is. Are you trained in psychology at all?"

"I had some courses when I was doing post-grad work in sociology."

"Maybe you could call her in and talk to her under the pretense of getting to know the students? Perhaps you will have some insights. I just can't bear to see her this way. Not to be trite, but it's like a bright light has gone out. I'm worried she might hurt herself."

"I understand your concern. If the girl may harm herself, perhaps some intervention *is* needed here." The woman went to her file drawer and pulled a file. After looking over a single page, which was the total of its contents, she said, "I actually have been trying to get to know the students one by one, starting with the first-year girls. I see that Miss Favringham is first-year."

"Yes," said Catherine.

"All right. I will call Favringham in, but if she tells me anything in confidence, I won't be able to pass it on to you in specific terms. You do realize that?"

"All I want is for someone to help her," Catherine said, feeling a bit of her worry ease. Then she remembered her request that the baron read E.E. Cummings to her students and his acquiescence to the idea.

She told the dean of her proposal.

"That sounds like an excellent idea to help keep her in touch with her family," the woman said.

From the page in front of her, the dean gave Catherine the baron's London telephone number. "I don't think it would be wise for you to confide your worries to him about his daughter at this time."

Catherine agreed with the dean.

* * *

The baron was thrilled with the invitation to read for her students. As he needed to be at Oxford on Thursday morning for a meeting of the trustees at St. John's, his alma mater, he proposed a reading on Thursday afternoon. Catherine said she would arrange to have tea and cakes served in the Somerville Reading Room, where she would have all of her tutorial students present. It would be a lovely, intimate setting.

The next thing on Catherine's agenda was to arrange for the tea and cakes to be served. Then she wrote notes to her seven tutorial students inviting them to attend the reading as part of their assignment for the seminar.

Catherine spent the rest of the day sketching out her lectures and tutorials for the next few weeks. She had taken on her post right before the term started and had only had the time to plan the direction she would be going vaguely. Now she was getting down to specifics.

Chapter Fifteen

At 5:00, her office phone rang, pulling her out of a state of deep concentration.

"Catherine?"

"Harry?"

"Yes. I'm ringing to see if you would like to have dinner at the college with Madeleine, Max, and me."

Floored by the invitation, she replied before thinking, "Won't I be in the way?"

"In the way of what?"

"Harry, I have eyes in my head. I saw you dance the Tango with Madeleine."

He only laughed. "Darling, the dinner is her idea. She very much wants to get to know you."

I'll just bet she does.

But she knew she would take up the woman's challenge. "I'll meet you at the Hall at seven o'clock then."

"No. I'll meet you at the porter's lodge at five before seven. We'll enter the Dining Hall together."

He rang off. Catherine felt a bit foolish, but Madeleine was what Hollywood would call a "knock out."

She checked the time. It was five o'clock. Just time enough for her to have a bath.

Returning to the flat, she informed Cherry of her plans for the evening.

"Oh! I was going to fix something new! A cassoulet of chicken," the maid said.

Catherine shuddered inwardly. She detested cassoulets of any kind. "You go ahead and fix it for yourself if you like. Then you can see how you like the recipe."

Cherry beamed. She ran the bath for her mistress and helped her undress.

"Could you pick out something that makes me look sophisticated?" Catherine asked her. "I'm going to be compared with some rather stiff competition this evening."

During her bath, she tried to relax and divert herself with thoughts of James Westfield's murder puzzle, but she had too many things going on in her head—worries over Miss Favringham, thoughts of Tony and Emily and what this would mean for Wills, and most of all Harry and the smashing Madeleine. Catherine had no doubt whatsoever that the woman was dangerous. This was war.

Before dressing, she sprayed herself with her new Shalimar perfume. Not too much, but just enough to be haunting. Cherry brushed her sable-colored hair until it shone and then gave it a fresh wave. Giving her mistress's makeup close attention, she also filed and painted Catherine's fingernails a wine color.

One did not wear evening dress for dinner in a college hall, so Cherry pulled out the next best thing--a three-quarter length chocolate-colored gown that hugged her slim figure in a princess line and flared at the knees. The sleeves puffed at the shoulder, creating the illusion that Catherine's waist was even slimmer.

Satisfied that she looked her best, Catherine sallied forth to her waiting taxi, cloaked in her sable fur. The night was foggy and damp.

Harry was waiting for her by the Christ Church College porter's lodge and saluted her with a peck on the cheek. Taking his arm, she allowed him to usher her to the Dining Hall.

"I have invited Baron Favringham to read E.E. Cummings at tea on Thursday in the Somerville Reading Room. He's a bona fide character—the father of my worrisome student. I think you would enjoy it. It will be a small gathering. Would you like to come?"

"Definitely. May I bring Madeleine and Max?"

If you must. "Certainly," Catherine said.

She spotted Madeleine immediately, looking like a goddess in seafoam green with her shoulders exposed and lovely. It hardly mattered that she was overdressed for the occasion.

Max's face lit up at the sight of Catherine. "How is Dot?" he asked immediately.

She thought of the letter she had received that day. "Finding London a bit dull at the moment."

"I've decided to go down to visit on the weekend," he said.

"I'm certain she'll be happy to see you," Catherine said.

Madeleine said, "Harry has spoken much of you. Apparently, you are his Watson."

Catherine's temper rose along with her eyebrows. Was she being intentionally insulting, or did Harry really say that?

Vichyssoise was served.

"It is rather the other way around," Harry said with a light laugh. "She is my Holmes."

Madeleine turned to Harry. "Oh! Sorry. Did I get that wrong? What field did you say her doctorate was in, darling?"

Catherine raised her chin. She hated being talked about when she was present. "It is a work in progress," Catherine said. "But my subject is modern British lit with an emphasis on poetry."

"But I was sure he told me you are a professor at Somerville," said the American woman.

"I have other qualifications. I never intended to teach at the university level."

Madeleine looked puzzled. "What made you change your mind?"

"Harry," she said, exchanging a smile with him.

The woman across from her pouted. A moment later, her face cleared, and she said, "He can be very encouraging, can't he?"

"Demanding, more like," Catherine said. Turning to Max, she asked, "Have you gained any new insights on Conrad since you've been studying here?"

"He's more complex than I imagined," said Max. "I knew he explored the darker side of human nature, but I just discovered that he made a suicide attempt."

"Huh!" said Madeleine. "I'll never understand why you chose Conrad. Personality-wise, you're polar opposites."

"Maybe that's why," Harry posited. "Nature seeks a balance. Max's sunny disposition causes him to be intrigued by people who see the dark side of things."

"Most writers and poets venture deeper into the dark side of things than ordinary mortals do," said Max. "I picked up your first book of poems, Catherine. I was amazed at the depth of what you saw and yet still managed to remain positive about."

"Thank you. As you can tell, I'm intrigued by light. The Impressionists have had a great influence on me."

"Ice cream art," pronounced Madeleine.

"Each to her own," said Catherine cheerfully.

Harry took charge of the conversation then, directing it into broader, less personal paths as he talked about the royal consort, Prince Albert, and his influence on the literature of his age.

Catherine was more than ready to leave when coffee was finally served. "I'm afraid I must fly," she said. "I have a rehearsal."

* * *

That night, the band had an audience: Emily. She had breezed in, dressed in a plum overcoat over black trousers with a basket containing beignets. Catherine resigned herself to the fact that Emily was going to break Wills's heart. She was completely taken by the jazz band.

The rehearsal went well as they tried new numbers, and Joe talked them into improvising during some of them.

"More harmonies make the music come alive," he said.

Catherine was happy to see signs that the American was more intelligent than she had imagined. Once she had heard he was a boxing champion, she had had her doubts. What kind of a person intentionally subjects himself to blows to the head?

Afterward, in the pub, Red informed them that he had lined up a saxophone, and had his ears tuned to hear about a new singer. They liked what Catherine had added to the mix and wanted to continue in that direction.

Alfie bought a round of drinks for everyone to celebrate winning a national maths prize. After that, the party became very jolly. Emily sat between Joe and Tony, looping an arm around each of their necks. They sang "Living in Clover," and all in all, it did not appear that anyone missed James Westfield at all.

Even though the Chief Constable had seen fit to release Wills, Catherine wondered if the police still considered him a suspect. As long as Phillip Westfield continued to hide in Monte Carlo, Wills seemed the only suspect handy. She couldn't see Red feeling passionate about anything other than jazz and politics. And she couldn't see Alfie being interested enough. Tony was his friend, although there was that quarrel Red had told her about over a woman.

She watched Tony with Emily, but he didn't seem to be harboring a passion for the girl. Maybe he was an accomplished actor. Joe was the one who couldn't take his eyes off of her, and that worried Catherine. Any connection between those two would lay them open to hate-filled gossip that could destroy both their careers. Society was certainly not ready to condone a bi-racial relationship.

She pondered this all the way back to her flat in the cab. When she arrived home, however, Cherry wanted to know how her dinner had gone.

"Madeleine was rather vicious," she told her maid. "But I held my own. I can't imagine how Harry puts up with her. She is terribly rude."

As she lay in bed that night, she tossed and turned, thinking of Harry and Madeleine. The American was clearly eager to own Harry. Was he weary of Catherine's doubts? It wasn't that she doubted *him* in particular. She doubted everyone, even Wills. The only one she'd ever trusted was Rafe. And look how that had turned out!

Harry was exceedingly good looking. Women would always seek him out. Would she ever be able to bask in his love to bloom in his attention? Or would she always be on edge, waiting for the next Madeleine to come along? Wasn't it far easier to depend on yourself?

For some months now, however, her heart hadn't given her a choice. Why else would she have unsheathed her claws that night? She didn't like herself that way.

* * *

Because of her inability to find sleep until the wee hours, Cherry had to awaken her at 9:00 again for her Thursday tutoring session. Another morning wasted! When was she ever going to get ahead with her curriculum planning?

Her 11:00 tutoring session went off very well with good discussion. Catherine had a growing faith in the ability of literature to bring the emotional reality of past events into the here and now. If only she could educate all the decision-makers of tomorrow!

After lunch in the Hall with the girls in her tutoring group, she went back to the flat to prepare for the afternoon visit of the Baron Favringham. She hoped to get a short nap. Catherine knew she looked positively haggard.

Cherry ran a warm bath to relax her mistress and promised to take messages from anyone who rang or called at the door. Catherine was thus able to have a luxurious two-hour sleep. Unfortunately, when she woke, she felt more tired than before.

She washed her face with cold water and allowed Cherry to do her magic with makeup. She wore a cheerful pomegranate suit with a white shirt and a navy hat, gloves, and shoes. Catherine guessed that the baron would appreciate a well-turned-out woman.

Not to mention Harry's preferences, of course.

* * *

Thanks to Jennie and the other scouts, all was ready for tea with poetry and Baron Favringham. All her students turned up, with the baron's daughter looking as though she did not want to be there. This surprised Catherine. She wouldn't meet her father's eye and wouldn't even converse with the other students.

Catherine glanced at the short biography the baron had given her. A bit self-serving, it held few surprises: Fifth Baron Favringham, a graduate of St. John's before the war, lieutenant in the medical corps during the war. Father of one child, Beryl Favringham, student at Somerville. Trustee for St. John's College. Member of the House of Lords—Advisor to the Chancellor of Exchequer. Patron of the literary arts.

She felt as though she should have arranged a bigger audience. Therefore, she was grateful when Harry, Madeleine, and Max arrived. She introduced them to the Baron.

"I was surprised you were doing Cummings today since he is an American," said Madeleine.

"Yes," said Baron Favringham. "However, he is a tremendous exponent of the English language." He looked over his audience. "It is a great privilege to be gathered with so many brilliant minds."

He settled in a large, comfortable chair near the tea table. Catherine introduced him formally, and he said, "Most of you probably know Cummings as an eccentric who shuns the rules of grammar. What you might not realize is that this practice makes him extraordinarily difficult to interpret orally. I have taken this as a challenge."

He read beautifully from the *Collected Poems* and had some of the young women sighing over the beauty of the Cummings love poems. He ended with the masterpiece "Somewhere I Have Never Traveled, Gladly Beyond."

Catherine was uncomfortable when Madeleine tucked her hand into the crook of Harry's elbow during the recitation. He moved forward, resting his elbows on his knees, thus dislodging her hand. The woman gave a little puff of exasperation.

The group applauded enthusiastically when the readings came to an end. Catherine thanked the baron, and the girls descended upon him, talking about their favorite Cummings poems, eating tea cakes, and drinking more tea. His daughter remained withdrawn.

Catherine went over to her guests.

"Well! That went over very well, I thought," she said. "I wasn't sure exactly what to expect."

"He's got at least half a brain," said Max. Madeleine giggled.

Harry frowned. "Which one is his daughter?" he asked.

"The lovely one in forest green."

"She looks like a study in tragedy," said Max.

"Yes, I'm more than a bit worried about her," said Catherine. "I don't want to see her waste her potential."

At that moment, Miss Favringham walked by their little group, next to her father. "I won't be able to, I'm afraid," she was telling him. "I'm engaged this evening."

"Oh?" he said. "Anyone I've met?"

"I don't think so. I'll introduce you if he shows promise," his daughter said.

A man in the girl's life? Someone prone to girls with melancholy. Catherine couldn't see it. Maybe she was just putting her father off so she wouldn't have to spend the evening with him.

The father and daughter walked out of the reading room, and the others began to disperse, as well. Harry suggested the four of them adjourn to the pub. Madeleine latched onto his arm and said it sounded like a splendid idea. Catherine decided not to submit herself to an evening watching Madeleine try to vamp Harry. It was becoming tiresome.

She said, "Well, thank you all for coming. I am behind on my work and must put in some time on it this evening. I believe I'll stay in. Thank you for the invitation."

Harry said, "I will miss you, darling. Have an early night then." He helped Madeleine on with her coat, and then they were off. Catherine was very glad she hadn't submitted to an evening of being baited by the American girl.

Chapter Sixteen

Friday afternoon, Catherine was finally putting the finishing touches on her curriculum plan when Harry called.

"I'm afraid I have some rather dreadful news. I took my pet policeman out for a pint and a spot of lunch at noon. It seems there's been an attempted murder."

Her heart fell. "Oh, no. Who?"

"Tony Bridgegate from the band."

She sat down with a thud. "That is so horrible!" Catherine cried. "How utterly beastly. I can't believe it. Why Tony? How?"

"No hint of a motive anywhere. Someone approached him from behind when he was walking home in the small hours last night. They tried to strangle him, but he got away. It was a near thing, apparently. There are some pretty beastly bruises on his throat."

"Gracious. Poor, poor Tony. I genuinely like him. He didn't see his attacker?"

"No. It was pitch black. I have no idea where he was or what he was doing out so late. He must have been quick to have gotten away."

"Oh, Harry, oh, this is just dreadful."

"One suspects it's the same chap who got James. If so, it certainly knocks brother Phillip out of the picture," he said.

Tears flowed down Catherine's cheeks, landing on her blotter. She reached for a handkerchief. "Where is Tony?"

"In his rooms at college. Of course, he's not going to be going anywhere by himself until this chap is caught."

"I wonder if this has anything to do with Emily."

"Emily? I didn't know he had any interest in Emily."

"He just worships from afar. According to Red, he and James argued about her. At a guess, I'd say Tony didn't like the off-hand way he was treating her. But Emily never knew. I guess that Tony was trying to protect her from suspicion by telling me James wasn't involved with anyone."

"Interesting," said Harry. "Do you want to meet at the Bird and the Baby? Let's go over everything you know about Tony."

"That would be great. I'm starved," she said.

* * *

Catherine was very glad of her fur, for another freezing fog had descended. Rather than walking in it, she took a cab to the Eagle and Child.

When she arrived, she looked out for Harry and realized she had arrived first. To her surprise, she saw Red, Alfie, and Joe hunched around a table. She made her way through the crowd until she came up to them.

"Hello," she said. "I heard about Tony."

"I wonder who's going to be next," said Alfie with a deep scowl.

"You think someone is trying to eliminate the band members?" said Catherine.

"Have you got any other bright ideas?" Alfie asked, sneering. She couldn't see his eyes, but his careless posture and general listlessness led her to believe he was between doses of his drug.

"No. I don't even know where it happened," said Catherine.

"He'd been meeting some woman, I think," said Red. "He was

in the dark bit of park behind St. John's. We're canceling the performance tonight."

"That's understandable," she said. She didn't suppose anyone felt like playing, and with Tony *and* the sax missing, the band was a bit too thin.

Just then, Harry came up and greeted everyone. Catherine watched as they closed ranks against an outsider, all looking mutely into their pints.

She led Harry away, and they went to a miraculously empty inglenook in the back. He helped her off with her fur.

"I think you should tell me everything you can think of about Tony," he said. "But first, I'm going to feed you. Pork pie? Fish and chips? What would you like?"

"Steak and kidney pie, please. And a hot cider."

When Harry returned, carrying their dinner on a tray, he set the steaming pie before her. "Just out of the oven."

She took a bite and savored it. Luncheon seemed a long time ago.

"All right. So, Tony is conflicted," she said, sipping her cider. "He is studying music in college so he can go on to become the conductor of a major orchestra someday. But he has a standing offer from one of the top jazz bands in London."

She took another bite.

"That would mean giving up college and his dream of conducting," she said. "And one thing more—he would have to give up thinking he could ever win the affections of the woman he loves and the acceptance of her parents. They are aristocrats, apparently. They frowned on jazz musicians, of course. And a great many other modern trends."

"He told you that?"

"Yes. And Red just told me he thought he was out meeting a woman last night when he was attacked. It happened in the park behind St. John's. It's very dark there, as you know," said Catherine.

"And you think the woman was Emily, don't you?" Harry asked.

"It makes sense."

"Aristocratic doesn't come to mind when I think of Emily, exactly," Harry said.

"Her family is blue-blooded enough. Her uncle is a viscount," said Catherine.

"I'm sorry. I know William is keen on her, but I see her as rather a hussy, running after the band members like she does. Does the woman Tony told you about know of his interest?"

"Not as of when he talked to me about it. He was going to wait until he 'bettered' himself, I think," Catherine said. "He is obsessed with his unworthiness. I think he fears rejection more than anything." She reflected on Tony's good looks and talent. She disliked the idea that anyone could make him feel unworthy, but she understood his unfortunate position.

"How rotten for him," said Harry. "I have often found myself wondering how the Baron Tregowyn would take to me, however, so I suppose I can understand."

His words made Catherine uncomfortable. Her parents *would* disapprove of this son of a wool merchant, however prosperous he might be.

"You needn't think of my father. I don't care a button for what he thinks. I don't need their permission for anything. There is no danger that they would leave me penniless no matter what I decide to do. I am independent of them, thanks to my grandmother." Catherine grinned. "She was rather a grand old girl—an early grad of Somerville and a writer, too. Have you come across Samuel Taylor in your studies?"

"He was a popular novelist in the late Victorian era. Don't tell me he was your grandmother!" Harry exclaimed.

"Yes. That was my grandmother's pen name. Unfortunately, her books have fallen out of fashion, but she left me a tidy sum."

"She was a significant feminist if I recall," said Harry.

"Yes, she was a firebrand in her day. I held her in awe. She's quite a figure for me to live up to."

"I think she would be very proud of you," Harry said. "You can be rather a firebrand on occasion."

"So you see—my parents aren't a factor in my future," she said. "They have never cared two pins for what I do."

Harry's brows drew together. "You must be exaggerating!"

His reaction made her angry. "Don't try to reframe my reality!" she said. "You don't know the first thing about it."

"But you have led an exemplary life! How could they not be proud of your accomplishments? Any parent would be."

He doesn't understand, but then, how could he? It is wholly different from his experience. As for me, how could one miss what one had never had?

"I told you about my brother, Michael," she said. "All their parental love went into their relationship with him.

"We were raised by nannies while they traveled the globe. Then we were put into boarding school. When we came home for the holidays, they left."

"No wonder you were so attached to Rafe," said Harry with a heavy sigh.

She was growing impatient with this conversation. "Yes, well, let's not talk about it anymore. I had it no worse or better than many an English child. Apparently, Emily's parents don't feel that same detachment, however. They must be 'frightfully' class conscious, as she would say. If it is Emily, he's mooning after. I wonder how she ever thought things would work out for her and James. I've meant to ask her."

"I wonder if her flatmates could be of any help to us there."

"That's a good idea. Though I hate going behind Emily's back," Catherine said.

"We'll have to be careful about how we phrase our questions. Do you know Emily's schedule this week?"

She looked at her watch. "She's off work all week while they look into the disappearance of the morphine. We can ring her and see if she's home. Tell her about Tony if she is." Catherine had polished off her pie. "I'm ready if you are."

His brows drew down again. "I'm sorry. You didn't owe me that explanation about your parents."

"It is past worrying over these days. I am a very fortunate person, and, believe me, I don't take my independence for granted."

* * *

They found Emily at home.

"Have you heard the news?" asked Catherine gently.

She frowned. "What news? William hasn't been arrested again, has he?"

"No. It's Tony," Catherine said. "He was attacked last night in the park behind St. John's. He was nearly killed."

The color drained from Emily's face. "Crickey! Is he all right?"

"Apparently, he's sporting some bruises, but other than that, he's all right."

The girl stepped out of the doorway and let them in.

"Have you seen Tony since I talked to you?" asked Catherine.

"No. I wasn't planning on seeing him until tonight. I was just getting ready to meet the band for their break."

Catherine told her, "They've canceled their performance."

The young woman's face fell. "Oh, my. But I guess they wouldn't be much of a band without Tony and James. I suppose they're all at the pub."

"Yes. At least, they were. May I ask you a few questions before you leave?"

"If it will help," the girl said.

"It may. You know, we haven't discussed it before, but how did your parents feel about your relationship with James?"

"They didn't know about it. But it was just a bit of fun. I'm not looking to get married at the moment."

Catherine was surprised at this information. She asked, "Would they have objected, had they known? The jazz band and all that?"

Won't she meet my eye? What is making her nervous?

"Most likely. But I've been on my own for a long time, except for the long vac when I used to go back to Kenya. Now I don't go at all. And they rarely come here."

"Are you close to your uncle?" asked Harry.

"Not so you'd notice. He views me as a poor relation if he thinks of me at all."

"Red said Tony was out with a woman last night. Any chance it was you?" asked Harry.

Emily stiffened. "This isn't just questions. It's an inquisition! Tony wasn't with me. And I think you're wrong, Miss Tregowyn, about his feelings for me. I've flirted with him a bit, and it's no go with him."

"Hmm," Catherine said. "How odd." She tried to rearrange her ideas, but it was difficult. Like someone had just dealt her a knave. "That means there's a mystery woman out there somewhere, then. Have you any ideas?"

"I've never seen him with a woman at all," she said. "Are you certain he's going to be all right?"

"Yes."

"Is he in the infirmary?"

"No. At college," said Harry. "I think I might pop 'round."

"I'm off for the pub," Emily said, standing.

"Thanks for your patience," said Catherine. "We just have to try to get the whole picture."

* * *

"She's hiding something still," said Catherine as they walked together toward her flat.

"I agree. She doesn't strike me as altogether reliable. I'm not 100% sure that she *isn't* Tony's love light. Now. After I've seen him, would you like to go down to London to see a play tonight, since you're at a loose end? Take a break from all this?"

"I'm surprised Madeleine hasn't got your evening planned," she said, her voice arch.

He put a finger on her chin. "Now, don't be catty. She's part of my job."

Catty? He thought she was catty? He didn't know the half! She said, "Max told me the two of you were planning a weekend at Haworth."

He looked her over and grinned suddenly. "I've since decided that would be asking for trouble."

Catherine was very glad to hear this. "Wise man," she said. The angst she had felt ever since that fateful Tango lessened a bit, but she was still a long way from trusting him. Madeleine had everything it took to appeal to the opposite sex. And she was determined.

"But it's nice to know you care," said the infuriating man.

* * *

In the event, they didn't go to London. Just before Harry was due to call for her in his motor, Emily rang.

"They've arrested Joe," the young woman said in a voice close to hysteria. "They came right into the pub and arrested him! You've got to help, Miss Tregowyn! Help him like you helped William."

A sense of wrong dealt a powerful blow to Catherine's stomach.

Chapter Seventeen

Catherine hadn't any idea what she should do. Joe needed representation, that was certain. But Mr. Spence was the only solicitor she knew who handled criminal cases, and he was already engaged to represent Wills. Should matters come to trial, Joe would need his own representative.

"I'll see what I can do," she told Emily. "Do you have any idea what the police are basing the arrest on?"

"Only that he's black is my guess." The girl's voice was bitter. "They haven't taken me into their confidence."

Catherine needed more information before she could decide what to do. "Are you at the pub now?" she asked Emily.

"Just outside. At the public booth."

"Could you please ask Red to ring me?"

"Yes, if that would help. He's hopping mad right now. Ready to take on the world. Joe is his best mate."

"Let him call me then. I can't promise anything, but I may be able to help."

Before Red could call her, Harry returned from his visit with Tony. She told him the news.

"To tell you the truth, I have just been waiting for this to happen. I wonder what kind of evidence the police have?"

"I'm waiting for Red to call."

At that moment, her telephone rang. It was the bandleader.

"Emily says you may be able to help Joe," he said immediately.

"I can try to find him a solicitor. Do you know if he has money to pay for one?"

"If he doesn't, I do," said Red. "What makes you think you can find one that will represent an American Negro?"

"I have connections. I'll do my best."

Red thanked her and rang off.

Catherine decided to start with Mr. Spence. Perhaps he could give her a recommendation.

* * *

The solicitor confirmed her guess about his inability to represent Joe.

"If they decided this case is connected to the murder of Mr. Westfield, it would be a conflict of interest for me to represent him and Mr. Tregowyn," he said.

"That is what I was afraid of. And there is something I haven't told you," she said. "It might make a difference in who will take him on as a client. Joe, I don't even know his surname, is black. He's an American jazz trombonist. Very good at what he does. And able to afford the best."

There was silence on the line.

Finally, the solicitor spoke. "Yes. I'm afraid that might make a difference. Many of my colleagues might have a prejudice against him."

"Could I ask you to try to find representation for him? I don't know where to start," said Catherine.

"I will try," Mr. Spence replied. "But I can't promise anything."

"I understand."

"I will ring up some people I know in the morning."

"All right. Thank you, Mr. Spence."

"Well?" asked Harry when she rang off.

"He's going to try ringing up some people in the morning, but he agreed that it was going to be difficult."

"Confound it!" Harry said. "This is supposedly twentieth-century Britain!"

Catherine led him to the sofa. "Come, have a drink and tell me what Tony said."

"He wouldn't tell me the name of the young woman involved, not that it would have mattered much. She was no longer with him when it happened."

"So, we do have a mystery woman!" said Catherine.

"Yes. And Tony didn't see anything of the man who attacked him. He came up behind him as my sergeant said."

"Has he any ideas? Does he think it's connected to James's death?" she asked.

"That's the only thing he can think of. He doesn't know why James was killed, and he doesn't know why anyone would want him dead, either."

"At least this doesn't involve Wills. Alfie thinks someone is just trying to wipe out the band." Suddenly, the reality of the situation struck her. Joe was in danger of hanging. Catherine felt a deep chill. She went to the fire, stirred the embers, and added coal. It wasn't a waste of fuel. She intended to stay up until she got some sense of what was happening.

"Who knows? Someone just may be crazy enough," said Harry, running a hand through his pomaded dark hair.

"We're due for a break here," Catherine said, going to the drinks tray. As she poured a whiskey for Harry, she sighed with frustration. "So far, we haven't a clue. If these two incidents are connected, it lets out Phillip Westfield. But in that case, why did he run to Monte Carlo?"

"No idea. Maybe they're not connected."

Her rational mind would not accept this. "Harry, this is *Oxford*!" Catherine pronounced. "If this chap had succeeded, that would have made two murders in two weeks! Of people in the same band! There has to be a connection. Anything else is illogical."

Harry sipped his whiskey. "You're right, of course. This isn't Chicago."

"I wonder why Tony wouldn't give you the woman's name?"

"Doesn't want her dragged into it, he said."

For some reason, Catherine had the idea that the woman's identity was important. From the beginning, she had sensed that Tony was being the slightest bit cagey about her. Had the unknown female created friction between him and James? Or between him and someone else in the band? Or was the woman completely irrelevant, other than being the reason Tony wouldn't pursue a jazz career?

Catherine realized she was starved as well as restless. "Come into the kitchen," she said. "Let's find something to nibble on."

Though they sat up until midnight fortifying themselves on biscuits and cheese, they failed to generate any breakthroughs in the case.

* * *

Saturday dawned bleak and blustery. Catherine gave Cherry a French lesson while waiting for Mr. Spence to call. It was close to noon by the time the solicitor rang.

"I think I've got you a good man—a Mr. Der Wolffe. He will go up to Oxford this afternoon to meet with his prospective client. Will you meet him at the jail? He plans to arrive at three o'clock."

"I think it would be best if Joe's closest friend and housemate filled that role. He knows all the details about him. I'll ring him."

"I'm afraid I promised you would be there," Mr. Spence objected.

"All right. I will be there, as well. Thank you ever so much, Mr. Spence."

* * *

Catherine was beginning to be a little bit too familiar with the jail. She met Red there at quarter to three. He wore a tweed suit, which surprised her. His hair was tamed, and he even wore a fedora hat.

"Have you spoken to Joe?" she asked.

"Yes. He's completely bewildered. Unfortunately, I had a meeting that went until late Thursday night and can give him no alibi."

"Does he have any idea what the evidence is against him?"

"No. The police aren't giving anything away. It's my belief it's because they don't have anything *to* give away."

"Well, if that's the case, this solicitor should be able to get him out on that basis."

At that moment, a young man walked into the station, dressed in the latest word in gentlemen's haberdashery. He addressed the sergeant behind the front desk, requesting an interview with the prisoner, his prospective client.

Catherine watched as Red intercepted the man.

"Alexander de Fontaine, sir. Friend of Joseph Hamilton. I will be taking care of your fee." Red extended his hand.

"George der Wolffe," the solicitor said, shaking the man's hand. "Does Mr. Hamilton expect you to be present for our interview?"

"I don't believe so. But should you decide to take my friend on, I will be waiting out here to write a check for your retainer. This lady is Miss Tregowyn. It is she who spoke with Mr. Spence on Joe's behalf. She is also concerned in the case."

Catherine noted that the solicitor had an accent she couldn't place. It wasn't exactly British. She gave him her hand. He shook it heartily and bowed his head over it. "Miss Tregowyn. I am pleased to make your acquaintance. This looks like being a miscarriage of justice."

She saw he was primed for a battle. "I certainly hope you can prevent that. Thank you for coming. I appreciate it greatly."

When he had proceeded to the interview room to meet with

Joe, she asked Red, "Where do you suppose he's from? I couldn't place his accent."

Red was frowning as he looked after the man. "He's a South African, or I miss my guess. Hardly the man I would have chosen to represent a black man."

Catherine was astonished. Weren't the races in South Africa segregated by law? Was Mr. der Wolffe inserting himself into the case to make sure the black man was convicted? Surely not!

"He must be a very different breed of South African."

"I intend to vet him myself before I write him a check," said Red.

"Very well. I know you will look after Joe properly. My presence might be awkward since Joe hardly knows me. I'll leave you to it."

Catherine left the police station and headed for Blackwell's, where she lost herself for the better part of the morning. When she emerged from the labyrinth and caught the bus that would carry her back to northwest Oxford, she had three new poets tucked under her arm. She looked forward to immersing herself in the collections, hoping to find a subject for her post-grad dissertation.

Cherry greeted her happily with a luncheon of beef tongue sandwiches and fresh grapes. As she ate, Catherine perused the morning's post. There was another letter from Rafe.

Surely it wouldn't hurt to open *one* letter. This was the second letter in as many weeks. It had been forwarded from the London flat. He must have something particular to tell her. Maybe it was important. Losing the battle with her good sense, she slit the missive open with her knife.

Before she could read it, Cherry interrupted her.

"Oh, miss. I'm sorry, but I forgot to tell you. You had a telephone call while you were out." She handed her a slip of paper. "It was a man who just called himself Red. He said you would know him. Here is the number."

Putting down her letter, Catherine went to the telephone in the sitting room and rang the bandleader.

"We got lucky," he told her.

"Well, that's a relief," she said.

"Yes. The man is a South African, but after attending Oxford and reading for the Bar, he says he couldn't go back there. He is strongly opposed to the state-enforced institutionalized segregation. He welcomes this chance to defend Joe."

"That sounds good," she said. "Does he think the police have a case?"

"He is entitled to know on what evidence they are holding Joe, but so far they haven't given der Wolffe anything. Joe is due to be arraigned on Monday. We'll hear the evidence then."

"All right. Thank you so much for letting me know."

Catherine felt as though a stone had moved off her heart. Joe was going to get fair representation, and Red was standing firmly beside him. Sitting down at her desk, she penned a letter to Mr. Spence thanking him for finding Mr. der Wolffe. It was only as she was affixing a stamp that she remembered her letter from Rafe sitting beside her unfinished lunch.

Picking it up, she carried it to her chair before the fire. It was another cold day, even inside the flat, which didn't bode well for the winter months.

My dear Cat,

Once again, I take up my pen, not having heard from you. I wish I knew whether you were getting my letters. I got your new address from Wills, but perhaps he intentionally misled me? I am sending this to your London address, hoping they will forward it to you, wherever you are.

Once again, I attempt an apology. I have no memory of the night I offended you so badly, except that I got inexcusably drunk. It must have been pretty rotten for you to have cut me out of your life for good. I want you to know that I haven't had a drink since the episode with my de Havilland. That was probably inexcusable in your book, as well, but it made for a good bit of fun.

Wills tells me that you have taken up with Bascombe. On the strength of my long relationship with you, I feel to warn you. He is bad business. <u>I know his type</u>. You have gotten out of the frying pan in washing your hands of me, but you have hopped right into the fire. The man is an unconscionable player. He will break your heart for certain. He hasn't got the least idea of what it means to be true to a woman.

Believe me. I have only your best interests at heart. I will suffer for that drunken episode for the rest of my life, should you not find it in your heart to forgive me. You know that my heart is yours forever.

Always,
Rafe

Halfway through the letter, Catherine's hands began to shake. The cold from outside seemed to have entered the flat and gone straight to her heart. What was it that Rafe knew about Harry?

Standing, she clutched the letter in her fist and paced the sitting room. Oddly enough, she believed Rafe when he said he was hers forever. The problem between them was not that. The problem was that he could not hold his liquor. It had a poisonous effect on him, causing him to do and say things that were despicable and intolerable. And promise what he might, he could never stay away from it for long.

Finally, she threw the letter on the fire. How could she trust Rafe? He could very well have been drunk when he was writing the letter. Nevertheless, it had brought darkness with it. For so many years, Rafe had been an ameliorating force in her life. Granted, he had never been very reliable, but the idea of him had always been enough to make her feel loved, make her feel that somehow her existence mattered. She knew that his warmth had been her substitute for a family's love, and without it, darkness threatened.

Now, she knew that her sense of his light and warmth had been based faultily on ignorance of his true nature. Last summer, he had let her down for the last time. But she hadn't had to step out into the darkness because Harry had been there. But there was the matter of Harry's charming Madeleine. No matter what he said, she had watched him charm the woman intentionally. Was Harry false, too? Was she really all alone in the world?

No. She had Wills. But somehow Wills and his analytical mind were not a comfort. Plus, he was only now learning about matters of the heart, and she had a strong presentiment that his feelings for Emily were not going to end well.

Rafe's words ate away at her. Having been tied up with him for so long, she knew very little about other men, though she was twenty-three years old. And having been so dreadfully wrong about Rafe, her judgment about them could also be naïve. She felt blind.

Is Harry a player? Is the universe really the cold and hostile place it would seem to be without him? Is "romantic love" merely an illusion of light? Did it even exist?

Her mind returned again to Harry's absorption in the Tango with Madeleine, and her heart hurt. He could leave her at any time it suited him. There were no commitments between them. Indeed, they had left anything of that nature completely unsaid.

In the wake of this realization, darkness descended, and there was no one there.

Chapter Eighteen

Catherine could not shake off the black emptiness she felt. She tried immersing herself in the new poetry books but found that the words would not make it past her eyes into her brain, much less her heart. Casting the works aside, she tried writing a list of projects she needed to accomplish before the end of the term, but her mind was a complete blank.

Her panicking brain groped for a task to occupy it. That organ was in danger of turning against her if she did not keep it occupied. Going into her clothes cupboard, she began ruthlessly to pluck out frocks and gowns she had not worn for over a year, throwing them on her bed. The remaining clothing, she divided and rehung by color.

She did the same with her shoes.

Cherry came in as she was working. "Whatever are you about, miss?"

"Go through the things on my bed and take whatever you like for yourself," Catherine said. "Please prepare the rest for the church jumble sale."

"Dr. Bascombe is on the telephone."

Light flickered. But what if it was merely the illusion of light? Not real in the same way that Rafe had not been real. "Tell him I'm engaged and cannot come to the 'phone," she said.

Cherry's eyes widened. "Are you sure, miss?"

"Of course, I'm sure. Can't you see that for yourself?"

Cherry's face fell, and she immediately regretted her tone. "I'm sorry. You did not deserve that. I'm in a bit of a funk. But just tell him, please."

When Catherine had transferred her vague attention to her handbags, Cherry entered once more. "Miss Norwood on the 'phone for you, miss."

Exasperated, Catherine stepped over her rejected possessions which lay in a heap at her feet and went into the sitting room to take the call.

"Emily?"

"Miss Tregowyn, I'm sorry to bother you, but have you heard anything about Joe?" The girl's voice was thin and tremulous.

"I found him a solicitor—a Mr. der Wolffe. He came up today from London. He seems very certain that Joe will be arraigned on Monday. That means the Crown will state their case against him, and he will offer a plea. A trial date will be set."

"But William was never arraigned!"

"They must be certain they have the right man."

"Well, I'm not!"

"Do you have any idea where he was on Thursday night?" asked Catherine.

"Yes! As a matter of fact, I do! He was with me!"

Catherine forgot all about Rafe and Harry as her jaw dropped. "Have you any witnesses?" she managed.

"No one I know. We went to London. To the White Plum—a jazz club."

"Surely, someone there would remember you."

"They wouldn't admit us. We ended up at another club near Soho. Basically, a hole in the ground, but the jazz was good."

"The White Plum would probably remember you especially well. I am sure Joe was quite a novelty. And 'the hole in the ground' should, too," said Catherine, feeling a wave of relief wash over her. "You must phone Joe's new solicitor. Again, his name is

George der Wolffe. The London exchange may have his number. Or Red may have it. You must try to get hold of him today."

"I shall," said Emily, her voice stronger. "Thank you. I'm sorry to disturb you, but I'm ever so glad I rang."

"I am, too," Catherine said.

And she was. The realization that something could be done to keep poor Joe out of prison for attempted murder helped get her partway out of her funk, but the black void of loneliness remained.

She still felt chilled to the bone, and the fire in her bedroom was not doing much to warm her. Drawing herself a hot bath, she lay down in the long, comfortable tub and had a good soak. She wouldn't think about Rafe or Harry at all. She would think about the case. And Emily.

What would the repercussions of the girl's statement be? How long had she and Joe been going out together? Was Joe the real reason James had ended their relationship?

Emily's feelings for the black man would have been abhorrent to him. He would have been grossly insulted by her preference.

Cherry knocked on the door of the bathroom. "Dr. Bascombe has called in person, miss. I told him you were in the bath, but he said he'd wait."

Blast! "Thank you, Cherry."

Of all people, she wanted to see Harry the least. He would only tempt her to think that she could rely on him when, in reality, he could vanish from her life at any moment. Since Rafe's letter, the feeling had grown in her that Harry represented only a false light. Their attraction towards one another was only shallow. A mere physical attraction. She had not found a real love, if there was such a thing. Her doubts on that score were too bleak to think on. She supposed a man who had knocked about the world as Rafe had done *would* know many more things about men than she did.

Catherine took her time drying herself. She had finally succeeded in getting warm. Dressing in her black wool trousers and a turtlenecked jumper, she then arranged a red scarf over her head, tying it in a rose-shaped knot to the side of her forehead. She touched up her makeup, sprayed herself with the tiniest squirt of Shalimar, squared her shoulders, and went to meet Harry in her sitting room.

"Sorry to interrupt your bath," he said. He looked very attractive—all in black just as she was. They looked like a pair of cat burglars. "What have you been up to today?" he asked.

Nothing. Just plunging to the depths. "Oh, this and that. I did manage to find a solicitor for Joe."

"Excellent. Did you meet him? What is he like?"

"Oddly enough, he's a South African. By the name of der Wolffe. He's violently opposed to institutionalized segregation, so I think he should do well by Joe. Red was there, too. He's standing by him."

"That's all good to know."

"I got some even better news from Emily. Thursday night, she was with Joe at a couple of jazz clubs in London. The managements should be sure to remember them."

Harry whistled. "That girl gets around."

"I know. Poor Wills. But I had my suspicions."

"I did, as well, I must admit," he said. "Do you think Emily was stepping out on James?"

"I wouldn't be surprised," said Catherine. "I think this is what she's been holding back all this time."

Harry seemed his usual self. It would be easy to slip back into their relaxed shell of a relationship. With an effort, she resisted her desire to sit with him on the sofa before the fire, and instead took a seat in her wing-backed chair.

He settled easily into the one opposite her. She didn't offer him a drink nor ask him how he had spent the day. Instead, she waited for him to speak.

"I say, are you upset with me for some reason?" he asked.

"No," she lied smoothly. *Nothing you would even begin to understand.*

"Mind if I have a drink?" he asked.

"Help yourself."

Going to the drinks tray, he poured a whiskey neat. "May I fix you something?" he asked.

"No, thanks," she said. *Alcohol only offered false comfort. Rafe had become consumed by the need for it. I always hoped that one day I would be enough for him, and he wouldn't need it. That day never came.*

"Max went down to London to see Dot. He was going to take her to a show." Harry sat back down.

She wondered if Harry had that news from Madeleine or Max. Catherine restrained herself from asking with some difficulty. "She'll enjoy that. I only hope she doesn't end by running off to America."

"It *would* be jolly good fun; you have to admit."

There was a peculiar gleam in his eye as he grinned. She found herself distrusting it. Was he thinking of a jaunt to the States?

When she said nothing, he ventured, "I thought we might go to the pictures tonight."

How easily he assumes my evenings belong to him!

"I'm sorry," she said. "I'm already engaged."

As if she had planned it, the telephone rang. Catherine answered it.

It was Red, calling to tell her that Emily had rung with the news about the alibi for Joe. Then he said, "I don't suppose you are free tonight?"

"I am, as a matter of fact." Harry, unabashedly listening, raised an eyebrow.

"Shall I pick you up? We can have a meal at Carmichael's if you like."

"That sounds lovely."

"I'll stop by for you in an hour if that suits you."

"All right. I look forward to seeing you."

Harry had a sardonic half-smile. "Taking a jog to the Left, are you?"

"It's not America, but it sounds like jolly good fun for a bit," she said.

He stood. "Well, I'll be going then." To her surprise, he came over and kissed her resoundingly on the lips. "Have fun." He walked out the door.

Am I mad? What have I done?

Her heart pounded in her ears.

* * *

Red looked very nice for a Communist. He was not in evening clothes, but a very well-cut suit and top hat. Catherine wore a silver-green dinner gown and an emerald pennant Wills had given her upon his return from Kenya.

Carmichael's was bustling, and she was half-afraid Harry would show up with Madeleine. She kept her back to the entrance. They sat in the corner among the intimacy of paper lanterns.

"It feels strange not to have a gig on Saturday night," Red remarked.

"How is Tony feeling?"

"He hasn't got much of a voice," said the bandleader. "And it's going to be a time before those bruises fade."

The waiter delivered their onion soup, prepared the Parisian way with cheese baked on top.

"It is all very mysterious. Yet, I feel it must be connected to James's death somehow," she said.

"I think it's all to do with women," said Red sourly.

"Do you have any idea who Tony was out with on Thursday?" she asked. "I can't help the feeling I've got that it matters somehow."

"It probably does."

"Is it my imagination, or do you think women are at the bottom of all men's problems?" she asked.

"It's not your imagination. My mother was a siren in her day. She never made a very good wife."

"You speak of her in the past tense."

"She jumped off Tower Bridge into the Thames one night. She was high on cocaine at the time."

"How dreadful! I'm sorry."

"It was a while ago. You probably read about it. Everyone did. Ava, Countess of Mumford—aging society beauty."

"Oh. Yes," said Catherine, remembering all the fuss. "I didn't know the countess was your mother."

"She didn't much like being anyone's mother," he said.

Catherine felt the pain behind his words. "It must bother you that Alfie is an addict."

"It does. But he's well and truly hooked. He can't imagine any other reality. He's not much good at anything when he's missed a fix."

"So," she said, her tone as brisk as she could make it, "Have you signed the singer for the band? And the saxophonist?"

He nodded. "Ready to start as soon as we find out what's going on with Joe. Next Friday, I hope. I will miss you."

"This has been a rough couple of weeks for your band. Have you ever considered giving it a name?"

"Can't come up with one."

"The Red Revue Jazz Band?" she suggested.

He smiled that particular smile that made him seem handsome. "I like it!"

"And you could all wear red waistcoats or red ties," she said.

She forced chatter about the new music that had come out the previous week that they had both heard on the BBC. The waiter took away their soup bowls and placed bowls of mussels in front of them. Red had suggested oysters for the fish course, but they reminded Catherine too much of the times she had been here with Harry, so she had suggested mussels.

Now looking at them all at once, she felt glum. What was she doing?

"I say," said Red. "Are you all right?"

"Sometimes I have dark days," she said, deciding to be honest with Red. "Today is one of them."

He nodded. "I know the feeling. The world is in a mess. It will be until Revolution has evened things out."

Catherine gave a hefty sigh. "It won't," she said. "There will always be a privileged class. It will just change identity. There will still be have-nots."

She had sparked a fire in his eyes. All the way through the mussels and then the steak, he lectured her about Utopia. Were it not based on false assumptions, she could believe in it. *Are my assumptions about the existence of love and light false, as well?*

She plunged deeper into gloom. Finally, over his port, Red realized she was not responding in the way he had hoped. "I am just making things worse, aren't I?" he said.

"Not at all. You are free to believe what you like. We all have to make sense of things somehow. It's the essence of the human condition."

"You're right," he said, running a hand through his red hair. He did not use pomade, which meant leaving his hair curly. "How do you make sense of it all?"

"I'm a bit lost, I confess," said Catherine. "It's very dark."

"Has someone let you down? Bascombe, for instance?"

"It's just the idea that he potentially could let me down. I don't trust him."

"That's probably wise," he said. "He's too good-looking by half. That's the trouble with being beautiful. People expect you to be perfect when it's likely that you are even less perfect than most people. I heard that you were engaged to that nitwit who crashed his plane in the Thames last summer."

"It was rather more tentative than that. The engagement, I mean. Not the crash. I guess I latched onto Harry too fast; I expect too much of him."

"No human being is perfect, Cat."

I know that. But does that mean there's no light to be had?
She shivered. "I think I'd like to go home now, Red."

"I can't abandon you when you're feeling so quenched. I care about you too much. Why don't you come back to my house and we'll make a little music? I have a piano."

"I'm afraid I'm long past exhausted. I need sleep," she said. "Maybe things won't look so grim after a good night."

"You won't do anything stupid?" Red looked directly into her eyes.

"I'm far too cowardly," she said.

Chapter Nineteen

Sunday dawned bright and clear. Catherine had been right. Her poor spirits yielded to the light of the morning. She could feel the grip of her *Weltschmerz* melting away. It was the kind of morning that needed a poem after the darkness of the night before. Blackness fleeing before the light.

Dressing in her tweeds, she took comfort in their warmth. Cherry boiled her an egg, and she sat at her desk in the sitting room, determined to compose something. At moments like this, however, she felt dwarfed by Wordsworth.

She could only write what was real and true for her, however. She commenced composing a simple verse about the coming of dawn.

In doing so, she realized that no man could make the day happen. Only God. Why did she forget Him? *He* was a Being of Light. That was too much to expect of poor Harry.

* * *

She decided to worship by listening to the world-renowned Christ Church Cathedral choir that morning rather than singing in the small choir in Somerville Chapel. She set out at 10:15 to walk down to Harry's college. She would check in at the police station after services to see if Joe had been released yet.

Catherine gloried in the morning as she walked. A day like this enabled her to see the sharpness of detail in college architecture down to the last gargoyle, the structure of the naked trees along the road, and the contrast between the bright blue sky and what lay beneath it. She truly wouldn't mind the coming winter if every day could be like today.

Her problems had undoubtedly been made worse by too many dark, cold, miserable days in a row. She would just have to soak in all the light she could and make her own soul a source. That, more than anything, was why she needed the Cathedral Choir this morning.

It was worth the walk. The inside of the cathedral sparkled that particular morning. It was cold, but she had worn her heaviest fur. When the choir began to sing, she heard the voices blend and echo through the building as though angels were flying about the columns and the vaulted ceiling. She let the sound fill her up.

After the service, she looked in vain for Harry, and then, resigning herself to his absence, she walked to the police station. Joe hadn't been released, but the sergeant on duty wouldn't tell her if Emily or his solicitor had called on the police yet. They might not yet know of his alibi. A worm of anxiety tunneled through her hard-won cheerfulness. On inquiring whether she could visit him, she was told that he had already received the one visitor he was allowed that day. She turned dogged steps toward home.

The flat was empty as it was Cherry's half day. Hoping to sustain her fragile grip on joy, she put a call through to Wills.

Her brother agreed to visit her that afternoon. Catherine examined the small icebox to see if there was anything to eat. She found a couple of lamb chops. There were potatoes in the larder along with Brussels sprouts, apples, and cheese. All very easy for her to prepare and within her scant abilities.

Wills arrived just as she was hunting down the mint jelly in the pantry. She surprised him by kissing his cheek in greeting. They had never been openly affectionate with one another.

"Darling, I must just lay the table. Then we can eat. Nothing fancy. Just chops and veg."

He said, "I didn't realize I was going to be fed. I say, Cat, this looks like a feast to me."

"Haven't you been eating?"

"When Joe was arrested, I got my lab rights back. I haven't wanted to stop my research long enough to get a decent meal. It's so good to be back, though, of course, I'm concerned for Joe."

"You needn't be," she said. "He has an alibi for the night Tony was attacked and should be released soon." She didn't elaborate. It was up to Emily to tell Wills about her pash for Joe. Catherine couldn't bring herself to do it.

Being with Wills grounded her in reality. They still didn't know who had tried to strangle Tony or who had killed James. To keep the troubling topics at bay for just a little longer, Catherine asked Will about his work.

He was in the middle of explaining his latest experiment with a water-purifying solution when there was a knock at the door. When she answered it, Red was on the doorstep.

"Hello!" she greeted him. "Come in and meet my brother. We're just finishing up our meal. May I get you a drink?"

"Yes. Whiskey, please. Sorry to interrupt your day, but something rather strange has happened."

She introduced Red to her brother. "What is it?" she asked, taking his coat and hanging it in the vestibule cupboard. She poured the man two fingers of Harry's whiskey. "We can talk in front of Will. Remember, at one time, he was arrested for James's murder."

"Right!" said Red. "That seems eons ago. All I've been able to think of is Tony. Someone evidently knows that. I've had an anonymous letter. According to the writer, a copy has been sent to the police, as well."

He rummaged in his jacket pocket and drew out a piece of

heavy stationery, the kind used by people of consequence. Red handed it to her. To her surprise, she found it was typed.

> Dear Sir,
>
> I am writing out of concern for Anthony Bridgegate. It has come to my attention that he was most brutally attacked on Thursday night. I was with him earlier in the evening, but both of us wish to keep my identity a secret for now. What I need to tell you is that he related something to me that provides a motive for the attack against him. I am fairly certain he will not tell you of it himself.
>
> The trumpeter in his band called 'Alfie' is addicted to cocaine. This is a matter of great concern to Anthony as his brother died of an overdose. He has been trying to get Alfie to quit using it. So far, nothing he has said has reached Alfie.
>
> Undoubtedly, you are aware of Alfie's receipt of a significant mathematics prize recently. Anthony threatened Alfie that he would make his cocaine use known to the prize committee unless he quit. Evidently, Alfie took it seriously, as it is my opinion that he tried to strangle Anthony that night. The prize money he had received was substantial and, probably he feared he could lose it all.
>
> I know Anthony is not revealing this to the police. For some quixotic reason, he is trying to shield his friend. But you can apply to him for confirmation of what I am

```
saying. It is highly probable, of course,
that Alfie committed the act while he was
in a manic state due to cocaine use. I am
worried that he will try again.
```

There was, of course, no signature. Something about the letter nagged at Catherine, however. Was it the stationery? She didn't know.

"What do you think?" she asked Red. "Is it all right if I show this to Wills?"

Red nodded, and she handed the note to her brother, then said, "I think it's just what I suspected! Something to do with a woman."

"But what about Alfie? Would he do something like the writer claims?" Catherine asked.

"Possibly, if he were high. But Tony should have known better than to threaten Alfie. Being separated from his drug is an addict's worst fear."

Catherine sat down hard on her chair. Wills asked, "Would the prize committee have cared that Alfie was on cocaine?"

"Part of the contest was to see how fast the contestants could arrive at the proof," said Red. "The jolt from cocaine speeds up your brain. It might have given Alf an unfair advantage."

"I wonder what the police will think," mused Catherine.

"They still haven't released Joe," Red said. "Even with the alibi Emily gave him. They must have checked with the nightclubs by now. I don't understand it."

"Mr. der Wolffe must be raising the roof," said Catherine. She turned to her brother and told him her impression of the solicitor. "Mr. Spence found him," she added.

"Sounds like just who he needs," Wills said.

"And now we have a mystery person," she said, indicating the letter. "I'm positive it's a female and that she's the one Tony is so smitten with."

Red tossed back the rest of his whiskey. "Like I said. A woman's at the bottom of this. See if I'm not right."

Catherine stood and began to clear the dishes out of the way. *Is this a break in the case? Could Alfie have had something to do with James's death, as well?*

She wished she knew what the police were thinking. At that moment, she wanted nothing more than to discuss the situation with Harry. Maybe she would telephone him after Wills and Red left.

But the two men eventually found common ground in assailing British colonialism and stayed to chat until evening. Catherine was obliged to make them an omelet and toast for their tea. Joe was forgotten for the moment.

* * *

When her brother and friend left, she finally put a call through to Harry, only to discover he was not in. She left a message with the porter: "Developments. Call me when you have time. C."

But by eight o'clock, she still had heard nothing. Remorse over her treatment of Harry ate at her, but she pushed it down inside. Catherine tried to lose herself in her new poetry books, but they were so grim, she knew the time was not right for her to read them.

What she needed was another walk. She bundled herself in her fur and set out. A wind had sprung up, blowing the spent leaves down the road as she headed toward the Martyr's Memorial through the sparse street lighting. Her spirits rose as she absently followed the road which ultimately led to Harry's college. Passing the Eagle and Child, she decided to go in for a hot cider. Her hands and feet were growing numb from the cold wind.

As soon as she entered, she heard Madeleine's laugh. She was sitting at the table where she usually sat with Harry. He was there now and looked as though he was telling her one of his humorous anecdotes.

Her heart quailed, and she walked out without ordering her cider. She could only hope she hadn't been seen.

Harry certainly hadn't wasted any time seeking solace. Had she expected him to? Biting her lip hard, she continued on blindly at first. Before she knew it, she was across from the Town Hall and the police station. She decided to see if Joe had yet been released. As she walked in, she nearly collided with Mr. der Wolffe coming out.

She greeted him, reminding him of who she was and asking, "What news of Joe? Has he been released yet? Have you heard about the anonymous letter?"

The solicitor scowled. "He has been cleared for the attack on Mr. Bridgegate. However, Detective Chief Inspector has now decided to arrest him for James Westfield's murder, so he remains in custody."

"What?" demanded Catherine incredulously.

"Is there somewhere close we can talk?" the man asked. "I have been told you are a better than average amateur sleuth."

"There's The King's Arms across the street," said Catherine, all thoughts of Harry's actions blown away by this new information.

She and the solicitor entered the pub, and she finally ordered her hot cider almost without thinking. Once they sat perched at a high table in the back of the hostelry, she asked, "What have they got in the way of evidence?"

"Joe is an amateur champion middleweight prizefighter. The victim had been struck repeatedly on the chin. Westfield was known to taunt my client with racial slurs. There was also the matter of Emily. Joe admitted to me that he had been seeing her privately. Westfield had just found out about it and was insulted by her preference. He was the one who started the fight."

"I can see that happening easily," she said. "It may have been an accident that James hit his head on the andirons. But where would Joe have come up with the morphine? That argues intent. And though he may have been hot-headed, I can't imagine him planning to murder James."

"You are very perceptive. That is precisely what my client says. He admits to knocking him out. When he left, the man was unconscious but alive. He didn't inject him with morphine."

Catherine absorbed this scenario. Her spirits sank lower. "Well, I hope you are up for a challenge," she said. "That is going to be difficult to prove."

The South African peered into his pint as though it were a crystal ball. "The only prayer we have is in finding the real culprit. That is where you come in, I hope. You know all these people. And the police certainly aren't doing anything."

She felt the weight of his words. "I haven't had much luck so far," she said.

"What about the other members of this jazz band?" the solicitor asked.

"Alfie, Red, and Tony," she said on a sigh. "Tony was his friend, although Red claims they had recently had a squabble. He has the idea it was over a woman. But that's just Red. He thinks women are the root of all evil."

"And Red, himself?"

She sipped her cider and thought about this unwelcome suggestion. "I suppose it's possible. I haven't looked into Red as a suspect."

"I've heard he is a Communist. They can be pretty ruthless," said der Wolffe.

She smiled a little. "For a Communist, Red is a little naïve. I can see him leading a miner's strike, but I honestly don't think he'd murder anyone. Particularly his prized saxophonist. And there isn't a whiff of motive." She turned her glass in her hands. "Alfie, on the other hand, seems to have a ruthless streak. I fully believe him capable of administering an overdose. But motive? I haven't a clue as to what it would be."

"The Crown won't have to prove motive, but it is always helpful with the jury."

"We think James had begun to dabble in cocaine. We even

imagined he was getting it from Alfie. But that doesn't get us any closer."

Suddenly, the task before her seemed monumental. "Might it be a good idea to trace Alfie's supplier?" she asked. "Perhaps there is something in that direction."

"I may have to hire a detective for that. I don't fancy your running amok in the world of drugs and suppliers. You could so easily come to harm."

"I don't relish the idea much. But I have a colleague who might turn his hand to it. He's a professor at Christ Church. St. John's College might be aware of cocaine sources among its students."

"Fine," said the solicitor. "See if he'll undertake the task. And let me know if he's willing. If not, I'll put a private investigator onto it."

"Red might know also," she mused. "I'll see what I can find out."

"Have you any idea who wrote the anonymous letter?"

"No. Red and I have dubbed her the mystery woman, but we don't even know for sure the source is a woman."

"There are still a lot of unknowns here," der Wolffe remarked. "Joe will be arraigned tomorrow. Time is of the essence."

His chivvying began to panic her. Did Joe's entire defense rest upon her shoulders? "I realize that. I'm most anxious to help Joe, believe me. But I'm only an amateur, and I do have a day job."

"Sorry," he said. "I tend to become a bit intense."

"I will certainly do what I can." Starting with finding Harry in the pub and putting him to work.

* * *

When she arrived in the Eagle and Child, she found that Harry was still there with Madeleine. Inhaling deeply, Catherine approached their table with another cider in her hand.

"Hello," she said, hoping her tone sounded breezy.

"Welcome, Catherine," said Madeleine. "We are taking apart the minds of the Brontës."

"Well, that's an ambitious project for a Sunday evening," she said. "I need to borrow Harry for a moment."

"Borrow away," said Harry.

"Joe has been freed from his arrest for the attempted murder of Tony, but unfortunately, he is now under arrest for the murder of James Westfield."

She told him of her discussion with der Wolffe.

"So, the man has actually admitted to assault?" Harry said, his very attractive eyebrows raised. "I am sorry to hear it. It will be hard to disprove the murder charge under those circumstances."

"Yes. To that end, I have a little job of work for you, if you can find the time," Catherine said. "Der Wolffe has pinned hopes on Alfie as the murderer. He wants me to investigate. We want to start with Alfie's cocaine supplier. Could you look into that for us?"

"What about Phillip Westfield? Or Red, for that matter?"

"Phillip is still an unknown, I admit. Red has no motive. But Alfie isn't exactly a pillar of moral rectitude. I agree with the solicitor that he could bear some looking into." For a reason she didn't altogether understand, she forbore mentioning the anonymous letter. Perhaps Madeleine's presence had something to do with it. She wanted to be way away from the two of them.

"I'll look into it, then," promised Harry.

"Won't that be a bit dangerous?" asked Madeleine.

"That's why I asked Harry to do it," said Catherine. "He likes danger."

The blonde woman shivered. "I don't know if I like the idea of your mixing with that element," she said to Harry, putting a hand on his arm.

Catherine frowned and stood. "I'll leave you two to work it out," she said and walked away.

When she got outside the pub, she realized she was trembling.

Madeleine had assumed rights to Harry rather quickly. What had they been up to?

She clamped down on her imagination. Hailing a cab, she rode the rest of the way to her flat, trying to quiet her shaking hands.

* * *

When she arrived home, dispirited, Catherine decided to ring Red.

"Did you know Joe is now under arrest for James's murder?" she asked.

"No! We shouldn't discuss this over the telephone. I'll be right over."

The man arrived scarcely ten minutes later. Just the idea that she wouldn't be alone had managed to calm her.

"How did you hear this?" he asked before he was properly inside her flat.

"From der Wolffe. That's why Joe is still in custody. He's being arraigned tomorrow. Der Wolffe's given me an assignment. I'm to uncover the identity of the anonymous letter writer as well as finding Alfie's cocaine supplier."

"I don't see how those tasks are relevant to James's murder," Red said, helping himself to her whiskey.

"We're going after Alfie as suspect Number One. Der Wolffe rather fancied you, but I think I dissuaded him," she said.

"Thank you for that," Red said drily.

She told him about Joe's assault confession as Red made himself at home on her sofa.

"That's not good. Poor Joe. A saint couldn't have withstood James's taunts. I should have put a stop to them somehow."

She added coal to the fire. Her flat seemed to be freezing.

"Come here," he said. "Let's have a bit of a cuddle. That'll warm you better than coal."

Catherine wondered if that was a good idea. Then she remembered Madeleine. She went to Red and allowed him to put his arm around her shoulders.

"As a matter of fact, I already know Alfie's supplier. He's a bloke at St. John's. Another student."

"Was he supplying James, too?"

Red hesitated. "No, that was Alfie. After getting him hooked, he saw no problem in charging James over the going rate. But then the worm turned, and James started blackmailing Alfie by threatening to go to the college administration."

"The more I hear about him, the less I like Alfie," she said.

"He is rather detestable. But I'm not going after another trumpeter now that I've lost my trombonist. I scarcely got my new sax."

"The whole band is turning over," she said after a moment. "See here. The anonymous letter writer is another one who doesn't like Alfie. Do you think you could prevail upon Tony to tell you who it is?" she asked.

"He'd go to the stake first. I'm certain it's a woman. He's crazy over her, but I'd be willing to bet her parents wouldn't approve of him, so he's got to keep it quiet. That includes not letting her get involved in a murder investigation. I don't see how he thinks he can bring it off."

"Yes. He's told me that to be accepted by the parents of the woman he secretly loves, he must be a serious musician. Like a conductor of a famous orchestra. I find it very sad. Do you think she's someone here at Oxford?"

"I don't know how else he would have met her. Unless she's from his home in the West Country. But then, how could he have been with her on Thursday night?"

"You're right. She must be a student," Catherine concluded. "Therefore, she's at Somerville. My province."

"Do you think you can find out who she is?"

"The scouts might know. I have an 'in' there."

"Good. It could be important."

"Now," she said, getting up from the sofa. "Time for a diversion. Tell me something about Red. What do you think of poetry?"

"Not much use for it. But why don't you turn on the BBC? I could use some dance tunes right about now."

Catherine complied. They listened for a while until the jazz had done its work, mellowing them. Red moved the tea table, and they began dancing on the carpet. It was not the same as dancing with Harry. Her senses did not tingle, but she felt Red responding to the music from head to toe. He was an excellent dancer.

They had been dancing for perhaps fifteen minutes, and Catherine felt flushed all over when there came a knock on the door. She went to open it, knowing without looking that it was going to be Harry.

It was. Obviously hearing the music from the vestibule, he looked at her face.

"You and Cherry have been dancing again?" he said with a grin.

"Uh, no. Red is here. There's been a development in the case."

Chapter Twenty

The two men stood facing one another in the sitting room, music blaring. Catherine turned it down.

"Red," Harry said, his voice challenging the man.

"Bascombe," Red answered, his greeting sounding as though Harry was the very one he wished to see. Catherine was relieved.

"There's been an anonymous letter," she said. "One to Red and one to the police. Red, do you still have it?"

The band leader said, "Right here." Pulling it out of his pocket, he handed it to Harry, who began reading it.

"This is rum," he said. "Female, I think."

"Yes," said Catherine. "Tony's secret lady, we think. We've decided she must be a Somerville student."

"So, I would think. And a trained typist. Do many of your students type their essays? Mine don't."

"A few," she said. "I think probably more women type than men. Secretarial training. Many of them have done a course before coming to university."

"Well, this doesn't help Joe much in the current mess he's in."

"No. But it gives Alfie a motive for the assault against Tony. And he has access to drugs. His supplier is at St. John's. He might have been guilty of James's death, as well," said Catherine.

"What motive could he have?"

Red spoke up. "They didn't get on. James had some hold over Alfie."

"Ain't love grand?" said Harry with some bitterness. "Well, I'll leave you two to your entertainment. I'll let you know on that other matter, Catherine."

"Actually, Red has the information," she said, lifting her chin.

"Then, I don't see that you need me for anything," Harry said lightly. "I'll be off."

The hollow feeling inside her was back, and the progress Catherine had made that day drained away.

"So I was right," said Red flatly. "There is something between the two of you."

"We've been going about together for several months. But no commitments. Just a bit of light fun and solving another murder case. I ended a relationship of long-standing last summer. It's left me a bit gun-shy."

"It seems to mean a bit more to him, I'd guess," said Red.

"He has other irons in the fire," Catherine said airily. Harry's taunt had wounded her. "I had better call it a night, though. I have rather a lot of work to get through tomorrow."

"I'm going to keep looking into Alfie. I'm in a better position than you, being at his college. I'll let you know if I uncover anything."

"All right. I appreciate it, Red. Thanks for dancing with me; that was fun."

Kissing her forehead, he left.

* * *

Catherine took Veronal to help her sleep. It was the first time she'd needed it in over a year, but there were too many concerns clamoring for attention in her aching head. She needed a good night's sleep.

Unfortunately, she woke groggy in the morning when Cherry brought her tea. *Monday.* She had essays to read and a tutorial and lecture to prepare for. How in the world was she going to discipline her mind to go forward with her work?

Catherine began with a bath, but she made it quick. It was raining outside, so she wore tweeds with a pearl-colored jumper. Sitting at her desk, she pored through her student's essays. Miss Favringham's was more intense than anything she had heretofore written, but it was a clear improvement.

As Catherine read on, however, she began to worry about the mental health of her student. Beryl Favringham had begun to identify herself to an alarming extent with the war writers and what they had seen.

> *One wonders how they could face each day, each hour in such mortal dread. At any moment, they or the man next to them could have been blown to bits. That they could manage to convert such emotion into poetry is beyond comprehension. In most people, such fear would make one numb and hopeless.*
>
> *But is it not the same with all of us who sojourn through this war of existence? At any moment, all can turn to dust. We never know from moment to moment what will befall us, what horrid thing is just waiting, like a German shell, to destroy us. Poetry is a way of pinning that horror with words—possibly making it more objective and understandable. It is, after all, the common plot of our lives as human beings.*

Was this essay somehow a cry for help? Was Beryl talking about her own feelings? It did not sound like the work of a girl of nineteen raised in privileged circumstances. What was Catherine's responsibility in the matter?

She finally decided to see how the young woman appeared at their tutorial the next day. Maybe she would share the work with Dean Godfrey.

Catherine pushed on to the other essays, which demonstrated

greater depth than they had last week, showing that the students were wrestling with the difficult questions raised by the war. For someone raised in homes of the gentry, as most of these girls were, it would be distinctly uncomfortable to put a toe in the turgid flow of unfairness when the world no longer proceeded "according to Hoyle."

As far as Catherine could tell from her reading, people had felt before the war that things were as they should be, but the war had changed all that. The poet Wilfred Owen especially had expressed those feelings. The last decade and a half had been spent by advantaged people trying to understand or forget the horrible, decimating, and cruel turn of events that was the Great War. People took different roads through the confusion: drugs and drinking to forget, fierce denial as they tried to bring back the pre-war days, or becoming an agent for change like Red. What did young parents teach their children about the world and their place in it these days?

Her parents were certainly on the denial list. They hadn't taught her anything. For them, the war did not exist. She was left to find its horrible reality on her own and to work through a heavy confusion of thought. For her, the future was a great unknown. The only thing she knew for sure was that they couldn't go back. But she had never known the distress poor Beryl Favringham was experiencing.

Catherine intended to raise the subject of how this study of war poetry had affected their lives, so her preparation for class lay in composing a half dozen questions designed to elicit comments about how they had faced this question. How did poetry and literature help?

The writer James Joyce was born into an Irish society constantly at war with itself in the matter of faith—Roman Catholicism—and allegiance—to Ireland or the wider European world. His sensitive poet's soul wound itself around these questions, but at the same time sought to free itself from them. War of one kind or another seemed always to be with him, and he seemed always to be trying to escape it.

With her present struggle at the front of her mind, Catherine encountered a Joyce quote that settled her soul somewhat: *All things are inconstant except the faith in the soul, which changes all things and fills their inconstancy with light, but though I seem to be driven out of my country as a misbeliever I have found no man yet with a faith like mine.*

The quote taken from a letter to Augusta Gregory in 1902 fueled her passion for the art of this man.

She would find her own light between her and God. She needn't depend upon a man to replace what she had never had.

Catherine found that the day had disappeared by the time she took her head out of Joyce, and she had not written her lecture. There had been no telephone calls or visits. Cherry had kept out of her way, except to bring her the requested apple and cheese for luncheon.

* * *

When evening descended, Catherine tried to make sense of her day and decided she had actually accomplished much. Her heart and head were both in a better place. Poetry and literature had served a practical purpose. Just after she had eaten Cherry's chicken pie and veg, the telephone rang. It proved to be the exchange. She had a trunk call from London.

When the call went through, she heard Dot's voice. "Isn't it exciting about America?" she asked.

"America?" asked Catherine, puzzled. "I don't follow you."

"We're all going to America!"

Her heart sank. "You're going to America?" she repeated stupidly.

"But, ducks, you are going, too, aren't you? At least that's what Max said."

Catherine was confused. "I have no plans now, nor do I intend to make any. What are you speaking of?"

"Oh! I'm sorry. I ruined the surprise, I guess. Harry is setting up a guest lecture tour through the States next summer during the Long Vac. He's going after the funding. You are to be part of it, according to Max."

Catherine felt a little sick. "I'm not sure, but I think Harry and I may have parted ways. He fancies Madeleine, and I have gotten unintentionally mixed up with Red."

"The Communist bandleader? Are you kidding?"

"He's just trying to deal with an unjust world the only way he knows how."

"But darling, are you going to be one of those dreary women in gray cotton with big muscles doing your own laundry in a tub?"

The image made Catherine blanch. "What are you talking about?"

"Socialist art. Haven't you seen it?"

"No. Perhaps it hasn't made its way to Oxford. We're still in the thrall of Egyptomania."

"Well," said Dot, "I would have a look at it before making any life-changing decisions. It's grim."

"I am not a Communist, dearest. Nor do I intend to become one. I am a poet. I've spent a very rewarding day with Joyce."

"Oh, I am glad," gushed Dot. "What has happened to you and Dr. Harry?"

"I don't know. I was in a funk. I didn't know if I could trust him, and then I sort of proved he couldn't trust me, either."

"What a shatter, darling. Can't you mend things?"

"I don't know if I want to. Leaning on a man for comfort and joy is a dicey proposition."

"Well, I'm all for standing tall—you have to be when you're my height—but I think your head has got a bit wooly. Why don't you come down to stay with me tomorrow night after your tutorial?"

"Only if you let me talk about my lecture on Joyce for

Wednesday. I could do with someone to help me organize my thoughts."

"All right. We'll set the clock. You and I will discuss Joyce until eight o'clock. Then, the alarm will go, and we'll discuss Dr. Harry and America. Oh, and Max, of course."

"Sounds lovely. Perfect," said Catherine. "And, of course, I want to hear all about Max!"

The phone conversation had disturbed her tranquility, however. America? Lecture tour with Harry? Had that been what he was coming to talk to her about when he caught her dancing solo in her flat with Red?

What a lovely Long Vac that would be! Had she ruined everything? But what about her new resolutions to tend to her own soul without the aid of a man?

She ended by taking another sachet of Veronal.

* * *

Her tutorial turned out well, but she was disappointed that Miss Favringham didn't make it. The girls had made a spirited effort to uncover the sea change in literature after 1918, especially concerning women. They compared Owen and Canaan, showing how literature had reflected the very edges of recognized thought and opinion.

When it was over, Catherine was pleased, but also free to wonder about Beryl Favringham. Was she manic-depressive by any chance? What had the dean found out? Did the scouts know anything?

She picked up the girl's essay again. This time when she read it through, something pulled at her mind. Some little detail she couldn't put her finger on. Giving up, she filed the idea away in the back of her mind intending to have another look at it when she returned from London. She would also give serious thought about showing it to Dean Godfrey. For now, she jotted a quick note to the dean: "Favringham still showing signs of profound melancholy in her work. Missed another tutorial."

Catherine went down to luncheon in the hall and then dropped her note by the dean's office on her way back to her flat to pack for her overnight at Dot's. She was exceedingly glad to be getting away, even if it was just for a night. A lecture tour in America? No. She wouldn't tease herself any longer. She had gummed up her affairs in such a manner they didn't bear thinking of.

She decided all at once that she could work on her Joyce presentation down at her London flat that afternoon and join Dot when she was home from work.

Chapter Twenty-One

With her lecture finished, Catherine took a taxi from her own flat to Dot's after ringing her to see that she was home. Her head reeling from too much Joyce, she decided not to bring him up with Dot. Miss Favringham's essay seemed to have gotten jumbled in with her Joyce lecture. Reading it again, Catherine was more troubled than before.

Maybe she should bring up the subject with Dot. Her friend was level-headed and practical in spite of her fun-loving nature. She might have some insights. Catherine folded the essay and stuck it in her handbag. Surely Dot could give her an opinion on the young woman's state of mind.

Her friend had tea waiting for them, and they settled into the nook in the blue and white sitting room where Dot took her meals. In spite of her plan for their visit, they launched right into discussing the American tour.

"Harry and Max are going to arrange everything," Dot said.

Despite her best intentions, Catherine had not been able to resist thinking about the plan. "But university won't be in session during the Long Vac," she protested.

"They have what they call 'summer school' over there. Plus, they are hoping to court the interest of the communities as well."

"What colleges?"

As they discussed Max's list of institutions, Catherine felt herself turn restless. "It sounds marvelous, but I'm afraid I've put myself beyond the pale as far as Harry is concerned. He came upon Red and me last night dancing to the wireless in my sitting room. On Saturday night, I actually made arrangements for dinner with Red on the telephone while Harry was in the room. I had just told him I didn't want to go to the pictures."

"What were you thinking of?" Dot asked.

"Red and I have been working together over this case." She told Dot about Tony's close call and their plans to investigate Alfie. "And every time I see Harry, it seems Madeleine is there. She is determined to have him."

"I can understand how that would make you feel," said Dot. "She's a predator."

"There's more," Catherine said. She told her friend about Rafe's letter and how it had shaken her. "Rafe was more than a romantic interest. I realize it more and more. I sort of hitched myself to him. Unreliable as he was, he is all I knew of love. Any kind of love—romantic or familial. I miss that. But it was like being raised by an alcoholic. Intense emotion and drama."

"Let me guess. Harry doesn't engender those feelings. He's too steady," Dot said.

Catherine considered this. "Yes. You may be right. I guess when there's no drama, I don't really believe he cares about me."

Dot shook her head over this, reminding Catherine of a mother hen. "You need to get past that. I'll wager you've hurt him."

"You really think so?" she asked.

"I know it's just your insecurity, but love isn't all emotional scenes. Part of it is just steady happiness and contentment. Then there is the part that involves patience and working through things."

They moved over to Dot's sofa, patterned in a bold Scandinavian print. "How did you become so wise?" she asked.

"It's not wisdom, really Cat. I was just lucky enough to have a normal home where I got the love I needed. Believe me, I no longer take that for granted."

Catherine pulled herself up straight. "I guess it's time I grew up," she said.

"You're a splendid person, Cat. All the *Sturm und Drang* just makes you a better poet."

Catherine forced a laugh. "I ought to mention Rafe in my acknowledgments, then."

Dot said, "I think you've been reading too much Joyce. You know Carl Jung diagnosed him as a schizophrenic."

"Poor man. He put himself through a tremendous amount of grief." Catherine put a hand to her forehead. "That reminds me. I have a student who is having a tough time. Not eating, missing class, looking like something the cat dragged in. I don't know why. She wrote a brilliant essay, but it was very disturbing. Then she didn't show up for our tutorial again. I'm starting to wonder if she is manic-depressive. It's such a shame. She has a brilliant mind."

"You were a bit that way at university. There were occasions when Rafe had your emotions all over the place. It could just be a man."

"I suppose that's as good an explanation as any. Would you mind looking at her essay? Maybe you'll have some insights. I've been worried about her for some time. What if she's at risk for suicide? This essay could be a cry for help."

"I'd be happy to look at the essay, but have you spoken to the dean?"

"I have. She was going to talk with the girl. But I haven't heard anything about it."

Catherine stood and retrieved her handbag from the vestibule next to her luggage. She handed the essay to her friend and proceeded to clear the table and take the dishes to the kitchen.

"Her typewriter wants adjusting," murmured Dot. "Her 'e' is out of alignment. It's distracting."

Catherine came and looked over her friend's shoulder. Immediately, she noticed what her friend was saying. "Yes, it is."

Something stirred in Catherine's memory. She had seen that same problem somewhere else. Another essay? No. That wasn't it. None of her other students had typed their work.

She went back to clearing up, trying to force her mind to remember.

Oh well. It isn't important.

"This essay is very well done. But I see what you mean. She's definitely in the Slough of Despond, though immersing oneself in the Great War is enough to do that to most anyone. She is just first-year?" asked Dot.

"Yes. I've seen some of her poetry, too. She's an original thinker."

"If it's going to show up anywhere, it will show up in the first-year's, before they get too burdened or intimidated by the Greats," said Dot.

Catherine sighed. "I agree. I was so hoping to encourage her."

"Don't give up on her. And show this essay to the dean. It's my theory, and I'm not alone, that many of the Greats were manic-depressive. As such, they have greater access to the depths and heights of feeling."

Catherine drew a deep breath and said, "I will try to leave the responsibility with the dean, but I can't help but worry."

She came back to the sofa and sat. "I'm sorry that's enough of that! Tell me about Max!"

"He's a lovely man." Dot colored under her freckles.

"Tell me all! I need a break from all my concerns."

Dot grinned. "Max is fabulous. Completely different from anyone you or I have ever met."

"And you're thinking about going to the States?"

"Yes. American advertising is the most advanced in the world. Madison Avenue, New York. My boss has connections. He's going to line me up with them, and I'm going to see how they do things and what I can learn. Max will meet me there when you start your speaking tour . . ."

"It will probably be Harry and Madeleine . . ."

"And we're going to see some Broadway musicals."

"It sounds like great fun," said Catherine. "I'm glad you're so happy."

Her own spirits sank into the hollow well inside her. She tried to pay attention as Dot began talking about cowboys and things called roundups, rodeos, and branding.

"It all seems frightfully medieval," Catherine said.

"It does, doesn't it?" said Dot with a laugh. "Scarcely civilized and very physical."

"Whatever made a cowboy like that want to focus on nineteenth-century British literature?"

"He says it was a whole new world to him. He was captivated by it. Max draws parallels between the literature and the scientific and industrial achievements of the century."

"No wonder Harry likes him so well."

"Yes, they're mates."

They talked about Max and his family of six and Dot's desire to see the American West for herself. Finally, when the hour was late, they washed up the dishes and made hot cocoa.

"You will fix things up with Harry, won't you?" Dot asked.

"Right now, I'm feeling way too vulnerable," said Catherine. "And Harry is not pleased with me."

Her lips in a firm line, Dot looked reproachful. "Don't let your insecurities dictate your life. You're braver than that," she said.

"Am I?" asked Catherine. "I don't know anymore."

They went to bed shortly after finishing their hot drinks. Talking to Dot had been good for Catherine. All the issues were out where she could see them instead of churning in her middle. She left them there and slept soundly.

* * *

In the morning, Dot dressed for work in a hurry while Catherine got ready to catch her train. They breakfasted at the bakery on the corner and went their separate ways.

For some reason, Catherine did some of her best thinking on trains. She reacquainted herself with Joyce during her journey and decided that as soon as the lecture was over, she was going to ring Miss Favringham if she failed to show up. She needed to tell the young woman what she thought of her essay and give her a bit of encouragement.

Then suddenly, there it was. She realized where she'd last seen the crooked "e" in Beryl Favringham's essay. It was in the anonymous letter Red had received. Could it be that the girl had written and sent the mysterious letter?

Catherine's mind pitched into a frenzy of thought. If Miss F. had written the anonymous letter, then she knew Tony well. Was she his secret *inamorata*? Her father would most certainly disapprove of a drummer from a jazz band! Poor Tony. He was right. He had a huge task ahead of him if he thought he could prove himself to Baron Favringham.

And the young woman was certainly in Tony's confidence if she knew of his threat to Alfie. She obviously wanted to see the man arrested for assault. Had the police taken the letter seriously? Would it have more weight if Catherine could convince the girl to go to the police directly?

When she arrived at the flat with just half an hour to make it to the lecture hall, Cherry greeted her with a message.

"A Miss Madeleine Foster rang this morning. She wanted to know where and when your lecture was this morning. She wanted to attend. I didn't think you'd mind one more in the audience, so I told her. I hope I did right."

"Yes, Cherry. That was all right." Hurriedly applying a bit of makeup as Cherry waved her hair, Catherine wondered why on earth Madeleine wanted to attend her lecture.

She walked as quickly as she could, arriving at the lecture hall on the dot of eleven. Madeleine sat in the front row. Catherine briefly wondered if the woman was trying to intimidate her.

She spoke of James Joyce as cogently as one could speak of anyone as "off script" as the Irishman was, being the father of the "stream of consciousness" technique. She was very glad no one had access to her stream of consciousness!

Miss Favringham had made it to the lecture. Had her absence at the tutorial been due to Tony's misfortune? He must be on the mend if she was feeling better emotionally.

When the class finally ended, she tried to catch the student, but Madeleine intervened.

"Catherine! May I speak with you for a moment?" The siren was all in red again. Catherine thought that it must be her favorite color.

"Actually, I have some business to attend to . . ." But she had already lost sight of Beryl Favringham. Maybe she would be in the hall for lunch. "Perhaps we could talk later?"

"Your lecture was excellent. I'm not a Joyce fan myself, but you did him proud." Despite Catherine's unwillingness to chat, Madeleine was following her out of the lecture hall towards the dining hall.

"Thank you," said Catherine.

"This won't take long. I just wondered if you could put in a good word for me with your publisher? Harry told me what you did for him. I'm looking to publish in England, and I need an 'in.' When Harry comes to the States, I'm going to introduce him to my publisher there. I can put in a good word for you if you like."

Catherine tried to stifle her annoyance. "I would have to see your work before I made any recommendation. Perhaps we can talk about this when I have more time?"

"I brought a copy of my *Life of Emily Brontë*." The woman offered it to her, and Catherine took it from her.

"Thank you. I will look at it when I have the time. Now. I must fly. I need to speak to someone."

Turning away from the annoying woman, Catherine made a

beeline for Miss Favringham, who was about to take her place in the dining hall. The seat to her right was unoccupied.

"Miss Favringham! I was so glad to see you at the lecture. We missed you yesterday. I wanted you to share your extraordinary essay with the others."

The young woman still did not look her best. There were shadows under her eyes.

"I'm so glad you liked it. I worked rather long hours on it. I'm just getting my strength back after being ill."

She would not meet Catherine's eyes. Suddenly, Catherine saw herself as an unwelcome intruder in the girl's life. What if she were wrong? There must be dozens of typewriters out there with a misaligned "e." It was one of the most commonly used letters.

It would be better if she approached Tony rather than risk her student-tutor relationship with Beryl Favringham. Particularly here in the very public dining hall.

"Did you speak to the dean about me?" the girl asked, her chin up, her eyes bright with unshed tears.

"I'm afraid I did. I was very concerned. I thought she needed to be informed."

"You are a good tutor, and I admire you for that. But please refrain from interfering in my personal life."

With that, Miss Favringham pushed her plate away, stood, and walked out of the hall. Catherine felt like a beast. She should never have interfered.

After pushing her own stew around on her plate, she got up and left the hall herself.

***

When Catherine arrived back at her flat that afternoon, she rang St. John's College and left a message for Red to ring her back. She knew he didn't live at the college, but she had no idea how to reach him. She wanted to compare the anonymous letter with the essay. Plus, she needed to unburden herself to someone. Catherine felt guilty.

She spent the afternoon reading essays from her second-year tutorial students. It was difficult to concentrate. When she finally got through them, she consulted her watch. It was already four o'clock. It dawned on her as she waited for Red to ring, that she hadn't talked to Harry in days. Should she ring him?

Madeleine's strange behavior in putting herself in Catherine's way suddenly made sense. The woman had no idea that Catherine had heard about the proposed American trip from Dot. She might not even have known that Harry had planned to have her accompany him. Madeleine wanted everything to appear as though he were going to the States to see her. And she wanted to tell her first to wound Catherine.

Catherine could think of a few choice things she would like to say to the American. She was getting ready to swallow her pride and ring Harry when the telephone rang under her hand.

"Hello?"

"Cat, this is Red. Sorry. I just got your message."

"Thank you for ringing me back, Red. If it's convenient, could you bring that anonymous letter over or meet me somewhere with it? I want to compare it to something I have. It may have been written by one of my students."

"You're having me on."

"I'm serious."

"Meet me at the Bird and the Baby in half an hour."

* * *

Catherine took the bus to the Eagle and Child. When she walked in, she didn't spot Red, but she did see Harry with Madeleine and Max sitting at one of the high tables in the back. She walked over to them.

"I say! Wonderful idea about going to the States. Dot told me all about it," she said.

"When did you see Dot?" asked Max.

"I went down to London yesterday after my tutorial. I spent the night there. She's quite excited about it."

"Did she tell you that I'm making arrangements for you and me to go on a lecture tour?" asked Harry. He looked into his pint as he spoke, as though it was all a matter of indifference to him.

"She did. I must confess, I was a bit surprised. I think on something of that enormity, it would have been nice to be consulted first."

He looked up. His eyes, when they landed on her, were distant as though she were a chance acquaintance. At that moment, Red found her.

"' Evening," he said to the assembled group, putting a hand at the crook of Catherine's elbow. She introduced him to Max and Madeleine.

"Red is the leader of the band you have been enjoying," she added.

"I understand the black fellow has been arrested for murder," said Madeleine.

She felt Red stiffen.

"Let's find a table," he said to Catherine, ignoring Madeleine altogether.

She bade the others good evening and followed Red to another table in an inglenook.

"What are you drinking tonight?" he asked her.

"I'll have a shandy," she said. When he left, she looked over her shoulder at Harry's table. He was staring at her. Catherine looked away quickly.

Harry was angry. Something in her shriveled. She had no doubt she was responsible. But she couldn't deal with those complicated emotions now.

When Red returned, she asked, "Have you got it?"

He pulled the letter from his pocket. Unfolding it quickly, she ran her eye over the typed letters. Yes. There was the crooked "e," just as she had remembered. She remembered how odd it had seemed in the perfectly typed note.

She took a sip of her drink and then pulled Miss Favringham's essay out of her handbag. After checking it against the anonymous letter, she smiled. "It's a match. Almost as good as a handwriting match." She passed the two documents over to Red.

After comparing them, he said, "You're right. Tell me about this student of yours. It looks like she may be Tony's secret love. I'm not going to spread it about, but I do intend to bring it up with him. I want to know why he didn't tell us about Alfie himself."

"She's a baron's daughter, and a very stuffy baron, at that. Hardly one who would approve of her dating a jazz drummer, even if he is a St. John's man. She's also extremely bright. But I've been worried about her lately. I expect she has emotional problems."

"What do you mean?" Red asked.

She explained her worries over the girl's behavior.

"That's too bad," Red replied. "I think it best if I confront Tony about this. He's up and about now. You'd think that with Joe having been in jail for the assault against him, he would have spoken up if he thought Alfie was guilty. I wonder why he didn't?"

"Maybe he didn't think that he was. Maybe that's just the construction that Beryl Favringham put upon it."

"Hmm. In that case, Tony won't be too pleased about this letter," said Red. Suddenly, he brightened, "There he is now. Good to see him out." He waved his arm in the air, catching the drummer's attention.

Chapter Twenty-Two

Tony saw him and grinned, carrying his pint over to where they sat. "Fancy meeting you here," he said.

"Join us," invited Catherine. She thought he still looked a bit seedy with large black circles under his eyes. He wore a turtle-necked jumper that covered his neck and the bruises she expected she would see. "I'm so glad you are still among us," she said, putting a hand on his arm.

"Not half as glad as I am," he said, patting her hand. Then he sat beside her and viewed the documents still lying on the table. "What's all this?" he asked.

Red answered, turning the letter and the essay toward him. "The one on the left is an anonymous letter. On the right is an essay. You will see that they are both written on the same typewriter."

"Anonymous letter?" questioned Tony.

"Yes. It came to me, with a copy to the police. You may read it."

He did so. His face turned bright red, and he looked up at his leader. "I suppose the essay belongs to Miss Favringham. Cat is her tutor."

"Yes," said Catherine. "Can we assume that she is the lady

you told me about? The reason you want to go on and become a conductor instead of staying with jazz?"

"She is. But you can't say anything. Especially not to the police. If it gets about that I have a pash for her, her father will be most upset."

"It's evidence, Tony. You know Joe is being held," Catherine said firmly.

"But not for the attack on me. He's been arrested for James's murder."

"Hasn't it ever occurred to you that the two events may be connected? Alfie and James didn't get on. Alfie was his cocaine supplier. You know how explosive he can be when he is high. He could have easily killed James!"

"But no matter what Miss Favringham says, Alfie didn't try to strangle me. I would have known it was him!" said Tony.

"How would you have known?" asked Catherine.

"I just would have known," Tony said stubbornly. "Alfie wouldn't have tried to strangle me."

"But, you did threaten him?" Red asked.

"I did, and I told Miss Favringham about it. But you simply can't tell the police that!"

Catherine was at a loss. Could they ruin the secrecy about Tony's love life? Joe was no longer under arrest for that crime. But what about James?

Suddenly she wanted to talk it over with Harry. He was her partner in this. He would help her investigate Alfie. She looked over at him and caught him looking at her. He quickly turned away. She felt a swift jab to the heart.

"We'll just have to continue to examine Alfie ourselves, then," she said. "The police have the letter, but they must have decided it's a fake. Possibly to draw them away from the actual perpetrator."

"Or maybe that's one thing that led them to remove the charges against Joe," said Tony. "Maybe they checked, and Alfie has an alibi."

"I guess we'd better check, as well," said Catherine. "If we can't involve the police, we have to follow it up ourselves."

* * *

Sleep did not come easily to Catherine that night. She was determined not to become dependent on Veronal, so she lay wide awake, reliving Harry's turning away from her.

She tried thinking about the investigation instead. Red had promised he would speak to Alfie about the night Tony was nearly strangled. Beryl Favringham was to be left out of the equation. Catherine felt deflated. She had been so sure the connection had been an important one, but maybe it was just that her curiosity had been satisfied regarding Tony's romance. She was not very sanguine about its outcome.

Nor did she think things would end well for Joe and Emily, even supposing he did not kill James, and it was proven to the police's satisfaction. This, of course, brought her around to her and Harry.

She didn't know how to conduct a relationship. Rafe had been the only man in her life for so many years, and she had anticipated that he always would be. Harry had been a bachelor ever since he'd graduated from Christ Church seven years ago. What had ever made her think he would want more than a casual relationship? Had she pushed him away because Madeleine had made her realize he would always be attractive to the ladies and she couldn't trust him? She was simply incapable of trusting herself to make good decisions about men. There were good reasons for her to think that, and they all had to do with Rafe.

She remembered her breakthrough the other day. She was looking for a man to fulfill the place left empty by her lack of family. Catherine castigated herself. There was Wills. He was likely feeling blue about Emily. She should reach out to him. Resolving to do so, she finally fell asleep.

She slept later than she should, and she had Cherry's French lesson to teach that morning. Then at eleven, she hastened off to her tutoring session. It went well with good discussion and some astute observations by her second-year girls. When it was over, she rang Wills from her office. He agreed to meet her for a pub lunch near his work.

They met at The Cheshire Cat, a pub renowned for its meat pies with their towering crusts. She ordered steak and kidney pie, as did Wills. Catherine noted that he was looking fraught with his hair on end and his eyes red with irritation.

"You look like you've been working hard," she said.

"I'm that close to a solution to my problem. I can feel it. I just have to stabilize one of the chemicals I'm working with."

"Have you had time to spend with Emily?" she asked.

"No. Not since a few days ago when she let me down gently. I think she is involved with someone else. She didn't want to leave me dangling. That's what James Westfield did with her. She is certain he was involved with another woman the whole time he was seeing her."

"Now, that's interesting," said Catherine. "Did she say why she thought so?"

"No. She didn't give me specifics, and I didn't ask. Do you think this might have had a bearing on Westfield's murder?"

"You never know. I have to tell you that Joe Hamilton, the trombone player, is looking pretty guilty. He confessed to knocking James out but denies he administered the morphine. I don't think the police believe him. With what you're saying, it's possible a woman could have killed him. Maybe it was Emily, after all. Maybe she went back later. After Joe."

"It sounds like his flat was a regular parade ground," said Wills. "But tell me, how have you been? You're looking like you haven't had a lot of sleep."

"Thanks," she said with a forced laugh. "Actually, I haven't. I've been thinking too much."

"About this investigation?" he asked.

She shrugged. "Partly. But mainly about Rafe and the role he has played in my life all these years."

"He's played with your emotions, Cat. Don't tell me you're thinking about . . ."

"No. I'm finished with him. But I'm finding that I'm ill-suited for the single life."

"What about Harry?"

"For some reason, I don't understand, I've been pushing him away. It's hurting both of us."

"Well, you know I'm no expert on love," he said, "but I thought the two of you made a great pair. I like the chap."

"I think I'm at a turning point, Wills," Catherine confessed.

Her brother looked a bit uncomfortable, but he asked, "In what way?"

"I'm not sure exactly. Do you ever get the feeling that we've missed out on something important?"

He squirmed a bit in his chair. "You mean because of our parents."

"Yes. I'm twenty-three years old, and yet I'm having this horrible empty feeling like I want my mummy."

"Men aren't like that," Wills said. In an awkward gesture, he put out his hand across the table. Catherine took it.

"Maybe not," she said. "And maybe I'm just blaming some inner lack on my part on my parents."

"I think it's more likely just missing Rafe. Or who you thought Rafe was. I envied him, you know. He was more of a brother to you than I ever was."

She nodded. "I'm sorry. He was just so much fun."

"Whereas I always had my nose in a book."

"You were far more scholarly than I was as a child. I was a terrible tomboy."

Wills looked thoughtful. "You know, Rafe had a huge empty spot in his life, as well. Why do you think he came to our house for the holidays?"

"I know his father was a brute," Catherine said, remembering tales of outsized punishments Rafe had endured. "I hope he isn't going to become like him."

"There is that danger," Wills said. "How do you feel about your work?"

"I like it very much. I could be busier, though. If I decide to stay on, I'm going to ask for another tutoring group—maybe third-years."

"At least you're not in the position of most women and dependent on a man to support you."

She took a deep breath. "Yes. I do have a lot to be glad of."

When she said good-bye to her brother twenty minutes later, she felt marginally better. If anyone knew what she was up against, it was Wills. And she had been dwelling on it overmuch. She needed to accept things and move on. Going back to her flat, she put on the wireless and danced with Cherry.

Yes, indeed. Things could be much worse.

* * *

That afternoon, Tony rang.

"I say, Cat. Could you spare a couple of minutes? There's something I need to talk to you about."

Intrigued, she told him to come to the flat. He arrived with worry pinched between his brows. She asked if he wanted tea or a drink. He declined. Cherry took his coat and hat, and Catherine led him to her sitting room.

"This is probably the most frightful cheek, but I wanted to ask you to lay off Miss Favringham. I've had her on the telephone for nearly an hour this morning."

"I'm sorry. I've probably been overly concerned, but she has been dreadfully unhappy, you know."

"Yes. It's just that her father is unusually hard on her. She never feels she can live up to his expectations. Then when you start having expectations . . . well, it's more than she can handle right now."

"I'm sorry she feels that way. But I don't think it's expecting too much to want her to come to class and do her assignments. You know, Somerville is an elite school. We have far more applicants than places. If she finds it too arduous, someone else would be happy to take her place."

"She hasn't been coming to class?" he inquired, eyebrows raised.

"Or meals," she said.

"It's worse than I thought," he said, looking down at the clenched hands he held between his knees. "I wish she were of age. We could marry. I have plenty of money to support her."

"Perhaps by the time she graduates . . ."

"Oh, I know. That's what I'm counting on. I just hope we can keep things secret until that time."

"How long before you have your degree?" she asked.

"I'm done with my undergrad in the spring. Then I have to do my post-grad work."

"But, Tony, if you are going to wait until she's of age to marry behind the Baron's back, you don't need to worry about your job. You can keep playing jazz. You're so talented."

The telephone rang before he could reply. Cherry was in the room in moments and answered it.

"Yes, ma'am," she said into the receiver. "Yes, ma'am. I'll get her right away, ma'am."

Cherry placed a hand over the receiver. "It's the dean, miss. She says it's urgent."

Alarmed, Catherine took the telephone from her maid.

"Yes, Dean?"

"Favringham's roommate rang. I've just been to her rooms. She's left a note and disappeared."

"Oh, gracious," said Catherine. "What does the note say?"

"' I'm going away. I don't intend to return to Somerville. Please arrange to give some other girl my place next term. I don't wish to be found. B.F.'"

Alarm sped through Catherine's body. "Do you think it's a suicide note? Have you rung the Baron?"

"She left a separate note for him. He's driving up from London now."

"I have a friend of hers here. I'll ask him if he has any ideas about where she might have gone. If I hear anything, I'll ring you."

"You don't know where she might have disappeared to?" the dean asked.

"No. I'm afraid I don't. She thought I was pushing her too hard. She told me to stay out of her personal life," said Catherine.

The dean rang off. Catherine turned to Tony. "You probably gathered that Beryl Favringham has disappeared. She left a note. She doesn't want to be found. I feel terrible. This is all my fault for hounding her."

Tony was stiff and unsmiling. He paced the sitting room. "And the baron? He knows?"

"Yes. He's on his way. She left him a note, as well. I don't suppose you have any idea where she's gone?" Catherine sat in a chair but remained sitting straight up, her hands kneading her handkerchief.

"Not a clue. She only has access to a small account for pin money. She can't have gone far. I wish the baron weren't involved. He'll raise the very devil with everybody." Tony's eyes darted around the room, like a furtive animal in danger.

Catherine said, "Yes. But maybe the devil needs to be raised. She's not safe—a young woman alone with virtually no money."

"I agree. I had better leave. The last thing Beryl needs is for her name to be connected with a man. I suppose this has to go to the newspapers?"

"Only if we go to the police, or if the press gets wind of it some other way. A roommate or something." Catherine was cold and reflexively added more coals to the fire.

"If what Beryl says about her father is true, he won't want the scandal of a police investigation. I'm off. The baron doesn't know about me, and I want to keep it that way. Please keep me informed if you can manage that," requested Tony.

"I will, Tony."

As soon as the young man left, Catherine picked up the telephone. She rang Harry before she could stop herself.

"Hello?"

"Harry, this is Catherine. Remember Miss Favringham? The student of mine I was so worried about? Baron Favringham's daughter?"

"Yes? What's this about, Catherine?"

"She's disappeared. Not kidnapped or anything. She left a note."

"I don't understand. What do you expect me to do about it?"

"I don't know," she said. "I shouldn't have called. I feel so responsible. I knew something was wrong, and I guess I hounded her. I also called the dean about her. Now she's left, but she doesn't want anyone to go after her."

"But you can't leave it alone," Harry sounded resigned.

"A young woman—she can't be more than nineteen—traveling alone with no money to speak of. I'm terribly afraid she means to do away with herself!"

"Calm down, darling," he said evenly. "I don't understand why you've called me of all people. This doesn't have anything to do with your investigation, does it?"

She realized how much Harry didn't know. "It does! She's Tony's secret love. They've been meeting in private."

"And you challenged her about it?"

"I didn't. I just told her I was worried about her missing classes and being so obviously distressed. But she told me to leave her alone. I felt horrid. Then she went to the dean and complained about me. And now she's run away."

"Hmm. That does sound serious. She's obviously under some severe stress. What does Tony say?"

Catherine recounted how Tony had come to her to plead for

her to leave Miss Favringham alone and was present when the dean called. "He's frightfully distressed as you can imagine."

"Has anyone notified the baron?"

"The dean. He's on his way. I'm sorry I called. It was my first instinct. I didn't mean to bother you."

"Keep me informed," he said, his voice still formal. "Good night, Catherine."

She sank miserably into her desk chair. Why had she called him? It had seemed the natural thing to do at the time. Clearly, however, he didn't want to be involved. But he had slipped once and called her "darling." That was something anyway.

Catherine had to do something. Without further thought, she slipped into her sable fur and told Cherry she was going out. She walked to Somerville in the light misty rain and headed for the dean's office.

Dean Godfrey was preparing tea on her gas ring.

"Miss Tregowyn! What are you doing here?"

"I know the baron slightly. Perhaps I can be of some help. I'm terribly worried."

"As am I. Aside from worrying about Miss Favringham, I am worried about the college. This affair will reflect poorly on us, I am afraid."

"I knew how upset she was. I should have done more," said Catherine.

"You did quite enough," the dean said firmly. "She felt singled out. And not in a good way."

"You should know she was going about with a young man who would not have the baron's approval."

"Ah, perhaps she eloped."

"No. He was there with me when you called. He's dreadfully upset."

"Why was he undesirable?"

"He is firmly rooted in the middle class and is a drummer in a jazz band."

"Ahh."

"You might have read about him in the *Mail*. Someone attempted to strangle him the other night. Miss Favringham wrote an anonymous letter to the police, accusing one of the other band members."

"And this young man's name?"

"Anthony Bridgegate."

At that moment, the baron strode through the office door. He didn't bother taking off his hat or coat. "Have you found her yet?" he asked.

"We are not the police, my lord," said the dean. "But I am deeply sorry that this has happened on our watch. We knew she was under some sort of strain, but she refused our help."

"You said there was a letter?"

Dean Godfrey handed her his daughter's letter.

His face grew flushed as he read the note. By the time he finished, his skin was nearly purple.

"She says I am not to involve the police. She doesn't intend to be found, and she will never come home or back to Somerville. Something serious has obviously driven her to this. Miss Tregowyn, what are you doing here?"

"I had noticed how unhappy she had become in recent weeks. She was missing all her classes and many of her meals. I came to offer my assistance."

"Hmm," said the baron. He paced around the office once. Looking up, he said. "I agree with her about one thing. The police shouldn't be involved."

"But the newspapers . . ." began Catherine, thinking of the help they could be in a case like this.

"Will blow the entire thing out of proportion. She hasn't done anything wrong. There is no reason for them or the police or the press to get involved."

"Do you have any idea where she may have gone, your lordship?"

"I do. I made a list while my driver was bringing me up here. I am going to hire a private inquiry agent."

"Perhaps I can help," said Catherine. "I haven't any classes until next Tuesday."

The baron looked at her. "Perhaps that would be best. The fewer people who know about this, the better. And maybe you can convince her to return. I know she thinks the world of you, Miss Tregowyn."

His words lanced Catherine's heart. *Did* think.

He handed her a paper torn out of his diary. "The first lady is her old Nanny. She lives in Wales. She's not on the telephone, but that's her address."

"And these other two?"

"Chums from her boarding school years. She's still very close to them. One of them lives in Yorkshire close to our home. They've known each other for donkey's years. The other is from Surrey. I think it best if you arrange to visit them all. Little can be accomplished by telephone. And it may warn her so that she can go back on the run."

He read the addresses out of his diary, and she wrote them down, her heart sinking. She would be spending long hours on trains, perhaps to no purpose. Too bad she couldn't enlist Harry and his motor. She had burnt that bridge.

* * *

Once Catherine was back in her flat, it was close to nine o'clock. Should she ring Red? No. He needed to stay here to keep Joe's spirits up. Dot was also out of the question because she had to work. It would have to be the train. She got out her ABC. There was a train through London and on to Surrey in the morning. She doubted she could sleep, but she would have to try.

After asking Cherry to pack clothes for four days, she took a hot bath to help her relax. While she was bathing, the maid knocked on the door.

"It's Dr. Bascombe, on the telephone, miss. Should I tell him you'll ring him back?"

Harry. Thank goodness. "No, I'll come now. Just tell him to hold on for a minute."

After getting out of the bath, she swathed herself in a large terry cloth towel and padded barefoot off to the sitting room. "Sorry," she said into the receiver. "I was in the bath. But I'm so glad you rang."

"I couldn't get that poor girl out of my mind," he said, his voice brisk. "Have you any news?"

"Yes. I met with the baron and the dean this evening. The baron doesn't want to involve the police or the newspapers. I volunteered my services since I don't have class until Tuesday. I'm taking the train to Surrey tomorrow morning to see her close friend from boarding school."

"Who else does he have you looking for?"

"Her old nanny lives in Wales, so I will go there next if I have no luck tomorrow. Then Yorkshire for another boarding school friend."

"Sounds like the Baron's not afraid of sending you all over the kingdom. Does he know you're a baron's daughter yourself and not his personal slave?"

"I offered Harry. It's the least I can do. I feel I'm partially at fault for her leaving. I could see she was upset, and I was trying to help. She finally told me to leave her alone. I think she felt persecuted."

"And how do you think she'll feel if you seek her out?"

"Maybe she'll be ready to talk. I hope so."

"Well," he said. "Best of luck to you."

He wasn't going to offer to drive her in his motor. Her heart hurt. "Thank you," she said. "Good-bye."

Between her guilt over Harry and Miss F.'s disappearance, Catherine had another bad night. She was afraid to take Veronal because she had to get up early. She finally fell asleep at some time after two a.m.

Cherry woke her with her tea at 6:30. She dressed hastily in her traveling tweeds and brown cloche hat. She had just donned her sable when there was a knock at the door.

There stood Harry.

Chapter Twenty-Three

She all but launched herself into his arms.

"I'm here to drive you to Surrey," he said. "Is that all your luggage?"

"Oh, you perfectly fabulous man," she said. "Yes. That's it."

He stored it in his boot while she said good-bye to Cherry. In a moment, they were off, and her heart felt lighter.

"I'm sorry I was such a blighter," he said.

The air between them was thick with things unsaid. But Catherine couldn't say them. Just thinking of all she had to say fairly choked her.

"Well, I haven't been on my best behavior," she said finally. "I'm sorry, too. We need to have a discussion, but now's not the time. I've had very little sleep and I'm that worried about Beryl Favringham. I'm afraid she may harm herself."

"Suppose you catch me up on what's been going on. It's very strange how these two concerns of yours have come together."

They spent the next two hours talking about the case, the band, and Joe in particular. "So, he actually knocked James out?" Harry asked.

"Yes. And left him lying there unconscious if Joe is to be believed. The only thing I can conclude is that he did think he'd killed him and that no one would believe it was an accident that James landed on the andiron."

"He's probably right. And when James regained consciousness, he would certainly have notified the police and pressed charges for assault."

"He seems such a gentle soul," Catherine remarked sadly. "And Emily has such a pash for him."

"It won't be fair, but I expect the authorities will deport him over this, even if he's found innocent of the murder," said Harry. "So, when all's said and done, you suspect Alfie?"

"I don't have a lick of evidence. Red's looking into it and might know more. Miss F. might know more than she said in the anonymous letter. She wouldn't have said anything that could have pointed to her identity."

"That's another reason to find her. What do you suppose is her real relationship with her father? Any suspicion that he beats her or anything of that sort?"

"Why do you ask that? You met him at the E.E. Cummings reading. Did he seem that sort of man to you?"

"He was awfully full of himself."

"I agree. I guess I don't know enough to guess what he's like in private. I had the impression that he expects a lot of his daughter, though."

"Well, we're in Surrey. Any idea where this house is?"

"The girl's name is Hermione Dawlish, and she lives outside Guildford. The baron just says Fairfield Hall. We'll have to find a pub for directions, I guess."

Half an hour later, they pulled into the crescent-shaped gravel drive of the brown stone house. It looked to be hundreds of years old and was very forbidding looking except for the twin urns of evergreen shrubs that sat on either side of the massive front door. The two of them got out, and Harry used the knocker that sprang from a bronze lion's mouth.

A correct butler answered the door. "Yes?" he said.

Catherine took the lead. "I am Miss Tregowyn." She handed

the butler her calling card. "I am here to see Miss Dawlish. I've come from Oxford. This is Dr. Bascombe."

Harry handed over his calling card, as well. The butler studied them and then invited them into the vestibule. "I will see if Miss Dawlish is at home."

There was a small bench in the entry where Catherine supposed they were meant to sit and wait. The room was very dark. She couldn't imagine anyone fleeing here for comfort.

It was at least ten minutes before the butler returned. "Miss Dawlish will see you in her sitting room," he said. "Follow me."

The servant led them up two flights of stairs and into a large powder blue room furnished in Queen Anne furniture. There sat a young woman with her hair in a plait wound around her head. She was dressed for riding and rose at their entrance.

"I can't imagine why you're here," she said. "The only one I know at Oxford is my great friend, Beryl."

"It is about her that we've come," said Catherine. "She's disappeared. Her father thought you might have heard from her. She's a student of mine."

"Disappeared? Beryl?" Catherine watched her closely. Her fingertips to her lips, Miss Dawlish seemed genuinely astonished. "But I just heard from her on Saturday."

"Can you be more specific?" asked Catherine.

The girl rubbed at the frown lines between her eyes. "I'm afraid not. Beryl's communications to me were all in confidence."

"Would you change your mind if I told you that the man she was going about with was almost murdered on Thursday night?" Catherine asked. "She wrote an anonymous letter to the police about it. We have reason to believe she's in danger."

They believed she *was* in danger. From herself.

Hermione Dawlish bit her bottom lip, her eyes wide with shock. "I'm sorry to hear that. But if you're looking for her, she isn't here. And I don't know where she is."

"Did you know she'd been very unhappy of late?" Catherine asked softly.

The girl only looked down at her lap.

Catherine stood up. "If you do hear from her, would you ask her to communicate with the baron? He's very concerned about her."

"I can't help you. Again, I'm sorry. I'll see you out," the girl said, rising.

Harry and Catherine walked behind her down to the front door, which she shut firmly behind them.

"Blast!" said Catherine. "I'm not even sure she's not there."

"I don't think she is. Our Hermione is no actress. She was genuinely shocked at the news about Tony."

"You're right," she admitted, though it cost her to do so.

* * *

They decided, after all, to take the train from London to northern Wales where Bronwyn Collier, Beryl's nanny, had retired. "It's a long way, and the train is faster because the roads are so bad in Wales," Harry told her. "Bangor is on the main rail line, fortunately."

Once they had their train tickets, they found room to sit and eat luncheon in a Lyons Corner House. For the first time that day, Catherine began to feel awkward. How much did she need to explain to Harry? How could she explain when she didn't understand herself? But the tension between them was stretched so tightly, she couldn't bear it any longer.

"Madeleine wants me to introduce her to our publisher," she blurted out.

"Yes. Her book on Emily Brontë is dashed good. I think you would enjoy it."

"I have trouble seeing her as a serious scholar," Catherine admitted. "Every time I see her, she's making a play for you."

Harry's eyes twinkled, "Don't tell me you're jealous."

Her voice was serious as she said, "It doesn't help that the first time I saw her, you were jolly smitten."

He shifted his flatware into precise alignment. "Ah, yes. The Tango. She was rather dramatic over that."

All the hurt she had felt coalesced within her. "As were you!" accused Catherine before she could help herself.

"Stop there!" he said. "Tell me, is this what has had you so upset with me?"

Instantly ashamed of herself for behaving like a shrew, she stirred her unappetizing stew. It was a moment before she could answer. "I think I was just looking for something to pin my insecurities on," she said at last.

"Insecurities? But why were you feeling insecure? Madeleine doesn't mean anything to me! How could you pit months of devotion on my part against one fleeting little dance?" His normal casual air had fallen away like a veneer, and there was anger behind his question.

"You wouldn't understand," she said. "I'm not certain that I do, though Dot has had a go at psychoanalyzing me."

"Oh? And what does Dot say?" She felt the heat of his glare.

"Harry, I don't know if I can explain without making you angrier. I don't like it when people get angry with me."

"Are you falling in love with Red?" he asked, his voice hard. "Do you have a penchant for cads? Is that it?"

She flared, "This has nothing to do with Red. It could have been anyone who was handy."

"You need to be adored, is that it? And my attitude of adoration wasn't sufficiently abject?"

"I knew you wouldn't listen," she said. "I'm not going to open up to you when you are in this frame of mind."

"Fine," he said, throwing down his napkin. "It's time for our train anyway."

"If you think I'm going to sit in a railway carriage with you all the way to Northern Wales when you are in this mood, you are mistaken. I'll go by myself. I don't need you," she informed him, raising her chin in defiance. In an impulse to sever herself from his disapproval, she felt to cut herself off from him completely. "I don't need you at all."

"You're right. Your insecurities are so great that you willfully misunderstand whatever I say. You are running from me, Catherine. All I can say is 'Godspeed.'" Standing, he threw some currency on the table, took his suitcase in hand, and walked away from her.

Her heart contracted into a small, hard knot. She rose and stumbled a bit as she walked out of the restaurant. She knew Harry would leave her. She had always known he would leave her.

Catherine made her way unseeingly to the platform from which her train was to depart. After boarding, she suddenly felt desperately tired. She was glad they had booked a private compartment. All the way to Bangor, her destination in Wales, she slept as her body shut down over her pain.

She was alone.

* * *

Catherine had never been to Northern Wales. It was far more aggressively Welsh than the south of the country. The signs were in Welsh, and even if she'd wanted to, she couldn't imagine how to pronounce them. It was evening, far too late for a call, so she booked herself into a railway hotel.

Automatically, she looked about the small and shabby room. She was cold to her marrow. Turning on the electric fire in the grate, she couldn't bring herself even to undress in the cheerless room. She bundled herself, tweeds and all, under the thin quilt and slept until morning.

Catherine hadn't drawn the drapes, so she woke with the sun which didn't arrive this far north until nine o'clock. She wished that she could speak with Dot, but her friend would be at work by now.

Instead, she tried to comfort herself with a bath, but the water was only tepid, and when she had finished, she was colder than ever. In fresh linen and a new jumper, she donned her tweeds again. There was tea and toast available downstairs. After she had partaken of the meager breakfast, she took a cab to the address the baron had given her.

Mrs. Collier, Miss Favringham's nanny, lived in a small cottage in the shadow of the hill where stood the splendid Penrhyn Castle, which had been amazingly well preserved. It stood with its turret and five-story towers against a robin's egg blue sky. The morning was clear and cold, with a sea mist rising along the ground.

The cottage was neatly kept—white with red shutters and door. Catherine knocked.

A small woman came to the door, her white hair in a Gibson girl knot on the top of her head. She was dressed all in brown.

"May I help you?" she asked, her voice light and lilting, betraying her Welsh heritage.

Catherine handed her one of her calling cards. "I'm Miss Tregowyn, Beryl Favringham's tutor from Oxford. She has gone missing, and the baron has sent me to inquire whether you have seen or heard from her."

"You had better come in," the little lady said, her words heavy with resignation. Catherine dared to hope she at least knew something.

The cottage was not neat as a pin as Catherine had subconsciously expected. There was a cheery fire in the sitting room, which was in complete disarray. Stacks of books stood about on the floor, obviously too many for the packed bookshelves. Every surface was covered—china figurines, a tray with used tea things, and tall stacks of newspapers. There was a crumpled afghan on one of the two plaid covered sofas.

"I haven't tidied in a while," the woman said. "I expect you know I am Nanny Collier if the baron sent you." She gathered up the afghan and gestured for Catherine to sit on the sofa.

"Have you heard from Miss Favringham?" Catherine asked directly. "We are all quite worried about her. She hasn't been herself lately."

"Miss Beryl has been here, but she is no longer," the small woman said, her face closed in on itself with secrets. Her brown eyes were implacable. "I will not give away her whereabouts. She knew her father would send someone."

Catherine felt winded at this news. How could she possibly proceed?

"I'm sorry she feels the need to hide away. Could you tell me why? Is she afraid of her father?"

"Miss Beryl is not strong. And I'm not talking about physically. She takes things too much to heart."

Catherine wondered if her half-serious idea of manic-depression had hit the mark. She knew very little about it. Only what she had read in scholarly publications that had linked the condition to various writers.

"I know very little about her—only that she is a brilliant writer with an insightful mind and understanding."

"That she is, from what I know of such things. But she is as guileless as a newborn kitten. She isn't equipped for the life she has been pushed into by her parents. Not that I think they didn't mean well. But she's their only chick. Too much has always been expected of her—tennis champion, attendance at Oxford, marriage to some high and mighty aristocrat with a brilliant future. And, of course, they have wanted her to be a published poet."

She looked askance at Catherine. "I believe you put that idea into their heads. It was the final straw. Miss Beryl can't deal with everyone's expectations. She's been wound too tight, and finally, her strings broke."

A weight of guilt descended on her. "I'm dreadfully sorry. I wish she had talked to me about it. I didn't mean to add to her load. She seemed immensely capable to me."

"All she has ever wanted is to be loved. But her father and mother have always wanted too high a price for their approval, never mind their love."

The nanny smoothed the dress over her lap with small, neat hands. "I might not be the brightest penny, but I always loved

Miss Beryl with all my heart. That's why she came to me, and that's why I'll keep the secret of her whereabouts."

Sorrow added itself to the guilt she felt. Catherine could certainly understand the girl's feelings. They had a lot in common that way. But she had come all this way to find out what the girl knew. Maybe she had discussed it with her old nanny.

"Did she say anything about an attempted murder?" Catherine went on to tell her about Tony and the anonymous letter.

"She only said she was afraid she knew who did it. And that she had to come away.

Poor mite. Beryl has so many secrets. The best thing you can do is to leave her alone to sort herself out," the nanny said firmly.

"I wish she realized that once she's told her story to the police, she would no longer need to fear. Is she all right for funds?" asked Catherine.

"She won't go hungry. And she has a roof over her head. That's all she cares about at the moment."

The words chilled Catherine. The girl must have been desperate, indeed.

Mrs. Collier said, "I just baked some scones. Would you care for some with a cup of tea before you leave?"

"Thank you, but no. I couldn't eat a thing. I'm far too ashamed of my part in this. It's taken away my appetite. Thank you for watching over her." Tears prickled at the back of Catherine's eyes. She blinked them away. "She is lucky to have someone like you she could turn to."

"Aw now, don't you go and take it to heart. You couldn't know that such a brilliant child could be so overburdened."

"I pray she will come about," said Catherine. "And I'm sorry to have bothered you. Take good care of her," she added.

Feeling completely cast down, Catherine left the nanny's cottage and wondered if she should even go to Yorkshire now. She felt guilty of trying to ambush the poor girl.

She hoped the baron wouldn't go looking for poor Beryl by himself. She had an idea that the nanny was probably living on a pension from the baron, and he could make things very unpleasant for the poor woman if she wouldn't cooperate with him. Catherine was nearly certain the girl was secreted somewhere close to her nanny. Who else would she be baking scones for?

She would only tell Baron Favringham his daughter wasn't with her nanny and let that be the end of it. But first, she must ring Lady Jane Reed in Yorkshire.

Returning to her hotel, she inquired whether she might make a trunk call. The desk clerk said there was a telephone for the guest's use in the sitting room. He would ring the number for her and obtain the amount of the charges from the exchange. He would add the amount to her bill.

The sparely built clerk with his old-fashioned pince-nez led her to a cheerless sitting room with its view of the railway station and the pigeons scattered on its steps. After requesting the number and charges from the exchange, he hung up and left the room. Soon the telephone rang.

"I have Lady Jane Reed for you, miss," the woman on the exchange said.

"Hello? Miss Catherine Tregowyn here."

"Lady Jane, here. Do I know you?"

"Perhaps you know of me," said Catherine. "I'm Miss Beryl Favringham's tutor at Somerville."

"Oh, yes. She has written about you. But why would you be ringing me?"

"Miss Favringham has gone missing. I'm trying to help the baron find her. I'm most concerned about her. She was in a highly emotional state the last I saw her."

There was a beat of silence as Lady Jane took this in.

"Well, I haven't seen her. She's written, of course. Beryl's been an absolute mess since it was determined James was murdered. I was going down to see her next week. I have been seriously worried about her, and now to know she has gone missing!"

The mention of James took Catherine completely by surprise.

Then she remembered he was from Yorkshire. Had they known each other from their growing-up years? Like she and Rafe?

"Yes," she temporized. "The news about James was a terrible blow. She missed a lot of class."

"So I would expect. He was her closest friend *and* her lover. I'm surprised you know about him. It was a dead secret. I shouldn't have said anything. I was just so shocked at your news!"

"Don't worry," said Catherine.

"I think she would have gone to Nanny Collier."

"I'm ringing from Bangor, actually. She's not with her nanny."

"Then I have no clue where she went. Sorry. I expect I'll hear from her eventually."

"All I want to know is if she's all right," said Catherine. "Nanny and I are both worried about her emotional well-being."

"Yes, I am, too. Beryl takes things much harder than anyone else I know. I have often thought that she has no barriers between herself and the outside world. She feels everything—good and bad—more than most people."

Catherine gave Lady Jane her Oxford address. "If you should hear from her and could just jot me a note to let me know how she is, I would appreciate it."

"I shall," promised Lady Jane.

Catherine felt she owed the dean an update. She made another trunk call to Oxford, and let Dean Godfrey know of her suspicions that Beryl Favringham was well looked after by her former nanny.

"I think it would be best for Miss Favringham if we didn't let the baron know of my suspicions," said Catherine. "According to the nanny, she is trying to escape from what sounded remarkably like bullying to me. I will speak to him when I return."

The dean had to be convinced that this was the right course but ultimately bowed to Catherine's judgment for the time being.

Chapter Twenty-Four

Catherine had a lot to think about on her long train journey back to Oxford. The Welsh scenery was bewitching with its tiny storybook-like towns and green, green valleys. At one station, she saw a man with a pumpkin stall, his orange vegetables piled high before him. Another station had a man performing on the penny whistle. And then there was the muddy Rugby team that boarded after an obviously rousing game.

All these things were only on the periphery of her thoughts, however. She was still reeling from the news that Beryl Favringham had been intimately acquainted with James. Did she have anything to do with his murder?

That must have been the "rough patch" the baron was referring to, only that conversation had taken place before they knew it was murder. Since then, the girl had been a shadow.

She did not doubt that the baron heartily disapproved of the attachment. But if what Nanny said about young Beryl's relationship with her parents was true, and Catherine had no cause to doubt it, then the girl's relationship with James might have been a sustaining one. Something that had helped the girl to get through all her growing up years. Maybe James had given her the only real acceptance she had known.

This feeling was so familiar to Catherine that she wondered if she should write the girl a letter in care of Nanny Collier. It might help her to know she was understood. She could work on it now. Anything to keep her from thinking of Harry.

She took out a notebook from her handbag that she normally kept for her shopping list. Catherine decided she could write the letter now and recopy it onto stationery later. It might require some trial and error.

By the time the train reached Birmingham where she would change for Oxford, she had what she hoped would be a good letter:

My dear Miss Favringham,

By now, you will know from your nanny that I have been in search of you. My intent was not to pester you but to ascertain whether you were all right. I understand that you need to withdraw from your Oxford life for a while, and I will respect that. I do not intend to tell your father that I suspect you are near your nanny and that she knows where you are.

From Lady Jane in Yorkshire, I have learned about your attachment to James Westfield. I am so very, very sorry you have suffered this loss. Perhaps if I tell you of my own loss, you will know that I truly understand. It was recent, and I'm only now beginning to understand it myself.

I grew up with my great love, Rafe, much as I understand you grew up with James. My parents (unlike yours) showed no interest in me at all. Rafe gave me all I knew of acceptance and love from the time I was ten. It turned out that he was not the man I always believed him to be, but I only discovered that last summer. I put him out of my life, for he was doing actual harm to me by that time.

The pain has been almost unbearable. There is a huge empty place in me now, and I have come to realize there always will be. However, we can, if we reach for it, find a sublime acceptance from the heavens that can soothe our souls. It isn't always easy, but it's there.

As far as relationships with other men go, no one will be able to fill the hole that Rafe left. It should have been filled with parental love and was not. Now that we are grown into women, we should not even be seeking that kind of love from a man. Perhaps you have already learned this. I am having a tough time with it. But if I find someone patient enough, I believe I will learn to love as a woman and not as a child.

I am truly sorry that you have lost James in such a brutal manner. If you should ever wish to talk to me about this, I am available. I hope you will find the healing you are seeking. I will cease to bother you.

Yours sincerely,
Catherine Tregowyn

At a railway stationers, Catherine was able to purchase some stationery while she waited for the Oxford train. She made a fair copy of the letter, purchased a stamp, and sent it off care of Nanny Collier.

With all she could think of to do for Beryl completed, Harry crowded into her mind. By the time she boarded the train, she had realized that her problems with him had started with Madeleine and the Tango, but not precisely because she was jealous. It was rather because the woman in red had represented all other attractive women who might come into Harry's life. She had taken all her eggs out of the Rafe basket and was attempting to put them in the Harry basket. If she lost him, she would lose everything for the second time.

How much better to realize that unconditional love, if there was such a thing, could only come from above. Her relationship with Harry was only in the beginning stages, and she had weighted it with far too much baggage. Like Beryl Favringham, Catherine needed to lick her wounds and realize that her relationship with Rafe and Beryl's with James were unhealthy. Catherine, at least, had endowed Rafe with godlike qualities and expected way too much of him. When he had failed her, she had turned those expectations on Harry.

Harry certainly wasn't God. He was going to disappoint her sometimes. She had best learn and expect him to be just a man, a good man. He hadn't been put on earth to save her.

Could she ever explain this to Harry? Maybe a letter would be the way to do that, also.

The rest of the way to Oxford, she tried to do just that. By the time she arrived, she thought she had a good letter. She would sleep on it tonight. Meanwhile, what was she going to tell the baron?

* * *

The news that greeted her from the *Oxford Mail* headlines in the train station was quite unexpected: *Christ Church College Man Attacked in Monte Carlo.*

As she read the article, she couldn't help feeling a bit disappointed. It had transpired that Phillip Westfield hadn't been running from a murder charge, but from gambling debts owed to some unsavory East End lenders. They had traced him to Monte Carlo and administered a beating to him when he refused to pay them. He must have thought Harry had been sent by his lenders when he saw him in the pub. The barkeep must have misunderstood the telephone conversation Harry had with the police telling them he had located Phillip Westfield. That's why he had run.

So who had killed James? Was it Alfie, after all?

Cherry was happy to see her but sent her to bed with a hot water bottle, claiming her lips were blue, and there were huge black rings around her eyes. She brought her a scrambled egg and some toast on a tray. Once she had eaten it, Cherry turned out the light, leaving Catherine with the company of her own thoughts: Harry, James's murder, and the baron. Why were train journeys so enervating? With her concerns swirling in her head, she fell into an uneasy sleep.

* * *

The baron had told her he was staying at the Savoy. The next morning, Catherine decided to handle her business with him by telegram: *Sorry Stop Could not find your daughter at any of the addresses Stop Sincerely Catherine Tregowyn.*

If he wished to ring her, he could do so. Next, she rang the police and determined that they were still holding Joe. His trial date was a month away. Burning with frustration, she tried to think of something she could do. But there were essays to mark for the next day's tutorial. She thought sadly of her lost student, Beryl Favringham, and got to work.

In the afternoon, she decided she would ring Tony. She wanted to hear things from his point of view. He was probably out, but she could leave a message.

Apparently, he was in. The student who answered the telephone for his hall went to get him.

"Tony Bridgegate here," he answered.

"Hi, Tony. It's Cat."

"Cat! You're back. Did you find Beryl?"

"I did, and I didn't. Do you want to meet somewhere so I can tell you about it?"

"Let's meet at The Cheshire Cat. Less of a walk than the Bird and the Baby. I never had luncheon, and I'm ready for one of their pies."

She agreed and rang off. After putting on her sable coat and brown cloche hat, she told Cherry she was off.

Tony was looking hollow, and his skin was a bit gray.

"My friend, you aren't looking your best. Haven't you recovered from your attack?"

"I think I've recovered, but I've been sick with worry over Beryl. Please tell me what you know."

She gave him an account of her travels. "So, I'm fairly sure she's in Wales where her nanny is keeping an eye on her. Beryl told her nanny she thinks she knows who the murderer is, and she's afraid. But she's also overwhelmed with James's loss and your near loss and everyone's expectations, including mine, unfortunately. Whyever didn't you tell me about her and James?"

Tony set down his fork as though his hunger had deserted him. "I was protecting her. They went to great lengths to keep their relationship from the baron. But James is the whole reason she came to Somerville. It's here that I met her."

"Have you been seeing her in secret ever since his death?"

"Yes. While I would never have poached on James's territory when he was alive, I had no difficulties once he was gone. He was two-timing her with Emily. That made me think a lot less of him, I can tell you."

"You'd better be careful, Tony. You might be had up for murder if you talk like that."

"Don't you think I know it?"

"Your feelings must be exceptionally strong if you're willing to give up jazz for her," said Catherine.

"They are. I love Miss Favringham. Do you think she'll ever come back to Oxford?"

"I don't think she knows. In her goodbye note, she told the dean to give her place at Somerville to someone else. She can't take the pressure from her father anymore. As I explained, everything became too much on top of James's death. Her nanny said she's emotionally delicate."

"Yeah. I knew that. That's why I was so angry with James for his fooling around with Emily. She's not a patch on Beryl."

"But Miss Favringham told me she doesn't care for jazz."

Tony grimaced. "Yeah. That was a problem between the two of them for sure."

Catherine was trying to make up her mind whether Tony could

really be a murderer and possibly faked the attack on himself when Wills came up to their table. Catherine invited him to join them. She was uncertain enough of the drummer to be relieved.

"Cherry told me you were away this weekend," Wills said.

"Yes. Trying to find one of my students who has disappeared."

"Were you successful?"

"Let's just say, I know she's safe, and I know she doesn't want to be found."

Apparently, this was enough for Wills.

"I hear you had a bit of a dust-up," he said to Tony.

"Yes," the drummer replied. "I was able to break the hold he had on me. I had the impression he wasn't a terribly strong chap."

"Well, that certainly lets out Joe," said Catherine. "If he had had a hold on you, it wouldn't have been possible to get away."

"I understand he has an alibi," said Tony.

"Oh, really?" said Wills. "What's that?"

"Emily. They were at a jazz club in London," said Tony.

Catherine's heart hurt as she registered the shock on her brother's face. The news was clearly new to him, but he said nothing.

Oblivious, Tony smiled. "I think it's rather a joke that she was two-timing James while he was two-timing her."

"Oh, yeah," said Wills. "A barrel of laughs. Having been a suspect, I'm pretty sick of this whole business."

"You're right out of it," said Tony "If I were you, I'd just concentrate on your work."

"I intend to," said Wills. Having downed his pint, he left.

"Tony, think again. Are you sure it wasn't Alfie who attacked you and killed James? That's what Miss Favringham thinks. She wrote an anonymous letter."

"Yeah. Red told me." Tony went back to eating his pie. "I can see him wanting to kill me when he was high, but why would he have killed James?"

"Was Alfie James's supplier? Maybe it was something to do with that. If Alfie could lay his hands on cocaine whenever he likes, he may have access to morphine, as well."

"Makes sense," said Tony. "I can find out if he had an alibi easily enough."

"But can you do it without putting yourself in danger?" she asked.

"I'm fairly certain I can, yes. Believe it or not, I can look after my own skin."

"Thanks." She handed him one of her visiting cards with her office and home telephone numbers written on it. "Call me if you find out one way or the other. And thanks for meeting me. I hope knowing Miss Favringham is safe will allow you to rest more easily." She stood. "I must go prepare a lecture for Wednesday. I'm rather behind."

"You're my heroine, Cat. Thanks for finding her." He tucked the card in his jacket pocket.

Chapter Twenty-Five

Catherine found it next to impossible to focus with matters as they stood. The investigation seemed to be in limbo, and she was desperately afraid that Joe was going to hang simply because she lacked the imagination to conceive who else could have committed James's murder. But it was her own personal situation with Harry that weighed most heavily on her. As though to counteract this narcissism, she plunged into the cynical, graphic poetry of Siegfried Sassoon, one of the most powerful of the war poets who only escaped court-martial for his work because Robert Graves convinced the military that Sassoon was suffering profound shell shock and needed to be hospitalized.

Once she had plunged into this poet's world and experience, they overshadowed her own concerns. What was one man's life when the lives of so many had been ended every day for years for no discernible reason?

She was in danger of falling into another funk when Cherry approached her with a telegram. "This just came for you, miss."

Oh. The baron. She'd forgotten about him. She tore open the message.

Must see you about my daughter Stop Will be there in morning Stop Wire address Stop Favringham.

The missive sounded like a royal edict and immediately got her back up. She sent an immediate reply by telephone. *Tutorial in morning Stop Come 2 pm Stop Eagle and Child Stop Tregowyn*

The idea of entertaining the baron in her flat did not sit well. If he was going to come over grand, she'd rather have him do it where he wouldn't bully her. And, truth to tell, she'd rather have Harry there. But that was impossible until she mended things if they could ever be mended.

Red rang, and she recounted her travels. He was glad to hear that Beryl Favringham was safe if still unlocated. He invited himself over for a drink, but Catherine forestalled him. She was still tired from her journey and wanted an early night.

Cherry served her a fish fillet, fried potatoes, and peas for dinner. She finished her lecture, had a bath, and went to bed.

* * *

In the morning, Tony rang. They arranged to meet for lunch again at The Cheshire Cat, where he would tell her what he had learned about Alfie.

Her tutorial was lackluster without Miss Favringham. The girls felt her absence, especially when Catherine told them she wouldn't be returning that term. They discussed their essays, which were far from brilliant, and she left the session feeling that she was failing as a tutor.

At The Cheshire Cat, Tony sat nursing a pint in a corner booth. In front of him was a musical score he appeared to be composing. He was completely absorbed when she sat down with her shandy.

"Oh, Cat! Hello. I say, I think I'm onto something good here. The best thing, to get myself composing. Takes my mind off missing Beryl."

"Her father has summoned me," she told him. "We're meeting at the Eagle and Child at two."

"How jolly for you."

"Tell me about Alfie," she said. "Surely, the police questioned him after the anonymous letter."

"They did, and he has a solid alibi. He was performing that night as a fill-in trumpet for a band down in London. However, the Sunday James was killed, he's a bit sketchy. I can't imagine why the police haven't looked at him more closely. He was in and out of his rooms all day. No real alibi at all."

"Hmm," said Catherine. "That is a bit strange. How did you find this out?"

"Well, I found out about the London gig from his roommate. When I realized he couldn't have been behind the attack on me, I just confronted him about his alibi for James's murder." Tony packed up his score as he spoke. "He hemmed and hawed and finally admitted it was just an ordinary Sunday. He did some proofs in his rooms, went to the hall for lunch, then the library for a change of scene, then back to his rooms. Hall for dinner. Couldn't remember who he sat with at either meal."

"That doesn't look good."

"Not caring for a fellow and murdering him are leagues apart," said Tony. "We'll have to find more if we want the police to look at anyone besides Joe."

"I just keep coming up against his addiction," said Catherine. "And his easy access to drugs. There might be something there. I feel like there *should* be."

"Tell me again what Beryl's nanny said about why she left," Tony said.

"She said that Beryl was afraid. And that she was pretty sure she knew who the murderer was."

Tony ran the palm of his hand over the back of his head as he thought. "So, she wasn't talking about my attack. She was talking about the murder."

"Yes." Catherine could almost see the gears clicking in his head.

"Well, it couldn't be Joe she was afraid of because he's in jail." She saw the moment he lit on a new idea.

"No. It can't be," Tony said.

"Who?" asked Catherine.

"Have you ever wondered about Red?"

Her stomach clenched. "Red? Yes. I did wonder once. But I dismissed it. Why would Red murder James?"

"I don't know. Again, we need a motive."

A chill stole over Catherine. It was true. Red had never really been investigated. They had been so busy looking at everyone else, they didn't even know if he had an alibi for either incident. And as the leader of the band, he held many of their secrets. And all of his own.

She thought of the evening they had spent dancing to the wireless. Had she danced in the arms of a killer?

"No," she said decisively. "It can't be Red. I would know it."

"I still think we need to keep our eyes open," said Tony. "We can't afford to dismiss anyone who doesn't have an alibi."

Catherine said, "I still favor Alfie."

"He certainly is the least attractive of the two. Alfie is on the way to becoming broken." Tony shook his head sadly. "It takes more and more cocaine to satisfy him. One day there will be an overdose. I've been through all of this before. With my brother."

Catherine reached across the table and grasped his hand. "I'm sorry, Tony."

Consulting her watch, she said, "I have to go. I'm meeting the baron."

"I don't envy you that conversation."

"I owe it to Beryl to keep her secrets. Don't worry. I won't give you away." She stood and stifled a sigh. Poor Tony. She doubted there was going to be a happy ending for him.

* * *

The baron looked a bit out of place in a mere pub. Nevertheless, she was glad they were meeting at The Eagle and Child. He would have been too grandiose for her humble flat.

He stood as she approached, and she stifled the need to curtsey. "Good afternoon, your Lordship."

"I've been checking up on you, my dear. You are Baron Tregowyn's daughter. You do not need to kowtow to me."

"Good afternoon, then," she said, smiling.

"I hope you're going to help me further in the matter of my missing daughter," he said.

"I spent my whole weekend doing that, my lord. I had no luck, as I've told you."

"I'm certain that nanny knows more than she's telling. She and my daughter are thick as thieves. She lived with us until my daughter was sixteen."

"Miss Favringham did not go to boarding school?"

"Not until she was sixteen. I wanted her by me. She's my only child."

"So, she had a governess?"

"Yes, and Nanny Collier. Now those two women did *not* see eye to eye." He laughed—a low, rumbling sound. "What will you drink, Miss Tregowyn?"

"I'll just have a shandy."

"Ah, lovely. Just what a young girl should drink," he said. "I'll be right back." He got up and went to the bar.

She only just kept herself from rolling her eyes. *Young girl?* If she were classified as a young girl, he must think his daughter to be an infant still!

When he returned with her drink, he said, "I am so glad my daughter has you to look up to. It is so difficult for girls these days."

Catherine had to differ. "It has always been difficult, but things are improving. Women have the vote now. They can actually graduate with degrees from Somerville. They can work in several different jobs. My closest friend is a copywriter for an advertising firm in London. She does very well for herself."

"That's topping. Absolutely topping!" He beamed. "Do either of you have young men?"

"If we do, we're keeping the fact to ourselves," she said, hoping she sounded coy enough to keep the offense from the words.

"Ah, very ladylike! I'm afraid my daughter has an unfortunate taste in men. You know, since she is my only posterity, we need to be very careful in selecting a mate for her. He must be worthy of our name and position in society."

"But she can't inherit your title or your estate, being a female," Catherine protested.

"The estate that goes with the Favringham title is paltry. My wealth is mine to do with as I like. It came to me through the female line. Beryl will inherit our home and acreage—a tidy estate. It is essential that she marry a titled man. You can see why, of course. Our estate merits a title. Beryl certainly does. She's always had the best of everything. I want her to assume her proper place in the world."

His daughter's secret love affairs with James and Tony made sense now. Of course, neither man would fit into the Baron's scheme of things. Catherine was suddenly very glad to have been a neglected child rather than the victim of such an obsessive parent.

"If the war taught us anything, it taught us that life is short and unpredictable," he said. "We must grab onto it and make a difference by holding onto the old ways. The structure of our society is what made this country great. It is more important now that ever."

Catherine imagined that her parents felt exactly the same way. At that moment, she looked up to find Red standing by their table. Her suspicions of him caused her heart to lurch. "Hello, Red. Have you met the baron?"

"Our parents are acquainted." He held out his hand to the baron who had stood up. "Alexander de Fontaine."

At those words, the baron looked down at the hand extended toward him, and pointedly did not offer his own. "You . . . you devil! You have given your poor parents nothing but heartache!"

Red grinned with obvious insouciance. "I have, haven't I? They, unfortunately, do not see the writing on the wall. When the Revolution comes, the aristocracy will be obliterated."

As Red baited the baron, Catherine suddenly saw her friend in a ruthless light.

"Cat, my love," he continued. "I have a fellow coming to audition for the band at seven tonight. May I ask you to dine with me? Carmichael's? I could pick you up no later than nine."

"How about if I meet you there?" she asked. Though she couldn't blame him for scoring off of the pompous baron, given her suspicions, she was in no hurry to be alone in a taxi with this man. She had no problem at the prospect of dining with him in a public place, however. She wanted to sound out his alibis.

"Delighted," he said with a mock bow. Red walked off.

The baron's face was red with outrage. "You would dine—in public!—with a Communist?"

"He's by way of being my boss," she said, miming an apology. It was impossible not to goad this man. He was such a parody of himself.

"Your *boss*? What can you mean?"

"He's the bandleader. I do a bit of jazz singing on the weekends."

"And what do your parents think of that?"

"I doubt they care two straws," she said. "If they even know."

"And you are my daughter's tutor? What does Somerville think of all this? I shall certainly let them know my opinion!"

"Somerville is a very progressive college," she said.

"No doubt, you would have approved of my daughter marrying James Westfield or Anthony Bridgegate!"

Even in this crowded place, Catherine was alarmed at the wild gleam in his eye. For the first time, she wondered if the man was completely sane.

"Are you a drug addict, too?" he demanded.

"Certainly not!" Catherine said. "I do not approve of drugs. They can alter one's mental state in alarming ways, and addiction renders the body a slave."

"Well, thank heavens for that, at least. But I must insist that you have nothing to do with my daughter from this time forth."

"Your daughter is missing, my lord. I would not know where to find her were it my desire to corrupt her."

He stood and clamped his bowler hat onto his head. "No doubt you find me a figure of fun, you and your friends. But I promise you! I am not the least bit funny!"

After he had exited The Eagle and Child altogether, Catherine drew a deep, cleansing breath. *What a truly awful man! Poor Beryl Favringham!*

She suddenly missed Harry exceedingly. She would love to share this moment with him. What would he think of the baron's mental health?

Catherine looked for Red, but he had gone. It wouldn't do to sit around the pub on her own. Standing, she put on her fur and decided on a restorative visit to Blackwell's to soothe her mind.

The book emporium had its usual effect on her, and by the time she had finished her browse, it was starting to get dark outside. A bundle of new poetry books under her arm, she caught a bus at Carfax and rode toward home.

She shivered as she stepped into the street and walked swiftly the rest of the way to her flat. When she walked through the door, she took off her hat and hung it on the hat tree. Catherine was pulling off her gloves when she heard a soft, "Hello, Miss Tregowyn."

Looking up, she saw the lovely, sweet face of Beryl Favringham.

Chapter Twenty-Six

"Miss Favringham!" exclaimed Catherine. "What are you doing here?"

"Your maid let me in," the girl said. She looked better than she had since the beginning of the term. "After I received your wonderful letter, I knew I needed to speak to you. I knew you would understand. Nanny is very loving and protective, but she doesn't really comprehend my problems."

"Has Cherry brought you anything to eat? You must have spent all day on the train."

"Yes. She fed me a lovely sandwich and some fruit, and I've drunk a whole pot of tea."

"That's good." Catherine hung her fur in the front cupboard. Then she stood before the fire to warm herself.

"Please call me Beryl," her student said. "Or even Favringham. Whichever you like."

"All right, Beryl. I'd love to hear what you have to say. You're quite the dark horse."

"When you hear what I have to say, you'll have even more reason to say that." She took a breath, lifted her chin, and said, "You see, my father is a murderer. He killed James, and I'm sure he tried to kill Tony."

Though some part of her mind had begun to suspect this, she was still shocked to hear it from Beryl's lips. "How do you know?"

"I overheard him tell Mummy. Eventually, I guessed he was responsible for what happened to Tony, as well."

"Good heavens! Your mother? What did she say?" Catherine sank to her chair before the fire.

"You have to understand that my parents are completely delusional when it comes to me. She went along with him, but didn't want to know the details."

Catherine shook her head. "Oh, Beryl. Are you prepared to tell the police? You know they are holding Joe."

"That's why I ran away. Because I wasn't ready. But I was a coward. I've come back because I can't let anything happen to Tony."

"You're right. Oh, my dear. What a horrible thing." Catherine's heart went out to the girl who seemed so small cuddled on the sofa under her afghan. She suddenly had an overwhelming desire for Dot. She would know exactly what to do.

At that moment, she realized Cherry had forgotten to draw the drapes. Anyone could be looking in and see poor Beryl sitting there. Catherine got up and performed the task.

"How would you like to handle this?" she asked. "Your father is up here in Oxford today. I just saw him this afternoon. He's very angry with me."

Beryl looked suddenly weary. "I suppose he gave you one of his lectures."

"Yes. Red was there, and we made plans for this evening. If you think he didn't approve of James, you can imagine how he felt about Red."

"That's torn it," Beryl said. She got up and began to pace in a circle. "It was wonderful in so many ways to come to Somerville and hear new ideas. Before that, the only person who presented anything new to me was James. And we had to meet the last few years in secret over the school holidays. But it seems we didn't fool my parents. I came to Somerville to be with him. But he was not the man I thought he was. Still, parting ways with him was a wrench, and as you guessed, left a huge hole in my life. And then when I heard he was murdered, I had my suspicions about my father. I wasn't all that surprised when they were confirmed."

Catherine was wondering how the young woman could have let other people be arrested for the crime when she knew her father was guilty, but she held her peace.

"Tony was a huge comfort to me. I was thinking of confiding the whole thing to him, but then he was attacked. I think my father must have been having me followed, possibly when I was still with James. Suddenly, it was all too much. I just wanted Nanny. But then, I couldn't tell her either." A tear coursed down Beryl's cheek. "I'm such a child, still. Such a coward. I even wrote that anonymous letter to try to make myself believe Alfie had attacked Tony."

"Would you like to stay here with me for the time being?" Catherine asked.

Suddenly, the front door crashed open. Catherine hadn't locked it behind her.

"Father!" Beryl screamed.

"She told me she didn't find you!" the baron roared. "What kind of rubbish is she filling your head with?"

Entering, he grabbed Catherine's arm and twisted it behind her back.

The pain almost made her scream, but Catherine had to keep her head. She saw Cherry poke her head out of the kitchen. The servant was out of the view of the baron. She mimed speaking on the telephone while Favringham pushed Catherine ahead of him out of the front door.

"How handy that the canal is so close. Just a half a block away. I'm afraid you're going to have a little accident," he growled in her ear. "You should never have tried to interfere."

She tried frantically to free herself, but it only resulted in more pain as she staggered down the street. The night air was freezing, and she didn't even want to think how cold the water would be in the canal.

Beryl came screaming out of the front door behind them. "Father, don't do anything more! This is it! I won't stand by any longer."

For just a moment, the baron was distracted. It was enough, Catherine twisted out of his grasp and went running the other way toward St. Giles's.

Then, all at once, there was a broad chest in front of her. Arms went around her. It was Harry. She began to sob. At the same moment, she heard the klaxon of police cars as they roared up St. Giles's. At the sounds of a struggle behind her, she turned in Harry's arms.

The baron had torn himself free from his daughter's grasp and was running towards the canal.

"Stop him, Harry!" Catherine cried.

The professor went after the baron, proving to be the faster and stronger of the two. This time it was the baron who had his arm twisted around to his back.

"You utter fool!" Favringham cried. "Let me go, or I will make you pay!"

"The only one who is going to pay here is you!"

Beryl was crying, "He's a murderer. My father is a murderer!"

"Watch what you say, girl! There is a switch waiting for you at home!"

And then, miraculously, the police were there.

* * *

The fire was built up in the sitting room, and Cherry was plying her mistress with hot cups of tea. Harry had helped himself to the whiskey. The baron was under arrest, and both Catherine and Beryl had given their statements to the police. The girl was now in a state of utter collapse, sleeping with a couple of hot water bottles in Catherine's room.

"I suppose you had it all figured out, didn't you?" Harry said.

"I was beginning to suspect, but it was such an outrageous idea I didn't dare believe it until Beryl told me. What a dreadful man! Too much attention is certainly worse than none at all!"

Catherine told him of her confrontation with the Baron in The Eagle and Child. "It has to be the first time in English history that a black man was released from jail to be replaced by a baron of the realm. As you can imagine, Chief Detective Inspector Marsh wanted a lot of convincing."

"Poor Beryl," Harry said. "What an awful thing."

"Yes, her world has collapsed. But she had run away, you know. She came back only because of her worry for Tony. I'm not sure I would have been that brave. In fact, with regard to you and me, I have shown myself to be an utter and complete weakling. How can you ever forgive me?" she asked in a small voice.

"You haven't killed anyone, Catherine. Don't be absurd."

"But I was trying ever so hard to conquer my feelings for you. And then you showed up here tonight. Why did you come?"

"I came because you have woven yourself so tightly around my heart that I couldn't stay away from you any longer."

Harry drew her up from her chair, folding her into his embrace. "I thought you were trying to steel yourself against me. What I didn't understand was why. It wasn't silly Madeleine, surely?"

"She rather threw everything into relief." Catherine settled her head on his shoulder. It was two in the morning, but she had been wound so tightly she only now could begin to relax. "I have been such a child. I've written the whole thing out in a letter to you to try to make you understand."

"I don't know how you ever could have thought you were in danger from me," he said in a low voice that penetrated straight through to her heart. She let the feelings she had trapped ruthlessly inside her run free.

"I was determined to stand on my own feet," she said. "I figured out that I had been looking at Rafe's love or whatever it was he felt for me as a substitute for parental love. When I cut myself off from him, I had nothing. I was in a black hole." She inhaled deeply of Harry's scent—pipe tobacco and some kind of woodsy cologne. Pulling back, she looked into his eyes, which were soft with caring.

"I need time, Harry. I'm very fond of you, but I have to make sure I'm not just leaning on you for strength. I need to have a source of peace and light in my own soul."

"That is certainly the worthiest of goals. I am not in any hurry," Harry said. "You are the best thing in my life, and I'm more than relieved to know I haven't lost you to that bounder, de Fontaine."

"No. Red isn't any threat. He is just a friend."

"Will he carry on with the band now?"

"I am sure he will. I think it means more to him than he realizes. But he doesn't belong in this conversation."

"If we can arrange for the necessary grants, will you come to the States with me next summer?"

In answer, she stood on tiptoe and kissed him as though they had been separated for months. "I'll have to," she said at last. "I'm no good at goodbyes." She kissed him again. "Now, speaking of America, we must ring Dot."

"But it's the middle of the night!"

"She'll never forgive us if she has to find out about Favringham from the newspaper!"

"All right. But give me a moment to finish kissing you."

"Of course," she said. "First things first."

The End

Other Books by G.G. Vandagriff

Mysteries
An Oxford Murder
Cankered Roots
Of Deadly Descent
Tangled Roots
Poisoned Pedigree
Hidden Branch

*

Romantic Suspense
Breaking News
Sleeping Secrets
Balkan Echo

*

Suspense
Arthurian Omen
Foggy With a Chance of Murder

*

Historical Fiction
The Last Waltz: A Novel of Love and War
Exile
Defiance

*

Regency Romances
The Duke's Undoing
The Taming of Lady Kate
Miss Braithwaite's Secret
Rescuing Rosalind
Lord Trowbridge's Angel
The Baron and the Bluestocking
Lord Grenville's Choice

Lord John's Dilemma
Lord Basingstoke's Downfall (novella)
Her Fateful Debut
His Mysterious Lady
Not an Ordinary Baronet
Love Unexpected
Miss Saunders Takes A Journey
The European Collection (anthology)
Spring in Hyde Park (anthology)
Much Ado About Lavender (novella)

*

Women's Fiction
Pieces of Paris
The Only Way to Paradise

*

Non-Fiction
Voices In Your Blood
Deliverance from Depression

ABOUT THE AUTHOR

G.G. VANDAGRIFF is a traditionally published author who has gone Indie. She loves the Regency period, having read Georgette Heyer over and over since she was a teen. Currently, she has thirteen Regency titles in print, but she writes other things, too. In 2010, she received the Whitney Award for Best Historical Novel for her epic, *The Last Waltz: A Novel of Love and War*. She has also written Romantic Suspense, and her mystery fans are always urging her to write another book featuring her wacky genealogical sleuths, Alex and Briggie. Her latest work is a 1930's Golden Age mystery series.

She studied writing at Stanford University and received her master's degree at George Washington University. Though she has lived in many places throughout the country, she now lives with her husband, David, a lawyer and a writer, on the bench of the Wasatch Mountains in Utah. From her office, she can see a beautiful valley, a lake, and another mountain range. She and David have three children and seven adventurous grandchildren.

Visit G.G. at her website http://ggvandagriff.com, where you can read her blog, keep track of all her books and her work in progress, and sign up to receive her newsletter. She has an author page on Facebook (G.G. Vandagriff-Author) and on Goodreads and Amazon. She loves to hear from her fans!

Printed in Great Britain
by Amazon

Printed in Great Britain
by Amazon